Hannah March w̶a̶...̶...̶...̶...̶ough
on the edge of the Fens and was a student on the
University of East Anglia MA Course in Creative Writing
under Malcolm Bradbury and Angela Carter. She is now
married and lives in Peterborough.

THE COMPLAINT OF THE DOVE, THE DEVIL'S
HIGHWAY (shortlisted for the CWA Ellis Peters Historical Dagger) and DISTINCTION OF BLOOD, Hannah
March's previous mysteries featuring Robert Fairfax, are
also published by Headline.

Also by Hannah March, featuring Robert Fairfax,
and available from Headline:

The Complaint of the Dove
The Devil's Highway
Distinction of Blood

Death Be My Theme

Hannah March

HEADLINE

First published in 2000
by HEADLINE BOOK PUBLISHING

First published in paperback in 2001
by HEADLINE BOOK PUBLISHING

10 9 8 7 6 5 4 3 2 1

ISBN 0 7472 6627 1

Typeset by Letterpart Ltd
Reigate, Surrey

Printed and bound in Great Britain by
Clays Ltd, St Ives plc.

HEADLINE BOOK PUBLISHING
A division of Hodder Headline
338 Euston Road
London NW1 3BH

www.headline.co.uk
www.hodderheadline.com

One

Overhead, thunderclouds were massing. The sultry air was as tense and still as held-in breath.

Robert Fairfax, strolling along Royal Hospital Row, wondered if he would complete his prescribed morning walk before the summer storm broke. Convalescent as he was, he knew he should avoid a wetting. And yet at least it would break the monotony of this enforced leisure.

Two days, he reproached himself. He had only been here in Chelsea, in the rural outskirts of London, for two days – surely not long enough for boredom to set in. And how often over the past few years had he longed for a little free time to himself, to rest and do as he pleased? He had a comfortable lodging in a charming spot, with no one to answer to, and he had the latest volume of *Tristram Shandy* to read.

Yet the prospect of another four weeks spent vegetating here depressed him. When you got what you wanted, you didn't want it any more – a sour truth that he had often reflected on with amusement. He would rather not have had it proved to him so thoroughly.

Ungrateful too. For the illness from which he was recuperating had brought him, he knew now, as close to death as he had ever been. At the time it had seemed an inconvenience that had run out of control. It had begun with a tertian ague, which he had tried to ignore; until at last his pupils asked their guardian why Mr Fairfax was trembling so hard he could not hold a book in his hands. And then bed-rest – except that no rest was possible in that burning, shivering, sweating, hallucinating nightmare into which he had descended. And still what lucid part of him remained expected to shake the fever off at any moment, and kept forcing his body up out of the bed, and could not understand why the doctor and the nursemaid restrained him.

Blankness then. His employers – decent and kind, he had been lucky – had despaired of his life, he learnt afterwards. They had even been about to send for someone – friend or kin – to be with him at the last. But he had rallied, somehow, and found himself lying flat and calm in sweat-soaked sheets with a feeling as if he had just surfaced from the depths of a turbulent ocean.

Kinder still, his employers had insisted on his taking a month in the country to convalesce, before returning to his post as private tutor: they would pay his salary in the meantime. It was touching, and he knew he should consider himself fortunate in all ways.

And so I do, he said to himself, as he paused by the Spread Eagle Inn, idly watching a carriage swing cumbrously off the road and trundle into the inn-yard. Be honest, Robert: it is that business of sending for someone, is it not? For who is there? Somewhere two sisters, married, preferring to forget the name of Fairfax. Acquaintances, glad enough to share a glass if we meet, but whom I cannot call friends simply because this restless and rootless life of mine precludes such a thing . . .

Yes, that was the nub of the matter. A brush with death had brought home to Fairfax how little his life meant to anyone but himself.

Morbid thoughts. But they beat a path, at least, to an understanding of why he dreaded this month. Without occupation, he could only be aware of his ever-present loneliness.

With a physical shudder, Fairfax shook these thoughts off, and was brisk with himself. He was not a lover of rustic seclusion, that was all it came down to. Chelsea was less than an hour by chair from St Paul's, and the pinnacles of Westminster Abbey could be seen across the fields on a clear morning; but still it was not the city that he loved, with its ceaseless clamour and colour. Here there were meadows and nurseries rather than clubs and coffee-houses, and a slumberous country-town atmosphere drowsed over the spacious streets around the Royal Hospital and the fashionable resort of Ranelagh Gardens. His doctor had recommended the spot for air and quiet, and quiet it certainly was, Fairfax thought: why else would he be watching the arrival of a carriage as if it were a noteworthy event?

Well, the healthy mind could find exercise in any object, he reflected, and set himself to deduce what he could about the carriage's owner.

No aristocratic crest, but the smartness of the equipage,

the gleaming lacquer and mahogany, proclaimed wealth. The horses were young and well groomed, but some awkwardness in negotiating the turning into the inn-yard suggested they were not a well-matched team. The owner was no sportish squire then, for whom horseflesh was religion. There was little dust on the wheels or on the horses' legs, so their journey could only have been short: probably from one of the riverside mansions or villas that rich men built for themselves hereabouts, as a retreat from the city – which suggested a man who was or had been in business. The coachman, in plain livery, drove sedately, and was himself elderly.

An older man, then, of fixed or retiring habits, accustomed to driving even short distances, perhaps a bachelor; though a further reason to employ elderly male servants, rather than personable young ones, might be . . .

A young wife. Just as Fairfax thought of it, the coachman got down and opened the carriage door to a young woman. She was richly but conservatively dressed, dark-haired, her thin face strikingly pale. Getting out, her kid-shod feet avoided the puddles of horse-urine with mincing accuracy.

Now for the older husband, Fairfax thought, quite caught up in his game; and he felt like letting out a small cheer when the man stepped out of the carriage after the woman, frowning, fiftyish, crusty-looking, clutching a malacca cane in one large reddened hand.

Just then Fairfax became aware that he was not the only observer. A man was lounging against the pump on the other side of the cobbled yard – a giant of a man in truth, well over six feet tall and brawny to boot. His arms, thick as Fairfax's thighs, were crossed over a deep chest which an open shirt and carelessly tied neckcloth revealed to be as hairy as a bear's. The big man was watching the young woman with frank interest, and when she glanced his way, he swept the uncocked hat off his head and leered at her, with a half-mocking bow. His nut-brown hair was long and lustrous and untied, falling about his shoulders. The village Samson, Fairfax thought maliciously: strength in his hair, and his brains in his—

'Ah, so there you are, sirrah!' the gentleman from the carriage cried, as an ostler came hurrying to attend to the horses. 'I began to think we must wait till doomsday. Are they all as sluggish to serve at this establishment, or are you just the laziest?'

The gentleman had a rasping crow's voice, and a flinty eye, and he proceeded to instruct the ostler on the care of his horses with the hectoring sharpness of a man accustomed to having his most pedantic demands met. Meanwhile the hulking Samson had sauntered over to the lady, who stood looking about her with a cool indifference, and with another sweep of his hat said, 'They serve a nice drop of shrub here, ma'am, if you stand in need of reviving.'

The lady looked at him, expressionlessly, and rather to Fairfax's surprise said, 'Do I look as if I need it, then?'

'Mebbe,' the big man said, studying her sideways with a little swagger. 'Not that there's any improvement needed: damn me, no.'

All at once the elderly man was at his lady's side. His florid face had turned crimson, and the way he thrust it forward at Samson's suggested that whatever else he was, he was no milksop. Indeed, for all the lace at his cuffs and the embroidery on his waistcoat, there was something raw-boned and bullish about this gentleman. A self-made man, Fairfax thought, in some trade that involved getting his hands dirty, at least when he started out.

'Sirrah? Do you address me?'

'I suppose I do now,' the big man said with a lazy smile. 'But afore that, I was speaking to the lady—'

'And that you do not do.' The elderly man gathered the lady's limp white arm to him fiercely. 'Are you employed here, fellow?'

'I ain't now, but I was. I used to do yon lazy cove's job, and a lot more smartly too. Now I've got me a better place, but I like to call in, you know, and give 'em the benefit of my advice. And as for the advice I was just giving the lady here—'

'The lady – my wife – does not want your advice, or your insolence. I've a mind to speak to the innkeeper, and have him turn you out of here.'

'Oh, that'll be fun to see,' the big man said, laughing with great composure; and he continued laughing as the older man hustled his silent wife away as if from a terrible contagion. But there was a hard and speculative look in his eye as he watched them go; and when he stirred at last and turned, Fairfax was careful not to catch that eye. Quickly he strolled on as if he had never stopped. Well, after all, he thought, I am a convalescent.

He did such a good job of seeming obliviously wrapped in thought that he nearly collided with a grey saddle-horse that was being hitched to a post by its rider a little further along the street. With a murmured apology he blundered on, still preoccupied with what he had seen in the inn-yard.

Mighty high-handed and protective the old curmudgeon had been, practically propelling his young wife away. And mighty discontented she had looked, though there had been no appearance of finding Samson's attentions welcome either. How did people end up in such ill-assorted matches?

A simple answer, of course: they married for other reasons than love. Or they married for love and found it did not endure. So it had been with the woman whose last letter to him he still carried in his breast pocket after nearly three years.

Inaccurate to say he had fallen in love with her, back then: rather love had stood phantom-like between them, an unrealized potential. Both had seen the ghost, but had not spoken of it. She was married. Her husband was cold, domineering and mistrustful, though there was that sad perplexity in her that suggested he had not always been so; and her husband he would remain. Fairfax still sometimes glimpsed the ghost, and sighed over it, uselessly.

His steps took him down Queen Street towards the timber bridge at Stone Wharf. Here a network of streams and canals fed from the Thames into a long reservoir, divided by a reedy island. The water supplied the new buildings springing up on the west side of the city, and the chimneys of the pumping-house could be seen towards Tothill Fields, adding their coal-smoke to the thundery murk of the sky. A couple of watermen's punts, and the stiff-legged floating corpse of a dog, gave a less than reassuring impression of the purity of the water that was destined for the sculleries of the genteel squares; but leaving that aside, it was a tranquil scene, and Fairfax leaned on the timber rail of the bridge to admire it.

There: the first sound of thunder from the southern horizon, oddly musical, like an arpeggio on deep bass strings. Below him the canal was filled with the turgid colour of the sky. To his surprise, he saw a small cocked hat on its surface, floating gently out from under the bridge. A moment later came a high-pitched exclamation, and a splash.

A child, surely.

Fairfax ran, shoes pounding on the timber, almost skidding as he reached the bank by the underside of the bridge.

A small boy had fallen into the canal; and though it was not very deep here, and he had managed to get a hold on the stone support of the bridge nearest the bank, his eyes were round blobs of alarm.

Well, here is the wetting after all, Fairfax thought, wading in. The water struck very chill on his heated body: the boy was already shivering, though no doubt that was partly shock. Lifting him out was a simple matter: he could have been no more than eight, and was very slight.

'Bathing is tempting on such a hot day,' Fairfax said, setting the little boy down on the bank. 'But try a safer spot next time – and not in your best clothes.' For the little boy, whose fair hair was curled and tied, was dressed in a notably grand and expensive coat of lilac cloth trimmed with gold.

The boy's large eyes regarded him with a shy, wondering, and somehow uncomprehending expression. It had just occurred to Fairfax that he might be deaf when the boy's lips moved. He murmured something.

Thank you . . . ? It was not quite what he had heard.

'*Danke* . . .' The boy raised his voice a little. '*Danke, gnadiger Herr.*'

'*Keine Ursache,*' Fairfax said automatically, before his surprise sank in. A little German, or German-speaker, playing about the Chelsea waterways! Before he could speak again, the boy turned in agitation and pointed at the canal.

'*Mein Hut.*'

Wading in again, Fairfax retrieved the little tricorne. The boy thanked him more fulsomely, and began to explain in rapid German that Fairfax had difficulty following that he had fallen in because he was trying to reach his hat, and his hat had fallen in because he had been leaning out over the bank to see what he thought was a frog but wasn't a frog . . .

Suddenly the boy gasped and looked down at himself. Water was dripping from the flared skirts of the gorgeous coat.

'Oh, my beautiful coat,' he mourned. 'I hope it will not be ruined. What will my father say? I was allowed to wear it today, in honour of my sister's birthday, but I promised I would look after it.' He gazed up at Fairfax with a bright confiding look. 'It was a present, you see, from the Empress in Vienna.'

Die Kaiserin in Wien . . . Had he really said that? Fairfax stared at the solemn, round-cheeked face. Either the boy was an odd fantasist, or . . .

Well, no matter. The important thing now was to get him home where he could dry off, especially as there was another deep chord of thunder booming in the sky.

'I don't think the coat will come to any harm, if you go home and dry off quickly,' Fairfax said. 'Where do you live?'

The boy turned confidently to point, then hesitated,

scanning the waterways and meadows. His face fell.

'I know where it is, but I can't see it. It is called' – he struggled with the words – 'fi-fee-ro . . .'

'Five Fields Row. I know it. I am lodging quite near there myself. Come, I will show you the way. My name is Robert Fairfax.'

The boy nodded, in a curiously gracious and adult manner, but did not offer his name in return. Again Fairfax thought, as they set off: the Empress in Vienna . . . ?'

The boy had to hurry to keep up with Fairfax's long strides, but it seemed best to get him home as soon as possible. The thunder was growing louder, and the sky was a weird and ominous biscuit colour from horizon to horizon. Fairfax's charge certainly showed no sign of wanting to linger, and when they came to Five Fields Row, a street of tall, genteel townhouses pleasantly situated with open meadows at their rear, he broke into a run.

Then, with his foot on the first of the steps leading up to his house, the boy paused and looked back. His face was full of appeal. Water dripped from his coat on to the steps.

'I will come in and explain to your father what happened,' Fairfax said, with a smile that meant *and I will put the best complexion on it*.

'Papa has been ill,' the boy confided, reaching up to rap at the door, 'I must not give him trouble. I only meant to go out for a little while. I thought no one would notice.'

Vain hope. The woman who threw open the door immediately cried out in German, 'Wolfgang, where have you been? And what is this – you're soaked, come in quickly. Your father—'

The woman stopped. Fairfax, just about to say that he

could explain, stopped too. They gazed at one another. For several moments he suspected his mind of playing some trick upon him, for this was the very woman he had been thinking of earlier.

'Mrs Linton,' he said. 'Cordelia . . .'

Two

'Mr Fairfax. Good God.' With a perplexity that even had something angry about it, she added, 'You are quite unchanged.'

'You also.'

Not true, at least just now; for she had turned so pale as to look quite ill.

'And you are soaked too. Has the rain—?'

'A mere mishap,' Fairfax said, 'down by the canals. No harm done or meant, I think. The boy was not sure of his way, and I thought it best to bring him back. I confess I did not expect . . .' He tailed off. He was torn between being unable to look at her and being unable to take his eyes off her.

'Frau Linton . . .'

The boy was plucking at Cordelia's skirts. She seemed relieved to turn her attention to him.

'Frau Linton, is Papa astir?'

'He is, and quite anxious for you. Whatever were you about? Well, no matter – take off that coat, and I will hang it before the kitchen fire. And I'll see if I can find you some clean breeches and stockings.'

13

The boy wriggled out of his coat. Taking it from him, Cordelia said to Fairfax, 'Will you wait here a moment?' and hurriedly left them by a door leading to the basement.

'Frau Linton is very good,' the boy said confidingly to Fairfax. 'She speaks German very well because her father was a Hamburg German and he was a composer – but *psch!*' – the boy held a finger to his lips – 'not a very good one!'

'So I have heard,' Fairfax said, smiling. 'Frau Linton lives with you, then?' How unutterably strange he felt, seeing her again. A small voice within him wondered whether he was going to be able to bear it.

'She lives here. And we are lodging here until we go back to London,' the boy said, dancing on the spot. 'She has helped us a lot because Papa speaks only a little English and Mama has none at all except "Good morrow, sir" and "Past ten o'clock" and that is because the nightwatchman says it. And all I know is "Bugger French!" and that is what the street-boys say when they see someone whose clothes are foreign – but I *think* it is dirty!'

Fairfax couldn't help laughing at the boy's grin. 'It is certainly dirty,' he said, and then with a look of concern, 'You are shivering.'

'So are you!'

'Is that Wolfgangerl there?' A hoarse, stern voice spoke in German from the first landing at the top of the stairs.

'I'm here, Papa!' The stairs were large for his short legs, but the boy took them at a run, and embraced the dressing-gowned figure at the top. 'I was gone only a little while.'

'I have told you before about slipping out without telling anyone. And on your sister's birthday too—'

'Well, but Papa, it was so warm, and Nannerl was busy

14

with writing a letter to Uncle Hagenauer, and I was tired from composing, you know – and you always tell me I mustn't get dull and stale at work. And this gentleman helped me and showed me the way home, his name is Fairfax and he speaks German pretty well though not as well as—'

'Wolfgangerl, your mother and I were troubled to find you gone. You must remember you are far from home now, and among strangers. Kind though they may be,' the man said. 'Also—'

'Also I am anxious for you, because *you* should not be out of bed, Papa,' the boy said, reaching up and kissing his father on the tip of his nose.

'Ach, it is too hot to lie so,' the man said, in a softened voice. He turned and beckoned to Fairfax with a courtly gesture. 'Sir, will it please you to walk up?'

Still feeling rather as if he were in a dream, Fairfax followed the man and the boy into a comfortable first-floor parlour. A plain woman in middle age, dressed in apron and mob-cap, put aside her sewing and rose in shy confusion when Fairfax entered. Seated at a writing-desk was a young girl of thirteen or so, fair and pretty and with a marked resemblance to the boy. Below the window stood a small harpsichord.

'Here he is, my dears,' the man said. 'Herr Fairfax, I present Frau Mozart, my wife; Maria-Anna, my daughter. Wolfgang you already know. I thank you, sir, for the return of my errant son.' He frowned at the boy, who had taken up a walking-stick and was galloping around the room with it tucked between his legs like a toy horse. A trail of wet footprints marked the floorboards. 'And I hope you will come to no harm from it.'

15

'Oh, it's no matter,' Fairfax said, and quickly explained what had happened, making light of it. The man listened gravely, a cleft between his brows. The boy, seeing his father's expression, abandoned the stick and darted over to them.

'Papa, I would have been quite all right. But Herr Fairfax is a kind gentleman, and helped me,' the boy said, and to Fairfax's surprise gave him a quick, affectionate squeeze on the arm. 'And I hope you will do him honour.'

'But Wolfgangerl, where is your fine coat?' his mother said in a soft, mourning voice.

'Frau Linton is taking care of it, Mama. Now I am going back to my composition. Nannerl, have you finished there?'

The young girl, with a rueful smile, gave place to her brother at the desk. Hoisting himself up on to the chair, the boy gathered up some papers which Fairfax saw were sheets of music manuscript. Legs dangling, the boy looked raptly into space for a moment and then dipped his pen and began writing with quick, nervous scratches.

With the faintest of sighs, the man said, 'Sir, again I thank you. Permit me to present myself: Leopold Mozart, Vice-Kapellmeister to the Prince-Archbishop of Salzburg, and author of the *School of Violin-Playing*.' He gave a crisp little bow. Though clad in an Indian dressing-gown and cap and slippers, with a quantity of flannel wound round his throat, Herr Mozart was as decorous and correct as if he were at a court function. His was a narrow, severe, but intelligent face, with compelling pale eyes; and there was a sharp pride in the way he introduced himself. 'Please forgive the informality of my appearance, Herr Fairfax. I have been ill, and am instructed still to take care of myself. It is why we

16

have withdrawn here, for the goodness of the air, though I am impatient to return to London.'

'You and I are in similar case,' Fairfax said. 'But surely – I have heard of your children. It was in the London newspapers just last month. Wolfgang Mozart, prodigy of human nature, plays upon the harpsichord at sight and so on, together with his sister – they gave a concert, I think.'

'Several, to great astonishment and applause,' Herr Mozart said, with a complacent look. 'There would have been more, had not my illness forced us to retire for a space. Sir, will you take tea with us? It is, I know, your English habit at all times of the day, and so we keep the kettle always on the fire.' He rang the bell. 'My wife has taken greatly to it. For myself, especially with this malignant sore throat, I prefer another English drink that I have never come across before. It is called cider. It refreshes without heating the spirits, I find. Yes, we came to London in April—'

'Papa was mighty sick on the boat,' Wolfgang put in, lifting his head from his work with an impish expression.

'We all made copious sacrifices to Neptune,' Leopold Mozart said with a twitch of humour at the corner of his thin lips. 'But once on *terra firma* our welcome could not have been more gratifying. Within a few days of our arrival we were cordially invited to appear at Court before their majesties King George and Queen Charlotte. The Queen was delighted to talk with speakers of her native language, and both professed themselves full of admiration for Wolfgang and Nannerl's abilities, so much so that we were invited to give a second concert before their majesties, at Buckingham House.'

'The King asked me to sight-read a piece by Handel,'

Wolfgang put in, 'and also I played organ and violin to them and I accompanied the Queen with a flautist as well. She plays very well, and she gave me a kiss, and I am going to dedicate some sonatas to her. And the King is very jolly, all the time he says *Vot? Vot?* and it made me smile.'

'I was a little perplexed to find so many of the quality going out of town for the summer,' Herr Mozart said, seating himself and gesturing to Fairfax to do likewise. 'But I arranged the first public concert for the fifth of June, as I calculated that many great ones would have to return for the birthday of the sovereign on the fourth. I was not disappointed. I believe the reception was as enthusiastic as any we have had in the course of our tour, and that has not lacked triumph. We were most graciously received at Vienna by her majesty the Empress Maria Theresa, and by the French King at Versailles . . . Ah, Potivin.' A manservant had appeared. 'Tea, if you please. I will take a glass of cider. And Frau Linton, is she below? Will she join us?'

'I will gladly, Herr Mozart,' Cordelia said, appearing behind the servant. She carried a bundle of clothes. 'As soon as I have dealt with these miscreants. Wolfgangerl, run to your chamber and put on these dry clothes. And Mr Fairfax, I have some clean stockings here.'

'Oh, thank you, but I do very well—'

'No, no, I will not have you suffer for your wet feet.'

Herr Mozart added his persuasions, and invited Fairfax to step into his bedchamber across the passage and change. Feeling a little awkward and embarrassed, he did so; and not knowing what to do with his wet stockings, stuffed them in his pocket. He paused a moment before going back, reflecting on Cordelia Linton, and the way she seemed now to have recovered some of that jaunty self-possession he remembered. It was the thing – no, one of the many things – that he had liked about her. And so was the intense vulnerability that it masked.

Oh, but it was nonsense. It was three years ago, and really there had been nothing between them then: let it die. And after all, nothing had changed – had it? She still had a husband – did she not?

A crash of thunder that rattled the window-panes broke overhead as he returned to the parlour. Frau Mozart cringed and trembled. The girl, Nannerl, sat beside her and held her hand.

'The young lady celebrates a birthday today, I understand,' Fairfax said. 'Our English weather has turned unusually dramatic for it, but I'm sure the storm will soon pass.'

'We are to have roast fowls and plum tarts for dinner, to mark the day,' Herr Mozart said. 'In our retirement here, my wife has taken the cooking into her own hands – and I may say I have never tasted better, though I have been too poorly to do it justice.' He coughed into the flannel muffler.

'I confess I long for the kitchen today,' Frau Mozart said shyly, 'for it is in the basement, where I would feel safer.' She flinched as lightning seared the room with white.

'Don't be afraid, Mama,' cried Wolfgang, who in clean clothes was back at the desk and bent over his music manuscript. 'The rain will come in a minute, and when the rain goes, the storm goes.'

'Take some tea, my dear,' her husband said, as the manservant arrived with a tray, 'it will soothe your nerves. As for me, I have no fear of the elements, Herr Fairfax, not after the fear I knew in the past weeks. At the worst, it seemed my life was in danger. I stood before the terrible prospect of departing from this world, leaving my family alone and unprovided for in a strange country.'

'Oh, Leopold, don't speak of it,' his wife murmured.

'Well, my dear, such things must be spoken of, and they must be thought of. A man must never take his mind from his responsibilities. The world is mighty cruel in falling upon those who do. If it is slow to reward virtue, this world is marvellous quick to punish vice.'

A touch of pomposity and manipulation in this man, Fairfax thought; but a good deal of hard-nosed shrewdness too.

'But thanks be to God, the crisis passed,' Leopold Mozart went on, 'and this week I have felt my strength returning, though my physician says I must still proceed carefully, and avoid stress upon the nerves. There has been such need of quiet that the children have been forbidden to touch an instrument – the sounds, alas, so pleasing to a lifelong musician are intolerable when such a sickness invades. But Wolfgang has occupied himself with composition, when not running around like a monkey' – he shook a mock fist at the boy, who grinned – 'and that is a good exercise for his talents, until he can return before the public.'

'You will soon be well, Papa,' the boy said, darting over and kissing his father's nose again, 'and then I shall play *magnifique*. And you will never be ill again, because I will take care of you – and when you are old, I shall put you in a glass case with a lid to protect you from the wind, and always keep you with me and honour you.'

'With a lid, my son?' Leopold smiled. 'But will I be able to breathe?'

'It will have holes, of course,' Wolfgang said, dancing back to the desk.

With a twinge of guilt, Fairfax realized he had offered up no thanks for his own recovery from illness. Not that he had a deity to thank: perhaps that was the root of it . . . He looked at Cordelia, who was pouring the tea. Would she understand? He had a feeling that she would: but then he ought not to be having such feelings . . .

'Well, I was telling you of our progress,' Herr Mozart said. 'The public concerts were a great success. Your country is generous to musicians, Herr Fairfax: a hundred guineas was agreed as a fee for the concerts, and twenty-four guineas for a court appearance. That compares very favourably with the German courts, who are rather too inclined to think a snuffbox a sufficient reward.'

'At Aachen the Princess gave me a kiss, and that was all!' Wolfgang cried. 'Also she had a moustache.' His sister gave a single squeal of laughter, then covered her mouth with her hand.

'A poor return indeed,' his father said dryly. 'Not that we are chary of donating our services in a good cause. Wolfgang played an organ concert at Ranelagh Gardens – just down by the river here, as it happens – in aid of the Lying-In Hospital.' Frau Mozart put a hand to her cheek in embarrassment at this public mention of childbirth, and her husband went on even more dryly, 'A curious institution, but it seemed a good way to win the hearts of your very curious nation. I speak, sir, with respect.'

'You speak only to half of Herr Fairfax,' Cordelia said.

'He is half French, as I am half German . . . Mongrels both of us,' she added in English, glancing at Fairfax. He could not interpret the look. But it stirred feelings in him that he didn't know whether he wanted revived.

'Ranelagh was so beautiful, wasn't it, Mama? ' Nannerl said, still squeezing her mother's hand. 'And also Vauxhall Gardens, St Paul's Church, Somerset House, St James' Park—'

'And the King and Queen waved to us!' Wolfgang cried. 'They saw us from their carriage and they knew us again at once!'

'Gratifying indeed,' Leopold Mozart said with a sound between a purr and a snuffle, sipping his cider. 'What is it, Potivin?'

The servant was back. 'Fräulein Henlow is here, sir.'

'Ah! Our good neighbour. Have her come up at once. Fräulein Henlow lives in the house next door,' Leopold Mozart said to Fairfax, 'and has been an excellent neighbour to us. She has no German, but we make shift to understand each other with French. She cheered my wife with company when I was confined to bed, and each day she brings me a posset of her own recipe. It has relieved me, I think, more than all my doctor's ministrations.' He rose, prompt and correct again, as a young woman entered, and greeted her in awkward French. 'Ah, my dear madam, how do you do? It is fortunate you have not far to come, with this shocking storm.'

'Most fearful, is it not? But at least it will clear and cool the air for us. Oh, I hope I don't intrude on your company, Herr Mozart.'

The young woman, who was carrying a jug covered with

muslin, stopped and acknowledged Fairfax with a graceful dip of her head. Her French was correct but somehow very English, as was her appearance. 'English rose' was the expression that came to Fairfax's mind on seeing Miss Henlow. She had a refined, unshowy, but undeniable beauty. She wore the simplest of gowns, without the vast hoop that made getting in and out of doors such a trial for ladies, and her fair hair was plainly dressed, yet everything about her suggested elegance. Her complexion merited that overused word flawless, Fairfax decided – indeed, her face brought to mind all the stock in trade of the Cavalier poets, with their cherry lips and sparkling eyes. Except that he had always suspected those endless Jocastas and Belindas to have been blowsy harpies with teeth like a set of chessmen – whereas this Miss Henlow was the true article. He was interested to see on Cordelia's face what was surely a look of downright dislike.

'No intrusion, my dear madam – you know you are like one of the family here. This is Herr Fairfax, who has just returned our wandering boy to us. Please, be seated.'

Miss Henlow, after placing the jug on the tea-tray, sat down next to Fairfax and gave him a bright and somehow inclusive smile, as if they already knew each other and could be perfectly easy together. For some reason he felt uncomfortably conscious of having a pair of wet stockings in his pocket.

'Well, and how do you go on, Herr Mozart? I have brought your posset again, as you are kind enough to say it eases you; though I declare from your looks you are improving daily, and will soon not need it.'

'I progress, certainly. But the throat is still sore,' Leopold

23

Mozart said. The peculiar possessive wistfulness of the invalid, Fairfax thought – reluctant to let the illness go. 'And how is your excellent brother-in-law? Is he from home?'

'He is – and under shelter, I hope; but it was pressing business and could not wait.'

'Exemplary – and sad!' sighed Leopold Mozart. 'I hope he bears up, my dear madam, under his heavy loss? And yours also. A double loss.'

'He finds what consolation is to be had, sir – in reflecting that Catherine is surely in a better and happier place. And in the child, who is a true blessing, and thankfully is thriving.' She turned to Fairfax. 'My sister died but a month ago, Mr Fairfax, in childbed – her first. The child lived, and I have the care of him. It was a loss extremely painful to me and to my brother-in-law, who had not been married to Catherine two years, and adored her. I do not wear mourning: I do not approve of it, and neither did my sister.'

She spoke in English, and with a matter-of-fact plainness that he rather admired, suggesting as it did that it would be uncivilized nonsense not to tell him what they were talking about.

'My commiserations,' he said.

'Thank you. You live hereabouts, Mr Fairfax?' Such a cool, shaded voice: viola rather than violin, he thought, taking the cue from his surroundings.

'I am lodging in Chelsea, for a short time only, for the benefit of my health. Ordinarily I am a private tutor to a family in the City. Such has been my vocation for several years, now here, now there.' He realized he was speaking mainly for the benefit of Cordelia Linton – seeking to convey to her, perhaps, that he was just the same as when they last

24

met. And more – he found some wild part of him wanted to add: *and though you are utterly charming, if there is a tremble about me and a tinge in my cheek it is because of that dark, thin, troubled woman across the room, whose image I have carried in my heart so long and whom I . . .* What, precisely? Did he love her? And did he, in fact, wish that their paths had not crossed again like this, to stir all that turbulence anew?

'Indeed? My brother-in-law Charles is a devoted reader. I never see him without a book. Perhaps you would care to sup with us one evening. Naturally we are in no case for formal entertaining at present – but to have some company, and thoughtful conversation, would I think benefit Charles, and I'm sure you would find him congenial.'

'Thank you, I would like that.'

Miss Henlow smiled and went over to the desk, where the boy's quill was wagging busily.

'Well, Wolfgang, may I ask what you are working on? Something that I may try my hand at, I hope – though you must bear in mind that my execution is indifferent at best.'

Leopold translated, and the boy looked up excitedly.

'You could not play this on your clavier, Fräulein Henlow,' he said, 'because it is a *sinfonia* for orchestra. It goes so well that I shall soon be out of paper.'

'A *sinfonia* for orchestra,' his father chuckled. 'What think you of that, Fräulein Henlow?'

'I think your son will never cease to astonish me, Herr Mozart,' she said, looking over the finished music-sheets that the boy had thrust impatiently aside. 'Do people not suspect you of, shall I say, helping him?'

'They do, often,' answered Leopold, 'but when they see

what Wolfgangerl is capable of, they are soon disabused of that. But I shall certainly study and correct your *sinfonia* when it is finished, Wolfgangerl, so no silly mistakes, if you please . . . Now, what is this, Potivin?'

Coughing apologetically, the servant had reappeared with a letter, which he held between thumb and finger as if to dissociate himself from it. A gentleman calling, he murmured, wanting to see Master Wolfgang.

'What gentleman?' Herr Mozart was testy. 'Is he known to us?'

The servant, who had a long and appropriately fiddle-shaped face, gave a shrug that could have meant anything. Leopold Mozart opened the letter and frowned over it.

'It is in English. But I think I gather its meaning . . . Frau Linton, would you be so good?'

Cordelia read the letter out, translating as she went.

'"Honoured sir, I have marked with keen attention the arrival on these shores of your son, Wolfgang Mozart, by all accounts the greatest of musical prodigies; and as an amateur devotee of that most amiable of sciences, I beg leave to wait upon you, and witness the abilities of this marvel for myself. Habits of retirement prevented me from attending the public concerts which were given with, I believe, resounding success in London earlier this summer; and having heard by report of your withdrawal here, I could not forbear giving myself the trouble, against my usual inclination, of venturing forth from my establishment at Kensington to wait upon you. I have hopes of an immediate reception, but should this prove inconvenient, I am to be found at the Spread Eagle Inn, Royal Hospital Row. I am, sir, your obedient servant, Gabriel Chilcott." Well!' Cordelia handed the letter back with a wry look. 'He certainly congratulates himself on the trouble he takes in coming all the way from Kensington to plague you. Kensington, by the by, Herr Mozart, is a morning's walk from here.'

'Extraordinary,' Leopold said, pacing irritably. 'Really, there is presumption in it. I am here to recover, not to receive company – not in this manner,' he added, waving a courtly hand at Fairfax. 'This man turns up on the doorstep and simply expects to be admitted – and to be given a private recital, if you please, by Wolfgang! Crowned heads have seen fit to reward his performances handsomely, and yet this man – Chilcott? Who is he, Fräulein Henlow, do you know?'

'I know of him by name only,' Miss Henlow said. 'A gentleman of wealth, who lives very retired. And stands much on his dignity, I understand – he has a reputation for disputes with his neighbours.'

Fairfax was sure this was the man he had seen arriving by carriage at the Spread Eagle. Everything certainly fitted with what he had observed of him.

'It is mighty high-handed,' Leopold Mozart grumbled, pacing over to the desk and laying the letter down. Absently he stroked his son's small, intent head, bent over the music sheets. 'Well, I shall speak to him, at any rate – have him walk up, Potivin. I shall lay the case quite squarely before him, and make sure he understands that my children are musical performers, who are to be heard for the price of a ticket like any others. If I do not nip this in the bud, then every idle spectator will be turning up on my doorstep.'

Idle, however, was not a word that Fairfax would have applied to the man who was shown up to the parlour. For all the protests about fixed habits, this was no lily-livered dilettante. It was, as Fairfax had suspected, the same gentleman he had seen at the inn-yard. Fairfax noted again his powerful red hands, and added to the observation the way Mr Gabriel Chilcott came into the room with a ducking of his large head, as if under a low lintel.

'Sir, you must be Mr Mozart – the boy's father, eh?' Mr Chilcott's faintly truculent eyes roamed about, passed with a distinct lack of interest over the women present, and lighted on the figure of Wolfgang seated at the desk. 'And that must be the boy! Well, well.' He shook his head. 'He is *very* small.'

One could almost fancy, from his note of disappointment, that he was about to ask whether they had anything in a larger size. But then Mr Chilcott stomped over to the desk, again with that stooped thrusting as if passing through a low doorway, and peered over Wolfgang's shoulder at the music manuscript.

'Saints alive, 'tis true – he makes his own compositions!' Mr Chilcott turned to Leopold, narrowing his eyes. 'Unless you have simply set him this to copy, sir – is that the shape of it?'

Leopold, who had been frowning and fuming throughout this, said in choked English, 'Sir – I speak not English so well, but—'

'Herr Mozart, perhaps you will allow me,' Cordelia said. Rapidly she translated all that Mr Chilcott had said, adding, 'Shall I present your compliments, and tell the gentleman what you said before?'

'If you please,' Leopold said through tight lips, sitting down and fussing with the flannel at his throat.

A look of puzzled stubbornness grew on Mr Chilcott's

face as Cordelia explained, deftly and gracefully, that delighted as he was by the gentleman's interest in the talents of his son, Herr Mozart begged it to be understood that these talents were only to be displayed in a concert setting, and certainly not here where ill health required Herr Mozart to retire away from the pressures of company.

'Yet I see company here,' Mr Chilcott said, with a sweep of his hands – restless hands, Fairfax noted. When not gesticulating, he kept clasping and unclasping them as if their lack of occupation bothered him. 'I fail to understand why you deny me this simple request.'

Cordelia translated. Her eye strayed to Fairfax's, and he caught an answering gleam of amusement there. Damn it all, he thought, she was still that person: the person in a room whose eyes you instinctively met whenever there was a touch of the ridiculous.

'Sir, it is so,' Leopold said, with a visible effort of self-command, 'and would be so with anyone who sought a private audience in this way. My son is a musical performer – not a dog who does tricks.'

Just then Wolfgang took it upon himself to get up from the desk, and offer to shake Mr Chilcott's hand.

'Sir, I am pleased to meet you. I shall play concerts again as soon as Papa is better, and then I hope you will come to hear me.'

Cordelia translated, whilst Mr Chilcott after a surprised moment shook the boy's hand – it was quite swallowed up in his – and studied him with an intense and greedy fascination.

'Ah, that would be very nice, my young friend,' he said. 'But 'twould be more convenient for me to hear you here. I seldom stir, and more seldom to London: I too must be careful of my health, and my habits are strict.'

'Out of the question,' Leopold rapped back, even before Cordelia had finished translating.

'But what does the boy say? You may like to know, my boy, that I have brought with me a special present, for you, if you would give me a little concert. It is a hobby-horse, brand new, and beautifully made. What think you of that, eh?'

Cordelia translated this with a faintly uncomfortable look. There was no doubting the impression the mention of the hobby-horse made on Wolfgang.

'Sir,' Leopold said with a sigh, 'be assured that Wolfgang will return to the concert stage very soon, and that as soon as he does you shall have a ticket. Say where you are to be found, and a complimentary ticket shall be sent to you as soon as a date is arranged. That is the best I can offer. It would set a very dubious precedent if my son were to begin accepting presents for impromptu displays, from all and sundry.'

Mr Chilcott's already high colour turned to mottled purple as he listened to the translation.

'Hardly all and sundry,' he said, breathing noisily. 'I have been an admirer – an enthusiast – of the musical science for many years. I have in my possession several autograph manuscripts of Mr Handel, amongst others going back to the barbaric times before Purcell, which are the envy of distinguished musicologists. You may care to know that my taste was fostered under the most unpropitious of circumstances. As a boy I was a brewer's apprentice, and I would creep up from my basement lodgings at night, to hear my master's sister play upon the spinet; and when I was caught, I was soundly whipped for it. Whipped, sir. But I am master now. Now I am accustomed to having my wishes met. My worldly position is such that, far from being whipped, I tolerate no slight or insult from any quarter.' It was a strange mixture of pathetic appeal and prickly pride: Fairfax thought of the dark young woman he had seen at the inn-yard and wondered what it must be like to live with such a man.

Leopold raised his eyebrows as Cordelia translated. 'I offer no insult, sir,' he said. 'I can only repeat that it is not convenient.'

'The inconvenience to me, in having my carriage and horses made ready, and coming here quite out of my usual habit, all for nothing, is considerable,' Mr Chilcott said, his face growing more purple and his hands grasping air. 'And now it rains, I see, and I shall be half drowned. However, no more of that. My home is Brockleigh House, at Kensington, sir, if that is your only offer – though I repeat, it is not my habit to go amongst the public. I may shake hands again with the boy, I hope?' Doing so, he shook his head and sighed and added with a cunningly assumed look of regret, 'Ah, a pity about that hobby-horse, eh? That *Steckenpferd*. Well, no matter.' He had taken note of the German word. Cunning indeed.

Leopold Mozart rang for the servant and said nothing more until Mr Chilcott, with several sharp backward looks, had gone. Then he let out a pent-up breath and threw his hands up.

'A stubborn donkey! Really, the intrusion . . .' Leopold plucked at his lip, and looked uncertain. 'I hope I was not uncivil. I do not doubt that the gentleman is truly devoted to music. But my nerves are simply not up to such an imposition. And it is not fair on Wolfgang, after all . . .'

The boy was seated at the desk, tickling his own chin with the end of his quill, and gazing as if in a dream at the door where the visitor had left. Looking at him, Fairfax wondered what it must be like to be this child – fêted, sought after, and in some ways treated, in spite of his father's disclaimer, like a superior fairground exhibit. The wonder was that he was so apparently unspoiled by it all.

'You acted very wisely, Herr Mozart,' said Miss Henlow, who had observed everything with mild, calm acuteness. 'And now I shall trouble you no longer. No, no, I must go at any rate. I must see to little Arthur. I try to supply as much of a mother's attention as I can, Mr Fairfax, though we have a wet-nurse living in. Charles would not have him sent out to nurse. It would have meant another parting, which in the circumstances . . .' She waved a white hand, then gave it to Fairfax, with a surprisingly strong grip. 'Sir, when I have talked to Charles, may we extend that invitation to sup?'

'Gladly. I am lodging at Dr Stagg's house, in Royal Hospital Row.'

'Ah! Is that the name of my physician I hear?' Leopold said.

'My landlord. I didn't know you were his patient, sir,' Fairfax said.

Though it was no great surprise that Dr Stagg, under whose modest roof he had taken a room for the duration of his stay, had not mentioned it. The young physician never talked about his patients – professional discretion but also shyness, thought Fairfax. His first breakfast with the tongue-tied young man had been a long agony of forced remarks and abysmal silences, though after a few days they were rubbing along together a little better.

'I expect a visit from him soon – indeed, he is a little late,' Leopold said, consulting a gold watch. 'Twelve is his usual hour. Not that he sets me up quite so well as your delicious posset, my dear,' he added gallantly in French, bowing over Miss Henlow's hand, 'but still, he is an estimable fellow.'

'He is, certainly,' Miss Henlow said, and Fairfax thought he detected for the first time an unsettling of her composure, and a tinge on her cheek, as she went over to the desk and said goodbye to Wolfgang. 'It looks mighty ingenious, even to my eye,' she said, turning over the manuscript sheets, and kissing the top of his head. '*Au revoir*, Wolfgangerl.'

'The storm is dying,' Leopold said at the window, which overlooked the street. 'Oh – and there is your brother-in-law coming, Fräulein Henlow. He must have finished his business early.'

'Yes, so he must. Goodbye, Nannerl; Frau Mozart; Mrs Linton.'

Again Fairfax saw a look of plain dislike on Cordelia's face as Miss Henlow took her leave. Jealousy? Well, Miss Henlow's peculiarly lucid beauty and grace would make her stand out at the most elegant gathering – but for him, all the advantage lay with Cordelia. She was just as he remembered her; and yet that, he realized, was a misleading phrase, for he had carried with him a mere conception of dark eyes, strongly marked brows, downright chin, and long limbs, very dry and abstract compared with the heart-stopping reality.

He was staring at her. This would never do.

'I must go too.' He said his farewells to the family, Leopold loading him with thanks again. Wolfgang jumped up and gave his hand a squeeze and said, 'Come back to see us, Herr Fairfax!'

Well, he would have liked to, for they were mighty interesting and the boy charming. Out of the question, though, because it would mean seeing Cordelia Linton, and getting his heart miserably embroiled again, and that he did not want.

'I will show you out, Mr Fairfax,' Cordelia said, in her soft, guttural voice. She preceded him down the stairs to the hall, then without a word turned and went down the passage by the stairs. He stood a moment in blind wretched confusion, until he saw that she had opened a door there and was faintly smiling at him.

'This is my own parlour,' she said. 'If you are not absolutely sick to death of company, and I'm sure I shouldn't blame you if you were, but if you really think you can bear it . . .'

He was in before he knew it, and found himself looking at a large painting of a stiffly smiling woman with an impossible neck, dangling a cluster of cherries in front of a hideous pink-eyed child. It hung above the fireplace of the little parlour, and there was no avoiding it.

'Sublime, is it not? The lady is some ancestor of Mrs Randall's, I think, and so the picture must hang, though I notice she does not care to have it in her own drawing room.'

'The lady of the house?'

'The elderly lady of the house. A matriarch. I live here as her companion-help, housekeeper, and whatnot. The family are gone to Bath for the summer, so I was left here to guard the silver, and make sure these strange foreign lodgers of ours do not get up to mischief.'

'How long have you—?'

'Six months, a little more.' Cordelia was avoiding his eyes, folding and refolding some sewing that lay on the table. Haphazard piles of books stamped her personality on the room, which otherwise was plain enough. He was surprised also to see a pair of steel spectacles. 'I am an atrocious needlewoman. But what rational creature wants to *sew*? I fancy my sight grows poor, so I am trying the effect of these.' She snatched the spectacles up and put them on. 'They make me look like a little owl, do they not?'

He smiled, but with constraint, which she saw.

'I am rambling, and not answering your question,' she said, throwing the spectacles down.

'I have asked no question, and nor do I have any right to.'

'Not so. You asked how long I had been here – and that means, in this peculiar situation. You did not expect to see me living as an old lady's companion, I think.'

'I never expected to see you again, Cordelia.'

He remained standing, at a distance, but when he spoke her name it was somehow as if he had taken a step towards her. What he said was true. The last time he had seen her was in Stamford, where her husband had been a newspaper proprietor; an enterprise which he had quixotically abandoned, taking his wife off to the West Country, as far as Fairfax knew. She had written a last letter to him, and he, on the move himself shortly afterwards, had seen it as a last letter in every sense. But there was more to his words than a mere statement of fact, and the faint tremble of her hands showed that she knew it.

'I might say the same, Mr Fairfax,' she said. 'And here, I had supposed only that I would vegetate quietly. Nothing more dramatic than going on tea-visits with Mrs Randall. Our remarkable lodgers seemed a curious enough turn of events – but this . . . I never dreamed . . .'

She sat down suddenly and heavily, her hands to her face. Fairfax felt as if something within himself had been wrenched violently askew.

'I disturb your peace,' he said, with an irresolute movement.

'I have no peace.' She almost snapped the words out, then closed her eyes for a moment. When she opened them again, there was a softness, and even a tenderness in them that caught him off balance.

'Whatever did you do with your wet stockings?' she said.

'Oh . . . I put them in my pocket.'

She laughed, low and long, shaking her head.

'Just as well I didn't make you change your breeches.'

'The only answers I can think of to that,' he said, 'are not suitable for polite company.'

'We were never polite company, were we?' She waved a hand, her face darkening again. 'I speak of things long ago. I should not, perhaps. Is it true what you were saying to Emma Henlow upstairs? About your life?'

'My life is unchanged since last we met, yes,' he said cautiously. 'Older, no wiser. I have a good enough post at present, but of course it will come to an end and then I must look for another. And you? I repeat I have no right, but I ask it anyhow. What has happened to you?'

'Well. You may gather I am separated from my husband.'

He just nodded, determined to make no visible response.

'George and I returned to London. He took up his old avocation. He seemed a little happier, for a time . . . It's hard to convey what it is like, being with – and loving – someone who is more or less continually unhappy all the time. Yes, of course, you think it is your fault; but also you are seduced into thinking the world is at fault too, for making this beloved person so wretched. And when he takes up the bottle, and will not leave off, why, then you are understanding again – because you think as he does, and of course it is all unfair, and who can blame him for seeking solace that way? And so you live a strange sort of life in which the soul finds its joy in slight improvements. If things are a little better today than yesterday, then you are thankful for that . . . Of course it could not go on. It took a toll of George's health, which broke down at last. He was very ill, and almost died.'

Here was another brush with mortality, Fairfax thought. Death, the stranger at the door. Yet he had learned nothing from his own meeting with that stranger, and he did not expect to hear that George Linton had either.

'Well, it changed things. Or so it seemed. At first, when he recovered, we seemed to have found one another again. There was talk of new beginnings and so forth. And he did not drink any more. The trouble was that when the unhappiness returned, there was no bottle to soften it. And, at last, when we quarrelled, he struck me.' Seeing his face, she said quickly, 'Oh, it was the first and only time. I am not one of those women who go on submitting to that sort of treatment. At least, so I had always prided myself – a little smugly, perhaps. I am less cocksure now. Because when it happened, and he was so very sorry afterwards, there was a

37

part of me that said, "There – *that's* done. Perhaps now he will be all right!" And that was something I had not understood before.'

He had been unable to look at her for some moments, and when he did he half expected her to be weeping. Instead he saw a wry, angular, despairing smile.

'This has turned out to be a merry meeting, has it not, Mr Fairfax? Never fear, I have almost done. It was soon after that that we separated. He drank again, and did not care that it would make him ill, and somehow it was his not caring that decided things for me. I could not bear to be in the position of suffering for him and with him again, and told him so, and I left. I heard of Mrs Randall's wanting a companion, and I came here. I lied, of course – told her I was a widow. She would not accept a woman who is living apart from her husband, because such a woman is – well, neither fish nor fowl, I suppose, but certainly not respectable. There – I must hope you will not give away my secret, Mr Fairfax.'

'Do you think me capable of that?' he said, almost angry with her.

'No,' she said promptly. 'I think you capable of no unjust action. But if you were to resent me, or think me stupid or contemptible, because I am still neither fish nor fowl, then – then I should quite understand.'

'A reconciliation – is it . . . ?'

'Likely? Probably not. Desired, by both parties? I can't say. I don't know.' She shrugged. 'Stupid and contemptible, as I said . . . Why have you not married, Mr Fairfax?'

He did not know whether to groan or laugh at the question. Instead he was brisk. 'You know my material situation. No settled home, no connections, a precarious vocation without any solid prospects. Hardly propitious for matrimony.'

'Oh, come – for any woman worth her salt, that in itself would be no impediment.'

'Wouldn't it?' he said, holding her eyes; and though she did not answer, he felt he had caught her in an admission. But there was no joy in it – or only a dark and painful sort of joy: as with this meeting. He felt he should go.

'You're very pale,' she said, arresting him.

'Yellow as a guinea, I fear,' he grimaced. 'Legacy of the fever I had, that's all.'

'Are you sure? You said you'd been ill too – and now you have taken a wetting. Dear God, Mr Fairfax, I hope you are not one of these men who say they are well when they are not. You are lodging with Dr Stagg, aren't you? I hope you will oblige me by asking him to have a look at you – just to be sure.'

He smiled. 'A lot to ask. I loathe being prodded about by doctors, and being bled turns me sick. I confess I quail at the sight of leeches . . . You do not call me Robert.' He hadn't meant to say it, but out it came.

'No. If I were to do that, then I should not know where I was. Which I suppose is another way of saying I would be . . . lost. Do you see?'

Before he could summon a reply, there came a loud hammering at the front door of the house.

'I'd better answer that,' she said, jumping up. 'The Randalls' servants are gone with them.'

'The Mozarts' man—'

'No, it should be me, really . . .'

She brushed past him. The scent of her hair filled his

head for a dizzy moment. Hearing an agitated voice at the door, he stepped out into the hall after her.

A boy was there, in the livery and huge boots of a postilion. He was leaning against the door-jamb, out of breath. Cordelia turned, surprise in her eyes.

'Mr Fairfax, perhaps you can help. Dr Stagg is wanted, most urgent. The boy has been to his house, but the servant there said he was due here at noon. 'Tis strange, he is always most punctual.'

'I fear I can't say where he may be. He said nothing of his appointments this morning – never does. What's amiss?'

'Gentleman at the Spread Eagle,' the boy said between gasps. 'Old gent – comes in – upstairs – shout – tumble – next thing, flat on his back at the bottom – looking like a landed fish.' The boy gave an impersonation, more vivid than compassionate. 'Ask me, he's dead as nits – but there, they said fetch surgeon—'

'What gentleman?' Fairfax said, exchanging a glance with Cordelia. 'Arrived in a carriage-and-four – name of Chilcott?'

'That's him. Are *you* a surgeon?' the boy said hopefully.

'No, alas, but I'll come . . . This is curious indeed,' he said to Cordelia.

'I'll come too,' she said. Just then Frau Mozart's voice spoke timidly from the top of the staircase.

'Oh, Frau Linton, is Wolfgangerl down there with you? We are missing him again. My husband is furious, but I said he cannot be far . . .'

'He's not with me, Frau Mozart,' Cordelia said. 'But as you say, he cannot be far. I am just going out – I'll see if I can spot him. There's someone taken ill at the inn – the man who was just here. They're looking for Dr Stagg, so if he comes here, will you tell him he's wanted at the Spread Eagle urgently?'

'God in heaven! Very well, Frau Linton. What a day! Storms are always unlucky . . .'

Fairfax and Cordelia followed the clumping boots of the postilion the short distance to the Spread Eagle. The rain had stopped, but the wide street was awash with puddles, which the boy took an absent pleasure in splashing through.

'If Wolfgang has slipped out again,' Cordelia said, 'he will be wanting more clean stockings. Incorrigible child! And yet it isn't like him, really. He is usually quite biddable. I wonder what can have got into him.'

Fairfax had an idea about that, but kept it to himself for now.

The Spread Eagle, a place of massy stone and little warped latticed windows, had the sleepy air of a country inn on which the town had crept up unawares; but the old place clearly did a good trade, and was buzzing like a stirred hive when Fairfax and Cordelia went in. People had crowded to the foot of the great panelled staircase in the vestibule. Grooms were jostling each other for a look, and one chambermaid, having had a look, was going off into swoons from which another was trying to rouse her by alternately flapping her apron in her face and pinching her unmercifully.

'Here's a doctor!' someone roared out, for no apparent reason, on seeing Fairfax. An impressively gaunt and harsh-featured woman, who had been kneeling in the middle of the cluster of people, rose and turned to Fairfax with a frown.

'You're not Dr Stagg,' she said.

'No. I'm only his lodger, I'm afraid. I've left word at the

house where he's expected, but . . .'

'Dr Stagg's lodger! Dr Stagg's lodger's here!' someone cried, as if that would do just as well.

'I fear the gentleman is beyond help at any rate,' the gaunt woman said. She moved aside to reveal the figure of Mr Gabriel Chilcott lying flat at the bottom of the stairs. His arms were outstretched, as if he had been arrested in some whimsical attempt to fly: one foot was propped on the bottom step. His unpowdered wig was half off, and this added to the grotesque quality of the expression on his upturned crimson face – an expression of sheer, horrified, and incredulous shock.

'Dear God,' murmured Cordelia, turning her face away after a moment: it was hard to look at those staring eyes.

Kneeling, Fairfax felt for a pulse, held the glass of his pocket-watch to the man's lips . . . no good. Death, the dark stranger, had exchanged places with Mr Gabriel Chilcott.

'You know him, sir?' the gaunt woman said.

'We met him just this morning. He came to call on the Mozart family, over at Five Fields Row—'

'The foreigners,' a groom said eagerly, 'I know 'em – and that's rum, because there's a little foreigner here. He must be a foreigner, I reckon, because he'll only talk lingo.'

'Wolfgang!' Cordelia cried.

Two maids had hold of the little boy, and were caressing him like affectionate jailers. Struggling free, he ran to Cordelia.

'He saw what happened, I reckon,' said the groom, stout and crimson-faced. 'When I heard the gentleman go crashing down, I came running to see, and here was the boy on the stairs, gaping like a choked throstle. We've tried talking to him, but we can't get sense out of him – only lingo.'

The boy looked frightened and near to tears. Taking his hand, Cordelia addressed him soothingly in German.

'It's all right, Wolfgangerl. Here, blow your nose. That's well. Now come, what are you doing here? You were missed again. We just want to know what has happened.'

'Papa will be angry,' the boy murmured.

'No one is angry, Wolfgangerl. Just be truthful.'

Licking his lips, the boy spoke, falteringly at first, and then in a rush. 'I slipped out because – I wanted to go after the man and perhaps say I would play for him. It was the hobby-horse, you see – I so wanted the hobby-horse. Well, I hurried after him down the street and into the inn-yard. He stopped there and ordered the men to have his carriage made ready – very sharp and fierce he was – and then he went stamping in and I followed. I thought there might be an instrument, anything, and I could play it – or I might at least just see the hobby-horse – and he went upstairs and into the room at the top and I was going to go up and knock but then . . . then . . .'

'All right, Wolfgangerl,' Cordelia said, patting his hand. 'Be calm.' She briefly translated what he had said – there were gasps at this feat, as if she had done a conjuring trick – and the gaunt woman nodded.

'Bespoke it,' she said. 'He wasn't staying the night, but he wanted a room, he said, where his lady could rest.'

'And what then, Wolfgangerl?'

'Then . . .' The boy looked timorously round at the ring of goggling faces. 'Then I was halfway up the stairs, and the man came out of the room again – suddenly – his eyes were round, like he had seen a ghost, and his hand went up to his chest, so – and then he made a horrible sound and he fell. His face was all purple and he fell forward and went past me down the stairs, bump, bump, all the way . . .'

Squeezing the agitated boy's hand, Cordelia translated, to more gasps.

'An apoplexy,' the gaunt woman said, nodding with grim satisfaction. 'Poor gentleman, he has the look of it. My late father was high-coloured like that.'

Wolfgang was saying something more, in a voice barely above a whisper. Cordelia bent to hear him.

'What is that, Wolfgangerl? Come, don't be afraid.'

'There was a man.' *Ein Mann* – that at least needed no translation, as the responding murmur of excitement showed. 'He came out of the room at the top of the stairs, with the lady. She came down the stairs, but he didn't. He ran the other way – down the passage.' The boy pointed an unsteady finger. 'There's the lady.'

There she was, indeed: the dark, delicate-looking young woman whom Fairfax had seen arriving with Mr Gabriel Chilcott. She stood in the shadow of the staircase, at a little distance – a distance magnified by her apparent composure: it was almost as if what had happened had nothing to do with her.

'You speak of me?' she said. Pale, though, Fairfax noted – in other circumstances he would have said pale as death.

'Ma'am.' Fairfax bowed. 'Ma'am, I'm so sorry . . . but the gentleman is your husband?'

'I am Jane Chilcott, certainly; and that is the mortal remains of my husband.'

This chill pedantry startled him. But of course grief and shock made people act in strange ways.

'Mrs Chilcott should have a seat, and air,' he said. He glanced at the gaunt woman, whose commanding manner proclaimed her the landlady of the inn, though in all other respects it was as if she had taken a vow not to resemble the traditional buxom hostess in any particular. She nodded, and conducted Mrs Chilcott to a chair in the adjoining bar-parlour, impatiently shooing her servants out of the way.

Once there the young widow closed her eyes and daintily held her brow with one white hand. A delicate blue vein pulsed at her temple.

'You are sure there are no – signs of life in my husband?'

'I fear not,' Fairfax said. 'As soon as the doctor can be found . . . but no, Mrs Chilcott, I fear not. I am very sorry.'

'You need pretend no grief, sir. You were surely not acquainted with him, and so his passing can be of no account to you.'

'Briefly acquainted,' Fairfax said, taken aback again. 'I was at the Mozarts' lodging when he called there to—'

'To see the wondrous boy. That was his purpose in coming here, quite out of his usual habit. The matter was of no interest to me, which is why I remained here at the inn . . . That, I suppose, is the boy?'

'Yes. The boy says—'

'I heard what the boy said. He must be mistaken – or else you, ma'am, mistook his words. 'Tis a foreign tongue, after all.'

Cordelia raised an eyebrow but said nothing.

'My husband returned, somewhat sooner than I had expected him. He came into the room where I was resting, and before he could speak a word he suffered – I know not what. His face coloured terribly, and as if felled by some great stroke he staggered backward, collapsing and tumbling down the stairs. As the boy said, I think.'

'Yes . . . It must be a great shock to you, ma'am,' Fairfax said. 'Unless your husband had a tendency to such affliction . . . ?'

'He was of an apoplectic temper,' Mrs Chilcott said, 'and his physician had concerns about the condition of his heart, which is why he took such particular care of himself, and lived very retired.'

'I see.' Fairfax hesitated. 'The boy also said something about seeing a man who—'

'Yes, so he did, and it must be a mistake, I repeat. There are men aplenty about the inn, as you can see, and no doubt he meant—'

'He said a man came out of your room, Mrs Chilcott,' Fairfax said, as respectfully as he could.

She gave him a look that he could only interpret as disgust.

'Sir, I think I am hardly likely to have a man with me in a private room at an inn that I never visited before in my life, am I?'

Used to the high-handedness of the grand and the great, Fairfax nevertheless flinched a little before the iciness of her reply. She was so very dry, tart and crisp, this young lady. Some people were undoubtedly earthy, some fiery, but Mrs Chilcott's nature seemed to be of a piece with the diamonds and pearls that glittered at her ears and throat. *Noli me tangere*, he thought: touch me not, for I am Caesar's. Somehow he could imagine Mrs Chilcott living to a great age.

'Perhaps a manservant,' he began, then remembered that

he had seen their arrival at the inn: no servant except the coachman.

'The boy may have seen a manservant belonging to the inn, passing by,' Mrs Chilcott said, 'but certainly not coming out of my room, because there was no man in my room.'

'But . . .' Fairfax stopped, feeling a warning touch on his arm from Cordelia. Of course, he could not keep pressing the poor woman like this. After all, what Wolfgang had said, taken together with the condition of the body, did not exactly suggest foul play.

It was just that little Wolfgang was a boy who, he was sure, would not lie about such a thing. It was just that Mr Gabriel Chilcott looked like a man who had reeled and died after getting the shock, literally, of his life.

Fairfax took the landlady aside.

'Ma'am, can you shed any light on this matter?'

'I can only tell you what I know, sir. As the lady says, she and the gentleman arrived by carriage this morning. He bespoke a room, and she withdrew there while he went out. The next thing I knew, he had come back – and this had happened.' The landlady frowned and lowered her voice. 'I'm sorry for the poor creature, but I can't help but wish it could have been under another roof than mine.'

'You did not know the gentleman?'

'He had never been here before. But the apoplectic temper I can well believe: he showed himself very exacting. Oh, was the room thoroughly aired, and when were the curtains last brushed, and so on. And he complained of insolence from a ruffian in the yard – I'm afraid I knew whom he meant at once. Young Runquest. He doesn't work here any more, but he's always about. He'll be gone soon, thank heaven: has another position.'

'I saw him earlier, I think . . . Then no one belonging to the inn can have gone into Mrs Chilcott's room?'

'No occasion to, sir: there was no food or drink wanted, and the gentleman was firm on her not being disturbed. So she was just let be—'

'She came down once, though,' put in the groom, who had been hovering about with very little pretence of not listening. 'I saw her, when I came through to tell missus we were out of neat's-foot oil. Saw her go through to the taproom, plain as day: but I didn't think nothing of it at the time.'

Another curiosity.

'The boy said the man didn't come down here,' Fairfax said, beckoning the landlady to the foot of the stairs, 'but went that way – a passage?'

'Yes, sir, there's a passage to the left, leading to another stairway. It's a dark one – comes out behind the scullery, next to the yard – and only the servants use it as a rule. But there's a stairway down, right enough,' she said, with a backward glance at the widow, who was being comforted by Cordelia.

An escape route, then – if there was a man, and if Wolfgang wasn't mistaken. A strange business. The death of Mr Gabriel Chilcott itself didn't suggest foul play, but something wasn't right.

Fairfax stepped as respectfully as he could around the body – large and masterful still, not shrunken as men often seemed to be by death – and slipped up the stairs. The door of the room immediately opposite the top stood open. He looked in. A typical country inn room, dim and smelling of dust and beeswax and the acrid ghost of old chamber pots: heavy bed-curtains, a couple of high-backed tapestried chairs. It all looked quite undisturbed, and there was certainly, Fairfax noted, no sign of the promised hobby-horse. Thinking, if not speaking, ill of the dead, Fairfax detected a meanness and double-dealing in the late Mr Chilcott.

He explored the passage to the left. Two doors, one leading to an empty guest room, the other to a store-closet, and at the end, as the landlady had said, a dark winding staircase. He contented himself with peeping into it. The man, if man there had been, would have been long gone by now.

Coming down the main staircase, he found that Dr Stagg had arrived. The physician had thrown off his hat and was bending over the body almost before any of the gawkers and gossipers, still gathered around the foot of the stairs, had noticed he was there. This was typical of what Fairfax knew of Dr Frederick Stagg, his temporary landlord, who had the most unassuming manner of any medical man he had ever known. Even surgeons and apothecaries, lower in the social scale, often cultivated a grand manner, and few were the physicians who did not adopt the professional puffed wig, the silver-headed cane, the swagger and the pompous utterance. But on several occasions Dr Stagg had come into the parlour without Fairfax even knowing he was there, though he was quite a big man, stocky and fair, with blunt yeoman features. At the wrists of his plain brown coat he wore linen bands instead of the lace that his colleagues, in spite of its unlovely tendency to absorb blood, had a weakness for.

'A servant saw me in the street, and told me I was wanted here,' Dr Stagg said, glancing up at Fairfax. 'Too late, I'm afraid.'

'They thought to find you at the Mozarts' at noon, where I happened to be,'

'I was detained.'

Uncommunicative even for Dr Stagg. Meanwhile he was thorough in his examination, even though the patient was beyond his help. Fairfax briefly relayed Wolfgang's account of what had happened, as well as Mrs Chilcott's. He wanted to ask: *Is there more to this?* but there were still too many spectators, in spite of the landlady's roundly urging them to disperse, for him to be discreet.

'Well.' Dr Stagg stood up. 'A severe seizure of the heart. Certainly sufficient to kill him without the fall. Chilcott, you say? I know of him, but have never attended him. I wonder if there had been trouble with the heart before.'

'I gather so. He seems to have been a semi-invalid. Dr Stagg, that expression on his face . . .'

'It is dismaying, indeed. Well, there is no reason why he should not be covered now, and moved somewhere more suitable.'

'But is it not an expression of – well, the utmost shock and horror?'

'It has that appearance.' Dr Stagg, who habitually spoke in this cautious, cumbersome way, mopped his broad brow with his handkerchief: the storm had died without clearing the sultry air. 'But such sudden and mortal strokes often have – an unfortunate effect on the features.'

'To this extent?'

'Well, seldom perhaps.' Dr Stagg gave the dead man a

last, searching look, not without compassion, and then turned to Fairfax. 'A shock may indeed precipitate such a collapse – as may overexertion, overeating, fatigue, mounting distress of mind . . . any number of things. The fact remains, Mr Fairfax, that this man's death has a pathological cause. There is obviously no question of a blow or anything like that.'

Fairfax nodded. 'Of course. I suppose, then, there is no need for a coroner to sit upon the body.'

'I would doubt it. It might be as well to consult Mr Yelverton, the magistrate. But I fear that this is, alas, just one of the thousand natural shocks that flesh is heir to.' The doctor produced the quotation with one of his small, rare smiles, which gave him a shy and intensely young look, though he was about Fairfax's age. 'I had better speak to the widow.'

Fairfax was anxious to do that himself too, but he was unsure how to go about it. As Dr Stagg implied, there was surely no question of crime about this death, sudden as it was, and peculiar as the circumstances surrounding it were. There was little justification for him to go cross-examining the young woman who had just lost her husband. It was simply that some things didn't add up: notably this question of a strange man coming out of Mrs Chilcott's room, as well as the groom's account of Mrs Chilcott being seen downstairs. He mused on this whilst the landlady gave directions for moving the body – 'The gentleman can be laid in the Princess Room. The room was once occupied by Princess Amelia, and is the finest in the house' – and took the opportunity of rescuing Wolfgang, who had been taken into caressing custody again by the two maids. He looked wretched, and said he wanted to go home.

'So you shall, Wolfgang, very soon,' Fairfax said soothingly. 'Just tell me again – you are sure you saw a man come out of that room?'

The boy nodded miserably.

'Can you say what sort of man? He is no one you see here, is he?'

'No. I don't think so. I only saw him very quick, before he ran away. He was – well, not like the poor dead man. Different.'

'How so?'

'A white face not a red one. Not old. Thin like you.'

Fairfax grunted.

'He was more like – well, like the poor lady.'

'Mrs Chilcott?' Well, that was unexpected. 'Dark, slim, then? And how was he dressed?'

Wolfgang shrugged. 'Just in clothes.'

'Would you know him again if you saw him?'

'Yes, perhaps.' The boy tugged at his lip. 'But Herr Fairfax, I don't want to, you see. I didn't mean any harm.'

'You've done no harm, Wolfgang. Nothing that has happened is any fault of yours. And soon you shall go home, and we will make all well with your Papa.'

He found Dr Stagg commiserating with the widow, awkwardly. On his first day at Dr Stagg's, Fairfax had watched him extract a carter's rotten tooth with impeccable command, dexterity and authority; but once in a social situation, all those qualities seemed to leave him. Mrs Chilcott, though, looked on him at least with a more friendly eye than on Fairfax, especially when, as delicately as he could, he raised the matter of the groom's having seen her come downstairs.

'If you suppose me an *habituée* of taprooms, sir,' she said thinly, 'then nothing I say will convince you otherwise. What this can have to do with my husband's death, I cannot conceive.'

He was, in short, an unfeeling monster – even Dr Stagg gave him a frown; and when the landlady came to speak to the widow of the arrangements for the laying out of the deceased, Cordelia took him aside with a very sardonic look.

'I am aware of your past predilection for ferreting out villainy,' she said, 'but really, Mr Fairfax, the poor woman is just bereaved. And this is no murky matter of a man with a knife in his back in a locked room with a fish in his pocket and the letter M written in the dust.'

'What an imagination you have . . . You must confess, though, it is curious.'

'Hm. If I did not know you better, I would accuse you of being rather too ready to believe that a woman must always be up to no good. In fact, I *will* accuse you of it.'

'Well, before I refute the base accusation, answer me this: do you suppose young Wolfgang to be a liar?'

'Absolutely not. And before you say it, it is odd that the groom should claim to have seen Mrs Chilcott downstairs. Odd, but no more. There is no crime here, Mr Fairfax, but there is a suddenly bereaved woman – who is likely, surely, to be confused and inconsistent. As well as none too pleased at being interrogated by a complete stranger.'

'True.' He felt ashamed, but only a little, because he still felt he was right. Mrs Chilcott was keeping some sort of secret. But as Cordelia suggested, it was hardly the time or place to press her on it.

The landlady was giving orders for Mrs Chilcott's carriage to be made ready: she was to go home. Hearing this, Cordelia approached her again.

'Ma'am – forgive me, but you mean to go alone? Is there no one who can be sent for, to be with you . . . ?'

'No one,' Mrs Chilcott said.

'Then – perhaps someone could go with you. Just so that—'

'No: I thank you, ma'am. I would rather go alone, and be at home. We have a very good steward, who will know what to do. With the remains, and so on.' Her costive, patrician voice with its pitched-back vowels made this sound like the disposal of the leftovers after dinner. But there was something coiled and bristling about Jane Chilcott too: Fairfax suddenly came in for it. 'You do not suggest, I hope, that I convey my husband home with me in the carriage,' she said, turning to him sharply.

Unfair, as he hadn't thought any such thing. Though he thought about it now, and felt queasy.

'No,' she resumed coolly, 'I shall go alone. I am to be found at Brockleigh House, if I am wanted for any reason. I cannot think why I should be.' Though she had turned her back on him, that too was for Fairfax.

'As you wish it, ma'am. But you'll take a little brandy and water, I hope, to support you – Nancy, fetch the brandy, sharp now – and I'll make sure the carriage is brought right to the door.' The landlady was all efficiency. 'And don't trouble about your poor husband – you may rest assured that there will be a good, respectable woman to see to him, and sit by him tonight. I have known the loss of a husband, ma'am. All the comfort I can offer is that I bore up: in time,

I bore up.' In about ten minutes, by the formidable look of her.

As for Mrs Chilcott's response to her sudden widowhood, Fairfax was still intrigued. No tears, though that in itself meant nothing – stunned grief was often dry; but there was something covert, hidden, false in the air, and he couldn't help but sniff curiously at it, despite knowing quite well that it was, as Cordelia had hinted, none of his business.

Brandy, at any rate, he fancied too; and as one of the kind-hearted maids suggested that 'the pretty dear' – Wolfgang – should have a drink of small beer to revive him, they repaired to the bar-parlour. It was a place of low, soot-grimed beams, high-backed wooden settles so warped out of shape by age they looked as if the beery atmosphere had seeped into their very timbers and rendered them permanently tipsy, and more nooks and corners than it seemed possible for one room to have. Huddled in these, little knots of drinkers could be dimly seen through the fug of tobacco smoke, undisturbed by the commotion: clearly such a minor spectacle as the collapse of an old gentleman was not enough to draw them from the serious business at hand.

As well as the small beer, the maid brought Wolfgang a pastry to eat, and a high stool to sit on; and perched by the bar, his little buckled shoes swinging and his face wreathed in crumbs, the boy looked much more cheerful about everything. A gaitered farmer trudging in saluted him with 'Hullo, half-pint!' and added to Fairfax and Cordelia, 'Bright as a bee, your younker, ain't he?' which made Cordelia smile, and gave Fairfax so many undefinable feelings he was struck dumb for several moments – long enough to become aware of an angry female voice detaching itself from the general hum of the bar-parlour.

It came from the other end of the room, by the cold fireplace: it rose in shrill thirds, like an operatic heroine in trouble, then became a wholly unmusical screech of fury.

'Bastard! Double-dealing bastard! Don't you dare walk away from me!'

The man to whom these remarks were addressed was doing just that, or trying to. He was, Fairfax saw, that same towering Samson he had watched in the inn-yard earlier. The same, but without the swagger. His lips were pursed and his stubbly cheeks tinged with an incongruous pink as he tried to disengage himself from the young woman clinging to his arm.

'You leave go of me. I'm warning you, Tabby—'

'Don't you walk away from me! That's not right, Jemmy, devil take you, it's not right!' The young woman fairly screeched the words.

'Oho, you're a fine one to talk of right,' the big man said, turning a kind of fierce smile on her. 'You're a precious one, Tabby, ain't you? Ain't you the one that was a-hugging and a-cooing with that cove behint the stables this morning? Ain't you? Queer if you ain't, because I saw you, Tabby. So where's your squealing now?'

After an open-mouthed moment, the young woman cried, 'That's not true – I don't know what you're talking about, Jemmy, I swear! Oh, don't be a beast, Jemmy – don't talk like that to me. I'm your Tabby – you know it. How can you pretend—'

'You ain't my Tabby, and I ain't your Jemmy,' he said grimly, 'and *this*, according, is a mite out of place.' He prised her hand from his arm, and shook it off as if it were a particularly slimy species of toad.

'Bastard . . . !' The woman went on to such a torrent of obscenities that Cordelia instinctively covered little Wolfgang's ears with her hands, even though he couldn't understand them. Jemmy tried again to walk away. This time the woman flung herself after him, pounding her fists on his back.

He turned, taking the blows on his chest as easily as if he were washing under a pump. The young woman was slender, but she was putting everything into those blows, and Fairfax winced.

'Look at you.' The big man spoke with wondering contempt, while the hitting went on. 'Whatever possessed me in the fust place, that's what I can't fathom. Hey well, water under the bridge. You'd best sit you down now, Tabby. You've had your squeal, old dear. Take another drink, eh? All you're fit for, I'm afraid.'

The young woman paused, fists in air, in a sudden coldness of fury. Her voice was thick. 'You might think you can walk away, Jemmy Runquest. Done it afore, I dare say. But you can't, not this time, because it's gone past that. I'll drag you down with me, Jemmy, I swear, and I won't let go . . .'

'Oh yes you will,' he said, quite casually, looking disdainfully at the hand she laid on his arm, and then hitting out with a wide backhanded slap. She staggered, nearly fell. Before he had time for second thoughts, Fairfax sprang forward and placed himself between them. His eyes were level with Jemmy Runquest's chin.

'Don't touch her again, sir.'

The big man looked coolly down at him – a measuring look. Fairfax juggled several vivid mental images of himself flying backwards – over the bar-counter, crashing through the window – and wondered which would hurt least.

'Any business of yourn, friend? Can't think how it is, you know, but if I'm wrong, of course' – Jemmy's shovel-like hands twitched – 'I'm ready to be corrected.'

'You do not strike women.' All at once Fairfax was surprised by the flaring rage inside him. And he wondered for a moment whether it was really Cordelia's absent husband, not this present brute, that he was confronting. 'It is a coward's part, sir. Would you be thought a coward?'

'Oho. I see it.' A treacherous good humour was on Jemmy Runquest's face now. He glanced back at the drooping girl and winked. 'Well, good luck to you, friend. Confidentially, now, she topes too much, and she squeals altogether too much – but there is good sport to be had there, friend, if nothing better offers.'

He grinned, then snuffed the grin out like a light and swaggered off, clapping his hat on to his head with a great swipe as if dealing a death blow to some snared animal.

The young woman had slumped back on to the settle by the hearth. Her dishevelled hair only partly covered the livid mark on her cheek.

'You're hurt,' Fairfax said. 'There is a doctor here, if you—'

'What good is *he*?'

She gave him a glare, and the long, flat hostility of it took him aback, though the film of tears might have been partly responsible. He was surprised too by her beauty, which the rage had distorted: a full-lipped, sulky, feline, but somehow very natural, beauty. Her hair, abundant and with the glossy blue-black of a crow's wing, had a single dab of grey in it, though she could not have been above twenty-one. Her frock of sprigged muslin was pretty, old-fashioned, and spotted with drink. A mistress's hand-me-down, he thought, with a new impulse of pity – which she seemed supernaturally to sense, for she gave him an unequivocal gesture and picked up her glass of gin.

'Leave me alone.'

'Very well. If you're sure you won't see the doctor . . . You witnessed nothing, by the by, of the old gentleman's collapse on the stairs?'

She stared at him as if he were mad. She dipped her lips in her gin and grumbled to herself, 'Gentleman . . . Jemmy's no gentleman, not he, for all his fancy talk. But I'll gentle him, oh, I'll gentle him right enough . . .'

Cordelia beckoned him away.

'Come. You did your best. I fear there's not much to be done with Tabitha Dance.'

'You know her?'

'She used to be serving-maid at the Porteous house, next door to us. She was dismissed a few weeks ago. Drink, loose morals, *und so weiter*. Apparently she hasn't found another place. Tabitha does have something of a reputation hereabouts – deserved, I fear.'

It was on his lips to say that now *she* was believing the worst of a woman, but she anticipated him.

'Yes, I know, perhaps I judge harshly. But she *is* one for the men, no doubt of it. And the weakness for drink you can see yourself. It has greatly reduced her, poor creature.'

'What a world of acid satisfaction there is when one

59

woman says of another "poor creature".'

She looked at him narrowly, then poked him hard in the ribs.

'That lady is sad,' said Wolfgang suddenly. He had been watching everything with lucid, wondering eyes.

And it was true. For all the maudlin drunkenness, there was a profound sadness about Tabitha Dance: looking back, Fairfax felt it come from her like a wave. No sophisticate, he thought: a simple country girl at bottom. The way she scrubbed at her eyes with the heel of her hand was as childlike as anything Wolfgang might do.

'And the big brute, I suppose, is her latest beau?' Fairfax said.

'So I believe. She has been seen about with him a good deal. But his intentions, it would seem, are not honourable.'

'Looking at him, I doubt they ever are.'

'Well . . . The fact is, Mr Fairfax, that a woman always thinks *she* will be the exception, and will change the man's ways. Call it hope, or vanity.' Cordelia smiled quickly, but too late to cover the chasm of unhappiness.

They left the bar-parlour. At the front of the inn the Chilcotts' carriage was being brought round, and at the door the gaunt landlady, cradling Mrs Chilcott's arm, was murmuring gaunt consolation. Dr Stagg was there too, stocky and silent: also troubled-looking, Fairfax thought. The presence of death, perhaps – emblem of failure to a conscientious doctor, although most of the physicians he had known were phlegmatic about it, considering it the patient's own fault if he expired.

All at once there was a shout, a shrill squeak, a crash, the alarmed whinnying of bucking horses. Grooms swore and ran: the landlady pulled Mrs Chilcott back. The carriage was skewed over to one side just as if, Fairfax thought, a deep pothole had suddenly opened under it. Then he saw something lurching and twirling across the cobbles, like a huge coin set spinning. It was the rear left-side wheel.

Amidst the confusion, Fairfax noticed the landlady's look of gloomy resignation: first a dead body in the Princess Room, now this. But it was the reaction of Mrs Chilcott that he took especial notice of. Gone was the queenly chill. Fairfax would almost have said that the mishap to her carriage affected her more than the death of her husband. And when one of the milling grooms piped up: 'What a mercy you weren't a-bowling along the King's Road when it happened, ma'am!' the hysteria she had so markedly lacked came up and out. Jane Chilcott screamed, sobbed and shook. The landlady had to half carry her back into the inn.

The groom with the brick-red face was bending over the cobbles. He picked something up that looked to Fairfax like a metal dish, and held it up to renewed mutterings from his fellows.

'That's rum. Almighty rum.'

'What's amiss?' Fairfax said.

'Oh, not a great deal, sir. It can be mended soon enough, though we'd best send over to the smith to be sure. Is that wheel aright there, Tom? Ah. Thought so. Well, that *is* rum.' The groom scratched under his horsehair wig.

'What is?'

'Why, the crown of the hub's come off, sir. Just come right off. *That's* what's rum.'

Fairfax, who had broken two watches by overwinding

them and did not understand the technicalities of a meat-jack, tried to nod sagely. 'And that would happen because . . . ?'

'Why, because someone loosened it.'

Fairfax stared at him.

'Could there be another reason for the – for that coming off? Wear and tear, perhaps?'

'Oh, I *have* known it happen. That fellow who took a spill coming over Ebury Bridge, Tom, d'you recall? Only he was a one-hoss farmer with an old cart that should have been firewood years afore, you see. But as for a spanking vehicle like this – why, I don't reckon it's hardly been used.'

'That's a fact,' put in the old coachman, who had come tottering down from the box and was trembling all over. 'Poor master, God rest him, didn't hold with gadding about overmuch. But carriage and beasts and tackle and all had to be in the best of repair – he was particular about that. Particular about everything, God rest his soul.'

The younger grooms were taking the horses from the traces. Fairfax looked at the slewed carriage.

'If the wheel was interfered with,' he said, 'it cannot have been done before the Chilcotts came here, can it?'

'I doubt it. They'd never have got here,' the red-faced groom said. 'Just fancy that 'ere coach bowling along smart as you like, and then off comes the wheel – oh, 'twouldn't have been pretty.'

'Don't speak of it,' the tottering coachman said faintly, looking for somewhere to sit down.

'Then it must have been done here – while the carriage was in the coach-house,' Fairfax said. 'How could that be?'

'Easy enough,' the coachman said, propping himself

against the pump and holding on with both hands. 'If anyone was vicious enough to want to, mind. Once 'twas all settled, I went into the kitchen for a dish of tea. Naught stronger – not with my master. Particular about that he was.'

'So someone must have slipped into the coach-house and . . .' Fairfax looked helplessly at the groom. 'Could someone have done that?'

'Plenty of tools and tackle around,' the groom said, nodding solemnly. 'No difficulty there. And there's always such comings and goings about the yard, 'twould be no great matter to 'scape being noticed. But 'tis just as the old gaffer here shapes it: who'd be such a vicious creetur as to do it?'

Someone, Fairfax thought dizzily, who wanted the carriage to crash on its way home. A clumsy design, perhaps; but at the least there was cruel mischief in it.

At worst, it was murderous.

Fairfax went over to Dr Stagg.

'I think now, Dr Stagg, we have no choice but to speak to the magistrate.'

Three

Before repairing to the house of the magistrate with Dr Stagg, Fairfax parted from Cordelia and Wolfgang.

'Will he be needed again for questions?' Cordelia said. 'I truly think he's had enough for one day.'

'I hope not.' Fairfax took the boy's hand. 'I must bid you farewell, Wolfgang.'

'Shall we see you again, Herr Fairfax?'

'Hush, Wolfgangerl,' Cordelia said, pushing back her hair with an irritable hand, 'you mustn't ask such things.'

'I hope to – I hope perhaps to wait upon you again,' Fairfax said awkwardly. 'And – Mrs Linton.' It typified their relationship, he thought with sudden wretchedness, that there was no simple formula of goodbye between them.

Before going to the magistrate, he spoke again to the head groom and the landlady of the Spread Eagle. While the carriage was repaired, Mrs Chilcott was resting in the landlady's own parlour, she said.

'Call it resting, anyhow. The poor creature is half distracted. Who wouldn't be?'

'She has said nothing about this matter of the carriage wheel – about who could have done it?'

'She has not. And for my part, sir, I can assure you nothing of the kind has ever happened before at the Spread Eagle, not in my time. I have the utmost trust in everyone in my employ, sir: all are as shocked as I.'

So he believed; but while everyone was willing to help, useful information was thin on the ground. It might have been easier if the Spread Eagle had not been such a thriving place; but though it was not a main posting-stage, its position on one of the major approaches to London, its proximity to the popular resort of Ranelagh Gardens, its ample stabling and good beer and victuals made it the busiest spot in these parts. There was room in its big dim parlours for everything from dining farmers to trysting lovers: it hired out saddle-horses and post-chaises and took delivery of letters and parcels. There were a few habitual and recognizable denizens – notably, he gathered, Tabitha Dance, who had fallen into a tearful doze, and Jemmy Runquest, who was gone – but on the whole, a conflux of strangers was the rule at the Spread Eagle. As for the coach-house, it was a long, shingle-roofed building forming one side of the stable block, and it was open at both ends. Anyone – anyone who was not constitutionally ham-fisted like Fairfax, that is – could have slipped in and tampered with the wheel.

Why? The only answer was that someone had been at the Spread Eagle who had a deadly grudge against either or both of the Chilcotts. And one of them was already dead before the carriage was brought out.

It was all a very curious business. But it was at once clear that Mr Yelverton, the local Justice of the Peace, had no taste for curiosities – not human ones, at any rate.

He had a modestly handsome Palladian house down by

the river beyond the Royal Hospital – an Arcadian suburb where old mansions built by Tudor grandees mingled with the brick villas of City merchants amongst lush gardens. Inside, it was an antiquarian's dream or housekeeper's nightmare. Mr Davis Yelverton was a collector and connoisseur specializing in Roman and Egyptian antiquities – Fairfax remembered now seeing his name at the foot of some deathly dry monograph on Etruscan paterae – and the evidence of his enthusiasm was not confined to cabinets: it was everywhere. Fairfax was terrified of making a sudden movement and sending some priceless monstrosity crashing to the floor. Mr Yelverton had turned his attention to China too, so there was plenty of delicate porcelain to nearly knock over, and his walls were crowded with Italian Old Masters – baleful martyrdoms mostly, with saints languidly pointing out the arrows and flames that transfixed and burned them; but dominating everything were the grim relics of unmerciful civilizations. The magistrate received them in a morning room crowded with sightlessly staring busts, hideous animal-headed gods looking sideways, and fragmentary vessels that all looked as if they had been meant to hold blood.

'I must notify you, gentlemen, that I am sorely pressed for time,' Mr Yelverton said. 'I am making ready for a new expedition. To Italy. I depart for Naples in three days. There is, dear me, much to do. But of course I am yours to command.' So saying, he pulled a gold watch from his fob, with as much effort as if he were lifting a full bucket from a well. He was an elderly, sallow, emaciated gentleman, limply ensconced in a great wing chair: his face, small and pained and vinegary, was framed by a vast powdered pigeon-wing wig. There seemed scarcely strength enough in his lace-draped wrists to handle the slightest of his marble and bronze treasures.

Fairfax related the events at the Spread Eagle. The magistrate listened with sour, tooth-sucking impatience, his hand absently straying to a sheaf of papers by his chair.

'Dear me. I am sorry for the gentleman. Such a, hm, reminder. In the midst of life we are in death.'

He certainly was, thought Fairfax, who was finding the dusty debris oppressive. Rationalist though he was, he would not have spent a night alone with these antlered horrors for a thousand pounds.

'This was a natural stroke of mortality, I take it, Dr Stagg?' Mr Yelverton went on. 'There is no necessity for a coroner's inquest?'

'There was no violence done, sir, and I would attribute the suddenness of the collapse to the condition of the gentleman's heart,' Dr Stagg said. 'In which case—'

'In which case, there is really no need for me to be troubled in this way. I repeat, I am sorry for the gentleman, and his widow. I know him by name, though not in a happy connection. An acquaintance of mine became embroiled in a lawsuit with him: he was, I gather, inclined to such quarrels. But there, in the matter of his death, at least, I see no occasion for the law to be involved.'

Quickly Fairfax raised the matter of the mysterious man seen leaving Mrs Chilcott's room – but just as quickly Mr Yelverton cut him off.

'This, dear me, is a private matter, sir – the private business of private individuals which, unless a crime or the suspicion of a crime is present, is no concern of the law. I think you speculate, sir, and such speculation is' – he writhed fastidiously in his chair – 'utterly distasteful. I would only add that the testimony on which you rely is that of a child. A child who is also, surely, a seeker of attention, as he has apparently been encouraged to see himself as a showman's exhibit. Dr Stagg, may I trouble you to ring that bell?'

'Sir,' Fairfax said, 'I am convinced that the boy's account is to be believed. There is simply no reason for him to invent such a tale.'

'Boys,' Mr Yelverton said, speaking as if referring to some obscure species of newt, 'have been known to lie for sheer devilment. And that does not alter the fact that we may not enquire into the private affairs of these people when no crime has been committed . . . Ah, Runquest. I wanted you half an hour since. Where were you?'

Fairfax was startled to see Jemmy Runquest come in and make a manservant's bow. His eyes took in Fairfax with a flicker of recognition tinged with mockery.

'Errand for the housekeeper, sir.'

'Tut, she should know better. Well, lift me to the desk.'

Promptly, and with surprising gentleness, Jemmy Runquest bent and lifted Mr Yelverton out of his wing chair and carried him across the room. For a grotesque moment the old man, dainty legs crossed and dangling, arm around the brawny servant's shoulders, resembled some unthinkable bride. The legs, though, Fairfax saw, had reason to be delicate. Mr Yelverton did not have the use of them. Placing him in the desk chair, Runquest rearranged his master's limp shanks as if setting down a marionette.

'Now. The six large packing cases have been sent on ahead,' Mr Yelverton said, consulting a list written on vellum. 'The smaller cases are to be taken out of the store closet – make sure they are *thoroughly* cleaned. The smaller of the trunks likewise, and then stocked with personal linen. The larger is for bedsheets – there is no trusting Italian inns. Bring it down to the housekeeper. Return to me when you are done.'

'Yes, sir.' No hint of that swaggering mockery, at any rate, in Runquest's relation to Mr Yelverton. When the servant had gone, Mr Yelverton raised his eyebrows at Fairfax and said, 'A riding accident, sir, deprived me of mobility, and obliges me to rely upon a servant in ways out of the common. Satisfactory candidates are not easy to come by. That fellow has just joined my service, but I think he promises well. An uncultured brute, of course. But strong arms and an adaptable spirit are needed more than the graces, especially on our travels.'

Fairfax said: 'He goes with you to Italy?'

'He goes with me, and is, I think, sensible of his good fortune. He will see the Bay of Naples, and set foot upon the fabled slopes of Vesuvius. Such opportunities come seldom to a man of his station. And now, my dear sirs, I fancy you need not detain me longer. This regrettable death—'

'Is only part of the matter,' Fairfax said. 'The mischief done to the Chilcotts' carriage surely warrants investigation.'

'Perhaps it does,' Mr Yelverton said with a sigh, 'but really, sir, I don't see what you expect me to do. I agree that it signifies some malicious intent; criminal damage, indeed, a disgraceful proceeding. But if, as you say, you have made enquiries at the Spread Eagle, and can find no hint of what person or persons might have been responsible, then I fear the matter will end there. It is possible that the widow may have some notion of what was behind it, but I imagine she is scarcely in a state to consider the question just now . . . You will forgive the impertinence, sir, but precisely who are you?'

Fairfax gave an account of himself. Mr Yelverton's crab-apple look grew sourer at the words 'private tutor', but when Fairfax went on to tell of the assistance he had given to the law in the past, mentioning the eminent Justices Fielding and Welch, there was a change. He saw on Mr Yelverton's face the covert glow of a man who sees himself being saved some trouble.

'In that case, my dear sir, I would suggest that you conduct such enquiries into these matters as you see fit, and *if* you should come across anything requiring the intervention of the law – I lay stress upon the *if*, for you must understand I am a busy man – then by all means come to me. Bearing in mind, sir, that in three days I shall be gone from here. For my part, I am convinced there is nothing to be done. I fear I discern the outlines of a classic situation – you said the widow was considerably younger than her husband, I believe? Ah – just so. Well, contumely will always attach to her, I fear, because of that. She might have been a hundred miles away, and folk will still whisper that she connived at his death; she might have been a model of devotion, and still the gossip will be that she was glad to be rid of him. So the world wags. Bad faith, duplicity – as a magistrate I see so much of these that I expect nothing else from mankind. Just the other week an unfortunate came begging in this parish – a ragged sailor, lamed in the service of his country. He carried a written testimonial from the captain of his vessel, which had gone down in a dreadful storm off

Finisterre. Here, surely, was honest worth. I examined the testimonial. It was a clever fraud, forged by one of those broken-down clerks who perpetrate such things for a fee.'

'Screevers,' said Fairfax, who had come across such men in his own years of scraping and scribbling for a living.

'That is the cant term, I believe. The fellow was no lamer than you, and had never been within ten miles of the sea. And that deception was trifling compared with some I have known: beggars who have rubbed themselves with saltpetre to create suppurating sores, for instance, putting themselves to more pain and trouble than if they had undertaken the hardest of labour. Faced with such things, what can a man be but a Stoic? Or should we ascribe it, perhaps, to original sin?' A harsh playfulness now. 'Dr Stagg, what say you, as one who ministers to the ills of the body? Are our souls sick too?'

Fairfax felt sorry for the young physician, who looked very ill at ease being catechized thus. But Stagg, after the customary shuffle of his large feet, surprised him by saying, 'Some souls are, sir. Of that I am convinced, though I do not have your experience. From what I have seen . . . But of course, such things are outside my scope,' he tailed off, gruffly.

'Ah . . . ? Well, then I fear human nature has not changed much since the days of dear Seneca,' Mr Yelverton said, as if he remembered them well; and taking up a volume, looked fondly into it. As he did not trouble to glance up again, Fairfax considered them dismissed.

'Mr Yelverton once told me that he considered the Christian religion a sentimental imposture,' Dr Stagg said as they left the magistrate's neatly barbered grounds.

'Indeed? An uncommon admission.' Fairfax wondered what Stagg had made of that. On first coming to lodge under the young doctor's roof, he had assumed that Frederick Stagg would have the rationalist tendencies of his profession. But he saw several devotional volumes amongst his landlord's small store of books, and had been faintly embarrassed to hear, from Stagg's room at bedtime, an audible stream of boyish yet wrenchingly sincere prayer. An intriguing mixture, like the stiff correctness of manner that was occasionally broken by surprising and seemingly unconscious crudities, deep belches after meals, a graceless 'What?' to an unheard question.

'That's Mr Yelverton's business, of course,' Dr Stagg grunted, looking at the sky. 'Damned hot still. Storm didn't clear it. I had better call on Herr Mozart.'

'He seemed pretty well when I saw him.' Fairfax went on to explain how he came to have met the Mozart family. He skated over his previous acquaintance with Cordelia Linton. Somehow Stagg, though they got along well enough, was not a man he felt he could talk to about it. Emotionally, there was a drum-skin tightness about the man: confidences would just come bouncing back.

'Oh, and I met a Miss Henlow there also, their neighbour. Perhaps you know her – a most charming woman.'

'You think so?'

The words came out with such an abrupt jerk, and such a sharp and almost suspicious look, that Fairfax was puzzled. And then, seeing Stagg's flushed round cheeks, he was not puzzled.

'Yes, very charming, I think,' he said blandly. He didn't

73

think anything really. He had just been trying to keep off the subject of Cordelia.

Which was sad nonsense, as he already knew that he was going to accompany the doctor to Five Fields Row, and speak to Cordelia again.

She did not seem surprised to see him. There was even a tea-tray set ready in her parlour, with kettle singing on the fire beneath the picture of the broken-necked woman. Yet there was something absent about her too, that made him wonder whether he had overstepped some mark in coming back.

'Well, Mr Yelverton I think does not want much to be troubled with the matter,' he said. 'Though I am free to pursue it, or waste my time pursuing it . . . I saw that brute Runquest there. He has just been taken into Mr Yelverton's service, it seems, and goes with him to Italy very soon.'

'Indeed? That would explain his eagerness to disentangle himself from poor Tabitha. Well, she would do better without him – though I fear, from what we saw today, that she is too smitten to see it in that light.'

'It's a good place for him. Has he a very ill reputation hereabouts?'

'He has the sort of ill reputation that some men are proud of. Much boozing and bruising, and seducing and throwing over of little chits, and bragging about it all.' She sat at a distance from him, looking at her hands folded in her lap. ''Tis the more depressing because I do fancy that Jemmy Runquest has a brain in his head.'

'And Tabitha?'

'If she weeps over a man, then she can't have,' Cordelia

said. She added one of her quick, glinting smiles, but still the tartness took him aback.

'I spoke of your neighbour, Miss Henlow, to Dr Stagg,' he said after a moment. 'I had the impression that he was – not indifferent to her name.'

'That's very probable. He was a frequent visitor next door, and not always professionally, one gathers. Whether there was actually a suit, I don't know. Miss Henlow, naturally, has been much admired. But the transparent fact is she is utterly devoted to her brother-in-law's interests, more than ever now that he has a motherless child. I doubt whether Dr Stagg could conquer that, even if he were more eligible. Do not misunderstand me – I think very highly of him. But he has no family, no connections, and few graces; and it will take a great deal of lustre to dazzle Emma Henlow's eyes.'

'You do not like Miss Henlow,' he said – as much to prick her out of her abstraction as for information.

'I like her,' Cordelia said with a wan smile, 'about as much as a woman generally likes another woman who is serenely beautiful, elegant, and accomplished. And looks as if she has never in her life made a splash using the chamber pot . . . Oh, dear.' She laughed ruefully at herself. Fairfax was glad to see a return of that old saltiness. 'Forgive me. Yes, I am envious. But you know, it is not the beauty – I don't believe it ever is, for anyone: what one envies is the composure.'

'A strange life for her, though, surely. Housekeeping, caring for her dead sister's child . . .'

'You mean she might have so much more. And you have a suspicion, which you are too tactful to voice, about her feelings for her brother-in-law. Well, that is quite natural.

But all I can say is that the devotion between the sisters seemed complete. When Mrs Porteous was pregnant, and poorly with it – it looked to be a difficult lying-in – Emma came to live with them, to be a help and stay and so forth. I remember calling on them, and poor Mrs Porteous – she was a week from her time then – saying she could hardly have managed without her sister. She looked very like Emma, almost a twin resemblance indeed, though she lacked Emma's evenness of temper, and could be quite a fretful creature, God rest her. Well, when Mrs Porteous did not survive the childbed fever, and Charles Porteous was quite broken up, I dare say there was nothing more natural than that Emma should stay on and be the tower of strength that was, I fear, much needed. She loved her sister, must of course love her sister's child, and loves and honours her brother-in-law for her sister's sake. There, I am being thoroughly fair now, am I not? Certainly fairer than many an old puss hereabouts, who does not scruple to whisper that Emma Henlow's regard for her brother-in-law is more than sisterly, or sister-in-lawly, if there is such a thing.'

'Ah. I suppose such gossip is inevitable.'

'It is, and I do believe Tabitha Dance may have given a fillip to it. There were high words when they dismissed her – she can be quite a tigress, as you've seen – and I got the impression, from Charles Porteous, that she had cast some aspersions he found intolerable in a servant. And he is far from a severe man: prefers anything to discord, I think. But then he is in a ticklish position when it comes to scandal. His uncle is Sir Andrew Porteous, a very well-set-up merchant in the City. The wine trade – not that he drinks it himself, for he is quite the old Puritan, it seems, mightily pious and proper. I once went with the Randalls to dine next door when they had Sir Andrew to visit. He reminded me of one of those fierce old sobersides who chopped King Charles' head off. Meanwhile his nephew was like a fly in a glue-pot – never relaxing a moment: desperate to please, and desperate not to displease. He has a position under Sir Andrew in the City, and has I'm sure expectations that way, as the old man is childless, but plainly he must work hard to keep in his uncle's favour. And so you see he is fearfully vulnerable to any touch of scandal.'

'I see. And so Tabitha had to go.'

'Well, that's how it appears. Mrs Randall, you know, approves very much of the people next door because they are most *respectable*, as she says; and they are certainly too respectable to talk of their private affairs. Well, Mr Fairfax, this is grist to your infernally inquisitive mill, no doubt,' she said with an unsuccessful attempt at brightness, 'but I still do not see what dark misdeeds you think to uncover.'

'There may be none. But the carriage wheel shows that someone here had some evil intent towards the late Mr Chilcott, or Mrs Chilcott, or both. And Mrs Chilcott is certainly keeping secrets. None of my business, I know. But if it should prove that her life is still in danger . . . I weary you with these speculations.'

He was on his feet. Cordelia looked startled.

'Why do you say that?'

'The evidence of my eyes. Cordelia—'

She gestured him to silence. 'You must think me very changeable. I am not, indeed. But there is something . . . When I came back I met the post-boy. With a letter from my husband.' She nodded at a folded sheet that lay on the table.

Fairfax experienced a moment of disappointment that she had not crumpled or torn it up, then was angry with himself.

'I see.'

'You see the letter, but cannot, I think, see what I feel.' She tried to soften that with a smile. 'Which I am glad of, in truth. It would not be edifying. Like peering into a cess-pit . . .'

'Cordelia. What does he say?'

'Confidential communication from husband to the wife of his bosom, good heavens, not a thing to be broached, Mr Fairfax, even to one who I account a – a good friend and one who understands, perhaps, more than he should . . . Well, George speaks of "a readiness to forgive", that is the phrase above all that sticks in my memory, or should I say sticks in my craw? Whether it refers to my being ready to forgive him, or he ready to forgive me, I am not entirely sure. George was always a master of the imprecise phrase. I don't know what to think, except to wish that the letter had never come.'

'I see that it has disturbed you,' he said. 'Stirred up powerful feelings . . . And that it is surely best I leave you to – to think.'

She nodded. 'It's best. Not that that means . . . What it means is I know you understand. You do, don't you? It is one of the things about you . . . Probably what I need just now is a confidant. And for that role you are unsuited.'

'I am, certainly.' He was glad, anyway, that she acknowledged that. A confidant was a third party, neutral and unengaged. God, he was not that.

Murmuring a goodbye, he got out of there, only to find her coming after him, muttering that she would see him out. At the front door he found that the brassy murk of summer storm had given sudden place to brilliant, fresh sunshine. It flashed from the windowpanes along the quiet street, making him blink again. Vapour rose from the broad puddles in the rutted road, which reflected like flawless mirrors, presenting tassels of white cloud.

'When you look into a puddle of water like that, it almost looks as if there was another world parallel to this one, and you could step straight into it,' Cordelia said.

'The same world?'

'I always fancy it is like but different.' Not looking at him, she said, 'In that world, Mr Fairfax, where certain things are different because certain things never happened – in that world you would not be Mr Fairfax to me. You would be Robert, and . . .'

'You don't have to say these things,' he said, stiff with pain.

'No. And I wish and hope, for your sake, that you did not care a hang one way or the other. But I fear it is not so. So I say it. It is not giving you much. Not compared with the everything I would give, if . . .'

And *if*, appropriately, was the last word: she seemed unable to say any more, and he could not have spoken if his life depended on it. He pressed her hand, and she drew back into the house, and he went splashing and trudging blindly through the reflections of the other world, and so they escaped from one another.

Four

He felt as if his spirit were wrapped in an oppressive fog, and part of him wanted to fly from here at once and never come back. He was not obliged to be here: he could convalesce in any spot he chose. Convalescence, at any rate, was something of a bad joke now, suggesting as it did peace and calm and the avoidance of agitation.

And he couldn't leave – couldn't bear to break the knot that bound him to Cordelia Linton, torturous though it was; as she in turn, it seemed, could not break the knot binding her to her husband . . . What a world! Well, there was the mystery surrounding the Chilcotts too: his mind could find some relief in gnawing at that. And in a peculiar way it corresponded with his wretched entanglement with Cordelia. Something dark, skewed, toilsome about it: something not right. The expression of utter horror on Gabriel Chilcott's face as he lay in undignified death; little Wolfgang whispering *Ein Mann*; the carriage wheel wriggling across the cobbles. Glimpses – like viewing some intriguing drama by watching the shadows it cast on a screen.

Fairfax kept to himself that evening, retiring to his own room after dinner, though thus far he and Dr Stagg had beguiled the evenings together in the doctor's comfortable parlour, with chess and a glass or two of brandy, and a little talk – not much. Stagg remained such an awkward conversationalist, even after brandy, that Fairfax could almost suppose himself not welcome. Yet Dr Stagg had said with apparent sincerity that he enjoyed having the company: it was partly why he let out rooms. The house, he murmured, was too big for a single man anyhow. It was a pleasant, airy house at the end of Royal Hospital Row – Stagg was visiting physician to Charles II's great hospital nearby, and had a case of mementoes given to him by sentimental old soldiers: bullets from the campaigns of Marlborough, powder-flasks that had seen service at Dettingen and Culloden – and snugly fitted out, though very much in the bachelor style. A manservant and a cook-maid saw to Stagg's wants, and he kept a serviceable mare. The fruits of a modest but definite success, Fairfax thought as he turned in that night; and, thinking of his own frustrations, wondered if Frederick Stagg accounted himself a happy man. Somehow he did not seem so: Fairfax detected a dissatisfaction in those pale blue eyes, those large, strong hands that constantly, rhythmically tapped on the arm of his chair as he contemplated the chess board. And yet he had surely risen in the world: Fairfax guessed his origins to be of middling, if not lowly, sort; and the licentiate of physician was the highest doctor's qualification, above the surgeons and apothecaries. But perhaps Dr Stagg's discontent was all too recognizable. The malady lay in the heart, and Fairfax shared it: he felt it still lodged in him like a burr when at last he drifted into sleep.

It was still with him the next morning when he set out to walk to Kensington, though the brilliance of a summer morning played its usual trick of convincing him that life was not such a hopeless affair as it appeared in the weary midnight. Leaving behind the suburban gentility of Sloane Square, he was soon amongst sweet-smelling fields and orchards, with the sun making an enchanted veil of the horizon where the coal-smoke of London glowered. It was a scene to seduce even a confirmed city-lover like himself, and he found a pastoral tune turning in his head. In his luggage at Dr Stagg's he had brought the flute on which he tootled with an amateur's enthusiasm, but with the company he had been keeping yesterday he had kept quiet about it. He found himself wondering about that ordinary, extraordinary boy, Wolfgang Mozart, and whether those musical powers of his were a mere freak that would dwindle into mediocrity as he grew to adulthood. He had a great curiosity to hear him play, and could understand Mr Gabriel Chilcott's similar if somewhat overbearing desire.

Indeed, he thought, was Mr Chilcott so bad after all? What he knew of the dead man's character seemed to be all hedged about with negatives: exacting, quarrelsome, proud and possessive. And yet he was a music-lover – and what had Shakespeare said? 'The man that hath no music in himself, Nor is mov'd with concord of sweet sounds, Is fit for treasons, stratagems, and spoils . . . Let no such man be trusted,' Fairfax mused aloud, getting a benevolent grunt from a grazing cow in return. He would have to tell that one to Leopold Mozart.

He found Brockleigh House, the residence of the Chilcotts, amongst a cluster of wonderful and fanciful retreats built by rich men around the verdant skirts of Kensington Palace. Whether or not there was a hope that dwelling near royalty, like living next door to a tannery, would cause it to rub off on you, the spot seemed to have produced palatial ambitions in the builders. Brockleigh House, even with its miniature park and little pseudo-Gothic turrets, was among the more modest of them, but still to walk up its well-swept drive was to be conscious of not being very well dressed, dusty from walking, and in need of a very good reason to be there.

Which he had, though it was doubtful whether Mrs Chilcott would see it that way. He had to talk to her about the events of yesterday, which meant raising the matter of the man Wolfgang had seen leaving her room; also the question of why anyone would tamper with their carriage, and whether she had reason to suspect anyone of wishing to do her or her late husband harm. He did not expect her to welcome these questions.

He did not expect, either, to see the person who was emerging from the front door up ahead of him. It was Tabitha Dance. She was leaving, or being urged to leave, with some reluctance; and as he drew nearer, he saw the wigged head and long face of an elderly man who held the door just a little ajar, and wagged an admonishing finger at the girl, and then hurriedly pressed a small bundle into her hands before pulling the door shut.

Slowly and droopingly, Tabitha came away. She was looking listlessly into the bundle when he drew level with her. He doffed his hat, and her eyes flashed sourly on his, as if she thought she was being mocked. That pained him.

'Good morning. We met but yesterday, you recall . . .' He saw there was food in the bundle – apples, some broken bread and cheese. Seeing he saw, she closed it up quickly.

'I've come to see Mrs Chilcott,' he went on awkwardly. 'Is she in, do you know?'

'Not to me,' Tabitha snapped. Then, putting her head down and making to move past him, she muttered, 'I don't know anything about it, I'm sorry, sir.'

'No . . . But might I just ask you again – yesterday, you were at the Spread Eagle when Mr Chilcott died, and I wondered if you saw anyone acting suspiciously, or anything at all out of the common?'

'I only heard about it after. At the time I wasn't – well, I wasn't taking a great deal of notice.' He was glad to see the gleam of humour breaking through the unhappiness, though it was soon extinguished. The mark of Runquest's hand was still faintly visible on her cheek, a grim parody of a blush. 'So I really can't say anything, sir, and I've got to go.'

'Of course . . . You know the Chilcotts?'

'You'd hardly expect me to be on calling-card terms, I think, sir,' she said, contemptuous again. 'I've been to see an old friend who was good to me, and I can't linger, and that's about all of it.' She walked away from him down the drive, head down, hugging the bundle to her.

Thoughtful, he knocked, and was admitted by a footman – elderly, of course, as seemed to be typical of Mr Chilcott's establishment, but not the long-faced man he had seen at the door. Marble, gilding, brocade, ormolu all assaulted his eye in the hall and in the drawing room to which the stooping footman ushered him. Mr Chilcott, whatever his faults, had been no cheeseparing miser: he had testified to his wealth in thoroughly material fashion. It was impossible not to reflect with sad irony on how durable all this expensive tonnage was, compared with that perishable flesh that had tumbled down the stairs of the Spread Eagle.

And thinking of that unprepossessing man, it was impossible not to see the beautiful young Mrs Chilcott, seated in queenly black-silk state, as another of the old fellow's pricey acquisitions, destined to outlive him . . . He put away these tart thoughts and made his bow, then added another in hasty surprise as he saw that the widow had company – Emma Henlow, who gave him a nod of coolly pleasant recognition. More than he got from Mrs Chilcott, whose look was withering. She was seated in the shadow of a *petit point* fire screen, though no fire was lit on such a warm day, and Fairfax could only imagine that it functioned in reverse, and kept her chilliness off other people.

'Sir. I did not expect to see you again.'

'Ma'am. I came to offer again my condolences, as well as those of Mr Davis Yelverton, Justice of the Peace at Chelsea, who has asked me to make enquiries on his behalf into the matter of Mr Chilcott's death.' There, he thought, that said it all in one go.

'Again enquiries. One might almost fancy oneself in France, with police and spies forever on the watch, and the fingers of the censor pawing at one's private correspondence. Whatever became of the Englishman's liberty?' She has been rehearsing that one, Fairfax thought. 'I have only one or two questions,' he said temperately.

'One – or two? There is a difference. Oh, no matter. You had better sit down. This lady is Miss Henlow, who has *not* come to cross-examine me, thank heaven – or at least I hope not.'

'Mr Fairfax and I have met,' Emma Henlow said with a faint smile. 'As I was saying, Mrs Chilcott, I fear that I am the one taking liberties in coming here, as we have not been introduced. But when I heard what had happened at the Spread Eagle, I felt that I must trespass upon propriety, and come and offer you my condolences.'

'It is the talk of the neighbourhood, no doubt,' Mrs Chilcott said, eyes lowered: a delicate blue vein beat tremulously in one eyelid.

'It is known, as such a tragic event is sure to be; but I assure you, ma'am, any talk is only of the most sympathetic kind,' Miss Henlow said. 'It was sympathy, or fellow-feeling, that prompted me to come here this morning, and I hope you will not think that presumptuous. I cannot claim acquaintance with your late husband, but I met him briefly, as I was visiting my neighbours the Mozarts when he came there seeking an audience, and that made it doubly shocking to hear of his death so swiftly afterward. I do not indeed know what it is to lose a husband, but the sudden loss of a loved one – a dear sister – has been my own portion but recently, and I know the sad pains of bereavement. I also know how fruitless consolations can be, but I offer them at any rate, and those of my brother-in-law, Mr Charles Porteous. It is his especial wish that you be assured that any service we can offer you at this time, any assistance we can supply . . . It is conventional, I know. But very much meant.'

Mrs Chilcott inclined her head. The severe curve of her lips was a little unsteady: it was the first time he had seen a thaw in her frostiness. It did not surprise him that Emma Henlow should be the one to do it: it was admirable the way she combined warmth and briskness, though he could imagine what Cordelia would say to that.

'You are very kind,' Mrs Chilcott said. 'There is, as you

87

say, little consolation to be had – except, of course, that overriding consolation that every Christian must seek at such a time, in the certainties of our religion.'

'Of course,' Miss Henlow said, with a look that Fairfax found interesting – because it could only be called sceptical. 'Alas, we are fallible creatures, and not always able to lay hold of it.'

'I thank you, and your brother-in-law, for your offers of assistance likewise. As a woman suddenly alone and unprotected I might stand in need of them – but I am fortunate in having an excellent steward, long in my husband's service . . . Porteous, by the by, is a name I know. Could he be a relation of Sir Andrew Porteous, in the City?'

'Indeed: his nephew. You are acquainted with Sir Andrew?'

'Not acquainted. I know of him as an old business associate of my husband's. I will not say friend. My husband did not have friends.'

She stated it quite neutrally, as if mentioning that he did not keep dogs or drink coffee.

'Would you say that he had enemies, Mrs Chilcott?' Fairfax said.

She gave him a look as if she had forgotten he was there.

'Oh! Enquiries, of course. But you are beginning at the wrong end, are you not, sir? Surely I am the one under suspicion. My husband's body lies upstairs, you know, Mr Fairfax: my steward had him conveyed hither early this morning, and before we arrange for a funeral you will no doubt wish to examine him. Look for a tell-tale bullet-hole, perhaps, which will show that I shot him – silently, of course, and with a gun so small that it is practically invisible . . .'

'You misunderstand me,' Fairfax said, a little frosty himself now. 'I intrude on your grief only because there are circumstances surrounding your husband's death suggestive of some malice – to him, perhaps to you. It is plain, ma'am, that the tampering with the wheel of your carriage was done with evil intent. Unless we are to suppose some entirely random mischief-maker who goes about endangering people's lives in that way, then someone sought to harm you both yesterday. And that would suggest you may still be in danger. That is why I ask about enemies.'

'As to that, I am entirely baffled, sir. If anyone is my enemy in that way, it is probably in the nature of things that I would not know of it, but I cannot imagine that anyone could be.'

'But your husband? Forgive me, but I understand he tended to be contentious in his dealings—'

'Mr Chilcott and I had not been married above two years, sir. That is not very long, certainly not long enough for me to know him very well. Most of his life lay outside my sphere. So I really cannot help you.'

This seemed to Fairfax such a preposterous answer that he could only stare. In the meantime there was a knock, and the long-faced man he had seen earlier came softly in. The steward, he guessed: the snuff-brown coat with its old-fashioned long skirts, the apologetic flat-footed tread and the plain Cromwellian features all proclaimed the faithful retainer.

'I beg your pardon, ma'am, but the undertaker's woman is here. Shall I have her go up, or have you any special instructions for her?'

'Only that he be made – reposeful,' Mrs Chilcott said,

89

her breathing a little short. Fairfax recalled the dead man's face, the appalled and appalling eyes.

'Yes, ma'am. There is also the matter of measuring the servants for mourning clothes. Apparently a man can come in whenever you wish . . .'

'By and by, Minter. I cannot think of these things now.'

'Of course, ma'am.' The steward bowed and shuffled away. Fairfax met his rheumy eyes for a moment, and wondered about Tabitha Dance. But he chose not to mention the matter to Mrs Chilcott, not now. He surmised that the steward's gift had been made without the knowledge of his mistress, and he was wary of getting servants into trouble with their employers.

'It is, I well know, a sorely difficult time,' Emma Henlow said gently. 'One is required to turn the grieving mind to all manner of troublesome practicalities, just when it is least equipped to cope with them. I urge you, ma'am, is there no matter in which we can assist you? I hope I am not impertinent when I surmise that there are no near relatives to lend their aid.'

'There are no near relatives,' Mrs Chilcott said dully.

'In which case I beg you, any errand or instruction you have to make, let me be the bearer. I go about a good deal, and you have only to pen your requirements, and I shall be happy to be your messenger.' Miss Henlow gestured to a walnut writing-desk – one of many handsome pieces, but not the handsomest. That honour, Fairfax thought, belonged to a superb harpsichord that stood before the window.

'You are very good.' Mrs Chilcott gave a pained smile – the only sort of smile her face looked capable of. 'But I must reconcile myself to my solitary state, and the sooner the better. It is, as you remark, a difficult time – and in my case rendered more difficult by unworthy and impudent suspicions.'

That was for Fairfax, and annoyance made him blunt.

'I have spoken of no suspicions, ma'am. Only of concern that someone may have tried to do you injury. But as you say you cannot be of help in that, perhaps you are better able to speak of the other strange matter – the man who was seen to leave your room at the Spread Eagle at the time of your husband's collapse.'

'Now you are offensive, sir,' she said, and stalking over to the fireplace rang the bell with an angry jerk.

'I do not mean to be. I mean only to establish the truth.'

'Yet you have made up your mind to believe the fancies of a spoilt boy – a vagabond foreigner going about like a fairground tumbler.'

'We speak of Wolfgang Mozart?' Emma Henlow said. 'Oh, forgive me, ma'am, he really is not what you paint him. He is a delightful child, and there is nothing spurious about his claims as a musician.'

'A child, nonetheless,' Mrs Chilcott said. 'And as to his abilities, they are of no moment to me.' She went over to the harpsichord and rapped on it with her knuckles. 'To me this is mere lumber. I do not play, and neither did my husband, for all his musical enthusiasm. He could not play a note. I cannot understand the fuss about music: it has no utility, and its practitioners are usually ill-bred. A mere child, and one raised in such a world, is probably the last person I would credit. And now that is about enough, Mr Fairfax, of your insinuations.' The footman had creakingly appeared. 'Show this gentleman out.'

Well, there was nothing he could do but make his bow and get out of there. Miss Henlow was too cool to look surprised or embarrassed, of course, but she seemed to give him a glance of friendly understanding as he went: Mrs Chilcott kept her fine-boned profile averted. A difficult woman to feel sympathy for. Indeed he found himself feeling curiously sorry for Mr Gabriel Chilcott, simply on account of that harpsichord: a man who adored music but could not play a note of it, married to a woman who despised it. The smoothest life was a maze of cracks when you stood up close to it, he thought, as he followed the footman to the hall. There he spotted the steward, just about to enter a backstairs door.

'Sir. Mr Minter, I think? Will you do me the favour of a word?'

The old man looked wary, frightened even; but he came over with his deferential tread, nervously plucking at his long chin.

'I just wanted to ask you about the girl who was at the door earlier.'

'The girl, sir?'

'Her name is Tabitha Dance. You were kind enough to give her charity, I think.'

'I couldn't say, sir.' There was alarm in the old man's eyes. 'I really couldn't say.'

'Well, no matter. I know her but slightly, and I was merely curious at seeing her here. Has she some connection with the house, or anyone in it?'

'I couldn't say, sir. Forgive me, please. I mean no secrets, but it's – it's ticklish, sir. I have a very good place here – I hope you understand. And with everything so topsy-turvy

. . . I know the girl, and know no ill of her – that's all.'

'Of course. Oh, yes, of course, I meant no . . .' Well, he couldn't press the old man, who was obviously still haunted by the spectre of his late master's disapproval. Was Mr Chilcott so very demanding, and even tyrannical, as to inspire fear beyond the grave? Or could it be that Mrs Chilcott was the one who the servants trembled to displease? There was an interesting thought. 'Well, you will have much to do, no doubt, with the arrangements for Mr Chilcott's funeral.'

'Much. But there was nothing I wouldn't do for him in life,' Minter said with a sudden tremulous animation, 'and so it is in death, though I hoped never to see the day!'

Fairfax stopped. 'You were fond of your employer?'

'Fond?' The steward plucked and plucked at his chin as if he were trying to make it longer still. 'Why, to me Mr Chilcott was . . . Well, I'll say only this: I never hoped to see this day, but there's others who – who think different. That's all I'll say.' Minter shuffled away and came back again all in one movement. 'And I'll say this. My master was much put upon. It's a shame to think it, but – he was, and that's all.' Now he did go away, with a sound in his chest as if he were suppressing a sob.

Mr Chilcott much put upon . . . Here was another adjustment to be made to his image of that overbearing gentleman. Fairfax was still trying to make sense of it when, striking the high road out of Kensington, he heard rapid hoofbeats behind him.

'Mr Fairfax. How fast you walk.' Emma Henlow reined in her horse beside him. 'You almost outpace my poor nag.'

The poor nag, however, was a sleek and splendidly

groomed creature; and if it could be said with gallantry, he thought, the same applied to Miss Henlow. In sky-blue riding habit and tricorne hat, her fairness glowing in the sun, she managed to look both jaunty and ethereal. She dismounted lithely and walked beside him, leading the horse.

'Miss Henlow. I had not expected to see you there. It was a kind action.'

She waved an elegantly gloved hand. 'Not really. I was in two minds: one shrinks from intruding. But such a sudden and shocking event . . . And I know from experience that a death in the family embarrasses people, and they will do almost anything to avoid speaking to you of it. Which sharpens grief with the horrible feeling that the loved person somehow never existed at all. Well, I did not expect to see you either – and I am heartily sorry to have witnessed your being shown the door in that way. One must make allowances, of course, for Mrs Chilcott can hardly be in her right frame of mind.'

She did not look particularly sorry, Fairfax thought. In fact he did not know what to make of her, except insofar as he began to understand Cordelia's feelings about Emma Henlow. Such perfect equipoise, such a smooth way of covering every point of the conversation in advance: somehow you were made to feel superfluous. And yet she was a beautiful and charming young woman: perhaps he was feeling only what an undistinguished man of thirty-four with sweat running down the back of his neck tended to feel in such a situation.

'Well, it is no matter,' he said. 'I may go away, but those curious circumstances I spoke of will not. Pray, Miss Henlow, what do you know of a young woman named Tabitha Dance?'

'I will tell you,' she said, smiling faintly, 'but I think you should be plain about what you know, first, Mr Fairfax. From the very fact of your asking, I presume you know she was lately maidservant to our household, and that Charles was forced to dismiss her. Yes?'

'So I had heard,' he said awkwardly.

'Well, it is true enough. And it was a great pity. I liked Tabitha and believe she would have done well. Her way of living just now is, I know, sadly dissolute. But I think she was by no means badly raised: she has her letters, and was a good needlewoman, and very trim and tidy about the house. She would have made a respectable lady's-maid, and at first I thought we were fortunate to get her. But she has vices – or weaknesses, depending upon your view of human nature. The tippling and the amorousness might have been managed, just. But there was a sly insolence that could not be borne, least of all when it manifested itself in a house of mourning. I hope I am no more nor less mindful of my reputation than any other woman, Mr Fairfax. Idle gossip is one thing, mischievous gossip another. Mischievous, and downright vicious, is what I call any attempt to hint that I sought to step into my poor sister's shoes when the childbed fever took her from us. I am devoted to Charles, for two reasons: because he is an estimable man, and because I was devoted to Catherine, who loved him. Tattle-mongers have a very limited view of human feeling: they will see love affairs on all sides, but cannot conceive the intensity of love between sisters, or that it may be quite as enduring and powerful as the commoner passions. It is hard to conceive of a more tragical death than Catherine suffered, sir. The birth of her little boy was difficult and protracted, but perhaps not more than many women undergo, and in the first aftermath she seemed pretty well, though weak, and was able to nurse her baby, and take a little food. Then the fever set in. It was ghastly. I remember hugging little Arthur to me, and trying to pacify his cries, and feeling that it was the sound of his mother's screams upstairs that agitated him . . . Well. I can only say that when Catherine died, it was a happy release. She could not have continued so. But after such experiences, the insinuations of Tabitha were not to be tolerated. Charles was outraged at the first hint. She had to go. You understand, I think.'

'A dreadful ordeal . . . One is tempted to wonder what a benevolent Creator is up to in laying such burdens upon women.' It was the sort of irrepressible remark that had got him in trouble with employers in the past, but Miss Henlow regarded him quite neutrally; and even through that grim narration her voice had remained cool and steady. 'One's only hope is that medical science may in time learn to master these horrors.'

'Perhaps so. It was able to do nothing for Catherine, though she had the very best attendance in Dr Stagg – him I would trust above the grandest physician at St James.'

'You speak warmly of him.'

She gave him an acute look, faintly smiling again. 'I do. You have, it seems, very quickly picked up all the local gossip, Mr Fairfax. Could this be the work of dear Mrs Linton?'

He did not like the patronage in that, and said, 'It would be a pity if all conversation were to be labelled as gossip.'

'Most of it is. Well, we live in a quiet spot at Chelsea, and of course all news is eagerly seized on. My name was certainly linked with Dr Stagg's, first of all because I visit the sick and poor a lot – not because I want to play the grand, charitable lady, but because I truly like to do so, believing I have some skill in that direction. It gave me fruitful occupation when I first came to live here, and I aided the doctor where I could, and took an interest in his work. An unwomanly interest, some might say: I say it is surely better in all ways than doing trifling embroidery and painting indifferent watercolours. It may be that Dr Stagg misinterpreted that interest in a personal light; and any distress I may have caused him I am properly sorry for. But I assure you we are the best of friends now, and everything is perfectly easy.'

Again she contrived to make him feel there was nothing left he could say. He wondered if Dr Stagg used to feel this way in her presence.

'And now,' she said, stroking her horse's nose, 'I had better make haste, for I do not like to leave little Arthur too long. But I have enjoyed talking with you, Mr Fairfax, and I know Charles would too, and so let me invite you here and now to sup with us tonight. If you are otherwise engaged, do say so – but I hope you are not.'

He said he was not, and thanked her, and she said she would expect him at eight; and in a state of bafflement he watched her ride gracefully on. Enjoyed talking with you . . . ? He could almost fancy it mockery; and yet there was nothing arch about her. She was fascinating, and though he was not in the least in love with her, he could imagine what it was like to be so. Well, he looked forward to this evening, and to meeting at last Mr Charles Porteous. It seemed certain that Emma Henlow was devoted to her brother-in-law, whether in a platonic spirit or no, which piqued his curiosity about the man. And his ears had pricked up at Mrs Chilcott's mention of Sir Andrew Porteous as an associate of her husband's. That the families were linked in this way might mean something – though it was hard to say what exactly. He toyed with the notion that Charles Porteous might have some animosity against Mr Chilcott, on his uncle's behalf, which had induced him to slip into the Spread Eagle yard and sabotage the carriage . . . but it was such an absurdity that he did not toy with it for long. Obligingness to wealthy relatives could only go so far, he thought. All he was certain of was that he was missing something. And he could not quite believe that Emma Henlow had ridden over to Brockleigh simply to offer condolences to a woman she didn't know.

Well, at least it kept him from brooding over Cordelia, or at least from brooding over her more than twice a minute. The rate increased when he came at last, hot and dusty, to the purlieus of Chelsea, and quickened dramatically when he spotted Frau Mozart and Nannerl walking arm in arm ahead of him along Turks Row.

Yes, Frau Mozart said shyly, her husband was doing pretty well today; and Wolfgang was well likewise, and none the worse for the shock of yesterday. She hoped he would not have to go before a judge or an officer . . . ? No, no, Fairfax reassured her. It was Nannerl, twirling her parasol, and looking as prettily apple-cheeked and Austrian as could be imagined, who noticed his wilting condition, and suggested that Wolfgang would be glad to see his friend Herr Fairfax, and Papa to offer him some cider, if he cared to come in.

Surely, surely. Probably he should not kindle at the thought of perhaps seeing Cordelia again, but there was no help for it. And he did wish to speak to Wolfgang. Of Cordelia, at any rate, there was no sign at Five Fields Row, and he found Wolfgang rather distracted. The boy was seated on the floor amongst a litter of music sheets.

'But I finished the second movement, Papa – I know I did. Where can it be . . . ? Nannerl! You were copying out my symphony for me. I finished the second movement, didn't I?'

'I'm sure you did, Wolfgangerl. I sat beside you. And you said, "Remind me to give the horn something worthwhile to do."'

'Well, I cannot find the last page. I wanted to show the symphony to Papa and – *ach!*' The boy scattered the sheets with an impatient hand. 'It makes me so angry!'

'Ah, Wolfgangerl, method – time and again I have told you, method and order are needed in all your work,' said Leopold, who was seated in his dressing gown and fanning himself with the *Public Advertiser*. 'If you would aspire to be a good, solid musician, and worthy of the dignity of Kapellmeister some day, you must cultivate steady habits. The page will turn up, I am sure. Well, Herr Fairfax, and how do you do? I have been misled by reports of your English climate, I find. I swelter like a Moorish pasha. Take some cider with me, sir – it refreshes wonderfully, I find – and accept my thanks for going forth to retrieve this wandering boy a second time yesterday. We have had our words about it, have we not, Wolfgangerl? And I have chosen to accept that he went after the gentleman with the motive of being obliging, rather than any acquisitive notion of getting a hobby-horse.'

The boy gave his father a rueful sideways smile. Fairfax took the proffered glass of cider and gulped it greedily.

'The shock of seeing the poor gentleman's collapse was, I think, lesson enough, and he will not be so adventurous in future. I confess I was deeply dismayed at the news, and regretted that I had been obliged to be so unhelpful to the gentleman . . . but how is one to know these things? Fate is so capricious. He leaves a widow, I hear.'

'Yes, I have seen her just this morning. There are certain curious circumstances surrounding Mr Chilcott's death that I am looking into on behalf of the magistrate.'

'This business of the man that Wolfgangerl saw? All very strange. But my son is no liar, that I can vouch for, Herr Fairfax. And if there is some discreditable matter afoot, then I hope you will understand that I do not want him mixed up in it any more than can be helped.'

'Of course, Herr Mozart. I think there is nothing to fear on that score. But the truth of what Wolfgang witnessed – and I have no doubt of it – may be very important. So I must ask you, Wolfgang, now that a little time has passed and you are more collected: can you picture that man you saw? Would you recognize him again?'

Wolfgang thought for a moment, then nodded vigorously. 'I would know him. I wish I could draw what he looked like . . . But the nearest is you, Herr Fairfax. He looked a little like you.'

'But it was not Herr Fairfax, of course,' said Frau Mozart, displaying a certain confusion.

'That could hardly be, as he was with me at the

time – on the hunt for *you*, little rascal,' Cordelia Linton said, coming in and tickling Wolfgang's ribs from behind. She straightened, rather flushed, her eyes skimming Fairfax's.

Wolfgang wriggled away, giggling. 'Oh! Frau Linton, perhaps you know. I cannot find a page of my symphony and I have looked everywhere—'

'Meaning you have tossed your papers about, and given up,' said his father.

'A page of your symphony? Dear me, let's see,' Cordelia said. 'Why, I do believe I may have torn it up to light the fire—'

'Or to wipe your behind!' chuckled Frau Mozart – to Fairfax's astonishment: but the whole family seemed quite at home with this scatological joke, and laughed heartily.

'No, no,' Cordelia smiled, 'I have not seen it, Wolfgang, and believe me I would not use something so precious for – for lighting the fire. There are *some* papers that go on the fire, of course,' she added, looking straight at Fairfax. 'It is the only place for them.'

He felt his breath go short, and in spite of a fugitive exultation he could almost wish she had not said that. For where did it leave them, after all? 'Well, Wolfgang, I know that memory of yours: you will be able to recollect the passage, will you not?' Cordelia said.

'It will not be the same,' the boy said, pouting.

'Oh dear! Well, I came up to ask if you would like for us all to have supper together tonight. Mrs Randall has her butcher supply with me more beef than I can possibly eat, and it is a shame to see it spoiled.'

'And we still have some of yesterday's fowls – we could

101

combine, and feast!' Leopold Mozart said. 'Yes, it is an excellent notion, Frau Linton. Not, of course, that I have much of an appetite,' he added, regretfully remembering that he was an invalid. 'And what about Herr Fairfax? Are you engaged this evening, sir?'

'Alas, I am. With your next-door neighbours, indeed: Miss Henlow asked me this morning.' He had spoken without thinking, and now it was too late to retract. Cordelia raised an eyebrow, ironical – and displeased?

'Oh, a pity,' Leopold said, 'it would have been delightful.'

Yes. Nothing has ever gone right in my whole life, Fairfax thought, with outrageous exaggeration. And then he felt annoyed with Cordelia. Despite what she had signalled to him just now, there remained what she had said last night . . . and damn it all, she was still married. Then he had a wild wish to march across the room and take her in his arms and kiss her. The Mozarts, with their taste for earthy humour, would surely not be shocked. Oh, hell, hell.

'What time are you to go tonight?' Cordelia said. Her eyebrow was still lifted – and yet her expression . . .

'Seven,' he lied.

'Seven,' she said, nodding.

'Well, you must join us another time,' Leopold said. The manservant put his head round the door.

'Herr Doctor Stagg, sir.'

Fairfax offered to leave, but Leopold waved a hand. 'No need. My good doctor's examinations are quite modest, I assure you. He does not want to look at my – ah, Dr Stagg, how do you do, sir?'

Stagg came quickly in, murmuring greetings, and bearing down briskly on the patient. He felt Leopold's throat and neck with large, golden-haired fingers.

'I hope you have no objections to my regimen of cider,' Leopold said, in high good humour. 'That, and the posset that dear Miss Henlow brings me, are all that make my life tolerable.'

'I would advise against spiritous liquors,' Dr Stagg said, after Cordelia had translated, 'but a mild beverage can do no harm.'

'You do not mention Miss Henlow's contribution,' Leopold said, huffing humorously, 'but perhaps that is because she poaches on your professional preserves, eh?'

Dr Stagg hesitated, his cheeks mottled.

'I am sure nothing can be amiss that comes from Miss Henlow's hands,' he got out.

Poor fellow, thought Fairfax – with sympathy not pity. For they were in the same boat, were they not? – or at least, in vessels of the same queasy build. He was sure he was just as awkward when, the doctor having finished his examination, he took his leave along with Stagg, and said his goodbyes to Cordelia. Had he taken her meaning aright when she had asked what time he would come to supper next door – that he was to come and see her first? These perplexities of the heart were enough to drive a man distracted, and he would have said so, in comradely feeling, to any man less reserved than Frederick Stagg.

But then Stagg surprised him. Mentioning that he was going to make his next call on a poor family, he asked if Fairfax would care to see the other side of salubrious Chelsea; and Fairfax readily agreeing, they went along together, Dr Stagg leading his saddle-horse. After a few minutes of charged silence, Stagg began abruptly to talk of Emma Henlow.

'I gave the wrong impression, perhaps, just now. About Miss Henlow and her – her concoction. Normally I am no friend to laymen meddling in medical business. I studied hard and long to attain such skill and knowledge as I have, and even then I recognize that our science carries only the feeblest taper into the – the dark mysteries of human pathology. But I except Miss Henlow because she has never shown any presumption in that regard. She has never pretended to be more than a keen observer of human ills, and a cautious seeker of remedies – such as a doctor should be, in fact.'

'Indeed. She spoke of this when I met her today.' Fairfax added as casually as he could that she had invited him to supper tonight, wondering what Stagg's reaction would be.

There was none. Stagg went on as if he had not heard him. 'Of course I see no prospect of a day when women may formally practise medicine. Leaving aside the question of feminine modesty, there is the matter of temperament.'

'Yet amongst the poor there have always been the old wise women with their cures and simples.'

'Miss Henlow is not poor,' Dr Stagg said, as sharply as if Fairfax had said she was. 'She has an independent portion – not great, but such as to place her eligibly in the world. It is all the more gratifying that a young woman of such – eminent respectability should interest herself in my work as she does, and make no fuss about going into low and pestilential places, and witnessing harrowing sights. I regret – I regret deeply that I was led – or rather led myself to believe that that interest was other than it was. For it was, of course, disinterested. A disinterested interest – damn my eyes, you take my meaning. Under that misapprehension, I was bold enough to press upon Miss Henlow a suit that I should have been judicious enough to see was – was wholly inappropriate.'

Dr Stagg emerged from the tortuous coils of this statement breathing hard. He swiped off his hat and scrubbed at his perspiring brow with his sleeve, staring flatly into the distance.

'I . . . understood there was a connection,' Fairfax said tentatively, 'though it was none of my business to ask—'

'Oh, there is no connection.' Sharp again. 'That is quite a misunderstanding, sir. The matter was all cleared up very quickly and amiably, as of course it must be. Through labour and luck I have risen in my profession, but my family were not well placed in the world, sir. Linen drapers in quite a small way, in the West Country. A man must have more address than I can command to leave such beginnings quite behind, and besides . . . the thing was out of the question, in all ways, and so it was settled, and everyone is quite easy now. You are wrong, sir, to speak of connections.'

Fairfax, who had talked to some prickly characters in his time, and had a little of the hedgehog in his own nature, was not put out by this. He simply said, 'Your philosophy does you credit.'

'I don't know about that. I seek no credit for it, I assure you. I am not – I have no pride in myself, Mr Fairfax, only in my attainments. By taking great pains and being methodical, I have become a good physician. I cannot always cure, but I have never, I believe, missed anything, or made a faulty diagnosis. That's all I can say for myself.'

'Your skills were, indeed, most warmly commended by the lady.'

'Do you speak truly?' Stagg's look was almost agonized. 'You do not jest with me?'

'Of course not,' Fairfax said. It would be well nigh impossible to jest with this man, he thought.

'Well. Well, that is curious. Gratifying, I should say. You may know that I attended upon the late Mrs Porteous, in her last days.'

'Yes. The account I have heard was most painful. And after a safe delivery—'

'There is never any telling,' Dr Stagg said dully. 'A woman in childbed runs a higher mortal risk than a man stepping into battle. She may appear to have come through the hazards, and then . . . Well, I could not save her. There was nothing in the world I could do – damn it, nothing!'

He spoke with such angry vehemence that his horse tossed its head in alarm. Stagg moodily tugged at the bridle, repeating 'Nothing' in a bitter murmur. Fairfax studied him sidelong. All settled and easy now, he had said – but what lover ever truly reconciled himself to such a thing? Had failing to save Emma Henlow's sister been the crowning torment to a hopeless but persisting love? Did he torture himself with the thought that if he had saved the sister, his suit might still have had a chance? Small wonder Stagg was such an unquiet man, if so.

The house they had come to visit was at no great distance from the public gardens of Ranelagh, where gardeners and labourers could be glimpsed tidying and trimming the walks and arbours ready for the influx of fashionable visitors tonight; but it might have been a world away. It was at the end of a tumbledown row of riverside cottages. The hot summer day did not reach inside, where damp and ill light created a perpetual chill. Like a cave, Fairfax would have said, except that even beasts would have disdained such accommodation. An upstairs partition had been crudely made from half-rotted timbers bolted crosswise and laid with warped planking. Here on a straw mattress lay the woman of the house and two children, sick with a malignant fever. Scrawny and yellow, the children horridly resembled the monkeys that fashionable ladies led about on a silk cord. Downstairs, a man who looked to be in the first stages of the fever listlessly stirred a pot over a meagre fire; a grandmother who looked ancient but might have been no more than fifty hunched nearby, washing a few potatoes – in its way the most shocking thing of all, for Fairfax saw the root as little more than fodder. All, he noticed, had the same eyes: not a family trait but a kind of hollow stare that would have been mistrust, except that they could not even afford that.

Stagg's constraint seemed to leave him with these people. He was tenderly practical and reassuring, though it was plain there was little he could do. Fairfax did all he could, which was to leave money. As well as relief in getting out of there, he felt his presumption in going in. The poor were always to be viewed.

'You needn't fear,' Dr Stagg said, as Fairfax hawked and spat outside, trying to get the foul smell out of his head. 'I have been daily, and taken no infection.'

'And the infection of the spirit?'

Stagg shrugged. 'One becomes accustomed. 'Tis best to regard it practically. They have no fresh water, and they all piss in the same pot. For what it's worth, the woman and the eldest child will I think recover: the younger I misdoubt. But there is never any telling.'

Fairfax wiped his mouth. He felt ashamed of his weakness. Having known poverty himself as a young man, he had lodged in some of the most unsavoury quarters of London, where such desolating sights were common. And yet . . .

'It is unexpected, I dare say,' Stagg said, as if reading his thought, 'here in Chelsea, amongst the ladies' academies and the gingerbread villas. But the poor always ye have with you – so says scripture. Take your way from here along the river up to Westminster, and you will come upon as many haunts of want and vice as in St Giles. Indeed they fairly teem about the noble skirts of the Abbey, and the palaces of government. I have been much amongst them, as few doctors will.'

Again it did him credit, but Fairfax chose not to say so, as praise seemed to stir up that mental gust in him.

'And so, how does the young widow do?'

'She bears up, as the saying goes, very well.'

'And is under suspicion on that account? Oh, forgive me, sir, 'tis not my place to speak of it, but I cannot think what you and Mr Yelverton think to discover in this business. The gentleman was not killed by any agency but nature, and as for the meddler with the carriage, it might have been anyone. Even early in the morning the Spread Eagle was full of company: all the carriers in the district use it, and—'

'Early in the morning? You mean yesterday? I had not known you were there then, Dr Stagg.'

'No? Well, I did not think to mention it. I called there early, to pick up some medical journals that I have sent from the city. Nothing unusual. And I repeat, I saw nothing out of the common there. I would have mentioned it, but really it seemed . . .'

'Yes, of course. Well, you may be right, Dr Stagg. I must crave your indulgence – once I see a puzzle, I cannot let it alone. A vexing habit.'

They parted before the gates of the Royal Hospital, Stagg to make his daily rounds there, Fairfax to return home and take an afternoon rest. This prescription of convalescence usually irked and bored him: today he felt genuinely tired, and after some cold meats from his landlord's well-supplied sideboard he lay down and composed his thoughts, which were a tangle of perplexity and suspicion.

Suspicion, even, of the man under whose roof he lay. When someone failed to mention something, he was instinctively mistrustful. And yet he couldn't help feeling that Stagg was right: that he was investigating a blind alley. The alley took visual form as he drifted on the edge of sleep, and though he saw its dead end as a wall of blank stone, there were foggy shadows on either side of him, and something lurked there, he knew – something malevolent that did not want to be seen. The image melded into a dream, and in the dream, naturally enough, was Cordelia. They were all to one another, magnificently in love – almost perfect; and yet also in the dream was the knowledge that Cordelia's husband was dead, and Fairfax had killed him. He did not know how he had done it; but in the dream George Linton's face, which he had long been able to picture only as a vague mask of dislike, was superbly clear to him. A dead face, staring in horror as Mr Chilcott's had been, at the bottom of some dark place. And he alone was responsible – yet he kept protesting in dream logic that it didn't matter, because . . . *I did it for love*. That was the phrase he kept repeating, like a chant; and he wasn't sure that he didn't cry it out loud as he lurched into waking, covered in sweat.

It was nearly six, and a wonderfully mellow bronzy light filled his chamber. He felt absurdly elated and glad to be alive, and he dressed with care: his best velvet coat with embroidered buttonholes, silk breeches. Tying his hair with a new ribbon, he caught the faint sound of a footstep on the stairs. He disregarded it until, studying himself in the square of mirror above the mantel, he noticed a shadow between door and jamb. He waited a moment, then went quickly and opened the door.

'Ah. You're awake.' Dr Stagg stood stiffly there, blinking. 'I thought . . . I am having supper laid presently. You are going, of course, to the Porteous house, but I thought I had better make sure.'

'Yes. Shall I present your compliments?'

Fairfax said it simply to fill the awkward pause. Only when it was out did he see that it might be construed as a mischievous allusion to what Dr Stagg had told him earlier. Oh, but damn it all, the man was so smouldering and secret anyhow . . .

'My compliments. Yes – that would be appropriate, would it not? My compliments by all means.' There was a knock at the door downstairs: he looked relieved. 'I am wanted, perhaps. I'll leave you, sir.'

Fairfax finished tying his hair and picked up his hat, regretting the absence of gold lace on it. Descending the stairs, he heard a female voice, low but throbbing with agitation. He came down to the hall just in time to see the door of the parlour Stagg used as his consulting room closing, and to glimpse within the face of Tabitha Dance. It was pale but composed: there was a set expression of resolve on it that was somehow shocking, like a moment of nudity.

Well, he was seeing mysteries everywhere, no doubt: the worthy doctor treated the poor as well as the rich, and there was no reason why Tabitha should not be one of them. As for Stagg's hovering at his door . . . well, the thought had already crossed his mind that Frederick Stagg might be in a ferment of jealousy over the fact that Miss Henlow had invited him to supper, and if it were so, he thought, then he was going to have to come out and say something. Something to the effect that he had no interest in that lady (leaving aside the fact that he was even less eligible than Stagg) and that was because . . .

Because his heart was taken. Romantic and ridiculous notion. The heart, merely a sturdy organ that pumped blood about the body, was always being evoked; it leapt and ached, it yearned and cried, it was captured and offered and so on. He deplored the debased language one had to use for such a situation – and yet he felt its truth in (where else?) his heart, as he came to Five Fields Row, and there saw Cordelia.

She was standing outside the Randall house, at the foot of the steps. The evening glow was all around her. Her hair was a coppery flame. A molten silhouette, she waited for him. The glow faded as he drew nearer to her, replaced by detail.

'I thought—' she began. 'When you said—'

'Yes. I thought perhaps . . .'

111

They laughed a little tensely. It occurred to him that they both perhaps thought too much. But somehow he knew it would always be so with him and Cordelia – supposing there was such a thing as an 'always' between them.

'How are you?' she said.

'I do very well.'

'Good . . . You will have a very pleasant evening there, you know: Mr Porteous and Miss Henlow are both highly civilized. You probably suspect me of irony when I speak of Miss Henlow, but I do not. Not this time at any rate.'

'It was curious how the invitation came about. I never expected to see Miss Henlow at Mrs Chilcott's; but so it was, and on the way back—'

'Dear Mr Fairfax, you do not have to explain yourself to me: really I should hope not. And as for Miss Henlow, she is addicted to good works, you know, and so visiting a new widow would be quite in her way. There, now I *am* being ironical. Well, come inside. There will be talk else.'

In her parlour the light of summer dusk was like amber liquid. Even the hideous portrait was harmonized. A bottle of wine and two glasses stood on the table, beaded with light.

'I thought you might drink a glass of canary with me before you go,' she said, pouring.

'With all my heart.' That damnable organ again . . . He took the glass, and they stood facing one another. 'It feels as if we are about to toast something.'

'Long life to his majesty? Or the king over the water, like the Jacobites?'

'Oh, kings are all alike.'

'The same is often said of women.'

'A slander. There are none like you, I think.'

She gave him a troubled smile. 'I cannot pretend I dislike hearing that. Even though the truth—'

'I do not know what the truth is. Only what I feel. And what I felt today, when you referred to that letter . . . You did mean the letter from your husband?'

'I did. It is destroyed.'

'If I understand aright . . . And yet I don't understand, Cordelia. Not really.'

She took a deep drink of wine, her hand slightly unsteady. 'I destroyed the letter because I felt it was worthless. I felt my husband's avowals were worthless, and talk of reconciliation a mockery. And now you will ask me if I still love him. I do not think I do. But love is a strange, piecemeal thing. Bits of it are left behind after the substance has departed. Its mark, or its stain, is on so many things in your life. Some fragments are like gunpowder, and you fear they may go off and hurt you.'

'In fact your – your heart is not free of him.'

'Maybe so. But I want it to be – I do indeed. If it were just a question of what I want, why then . . . Well, I will tell you. I truly wish I had never married George, and I say that not as the usual carping of the wronged wife, but as the one true wish of my life. But that I am married to him is the one true *fact* of my life, and it will not go away . . . Are you of a religious turn of mind, Mr Fairfax?'

'No.'

'I thought not – indeed I suspect you may well be the most shocking free thinker. Well, I am no pietist either. It is not the sacredness of the bond that affrights me, at least I don't think so. But I am affrighted nonetheless. To

113

contemplate casting it all away – everything to which convention and respectability subscribes – to fly in the face of the world as a woman must who breaks those bonds . . . It scares me and I flinch.'

Fairfax thought ruefully, grimly, of the manners and morals that were observed just an hour's chair-ride from here, in the salons of London society. There assignations were made with a flick of the fan and a lift of the artificial eyebrow: wives entertained young lovers in pastille-scented boudoirs while their husbands pursued doxies in gilded rooms above chocolate-houses. Adultery was as much a fashionable pastime as the whist table and the Italian opera and the ball with its decorous exchanges of daintily stepping partners: the cuckold was the stuff of stale jokes and the Fleet Street print-shops displayed a hundred bawdy variations on the theme of the Lover Surpriz'd, behind screens, behind bed-curtains, climbing bare-arsed through windows, forever absurd and forever trivial.

And yet, for good or ill, with him and Cordelia it could not be so. The very depth of their feelings – and he had no doubt of hers now – prevented it, and held them in a seething stiffness of abstention.

All very noble and stirring, no doubt: tragical even; but she was so beautiful to him just then that it was also unbearable. Unbearable, too, the thought that he might press her, and she might yield – but being the people they were, there would be a disabling regret after. Our characters are cages in which we prowl, he thought.

'Well, it is harder for you than me,' he said softly. 'I have nothing to lose but my heart.'

She finished her wine quickly, stood quizzically regarding

her glass as if she could not imagine where it had come from. 'You know, there is nothing to stop you making sheep's eyes at Emma Henlow this evening. With matters as they are, I can hold you to no undertaking. There is really nothing—'

'Yes, there is,' he said, taking the glass from her and setting it down.

'Well. I had better not have any more wine, I declare, I shall become unmanageable and start singing and you will hear me through the party wall . . . Finish yours, though. Here: take another glass.'

He took the refilled glass from her hands, and held it up to her before drinking.

'Gracious heavens, you don't mean to make a toast of me – that is for pretty young chits and I am quite the most over-the-hill and slipshod creature, and very far from a toast, you know . . .' She ran down into silence, and their eyes held each other while he drank the glass.

'I had better go . . . The trouble is, I shall walk in there smelling of wine and be thought a toper.'

'I don't think so.' She came close to him, and moved her face back and forth a couple of inches from his, her eyes half closed. 'No . . . you needn't fear.'

The wine had rather gone to his head, at any rate – the wine, and the meeting itself, which had been intoxicating and befuddling enough. Feeling slightly unreal, he left the Randall house and went up the steps next door, preparing himself to be sociable as a man might prepare to walk the high wire.

It was a strange evening. Later he tried to determine how much of that was the result of his own mental state, and couldn't decide. Emma Henlow and Charles Porteous made him very welcome: he had no feeling of intruding or outstaying his welcome. And yet there seemed a lurking inappropriateness about the whole business. Neither the young widower nor his sister-in-law wore mourning: yet if they had been replete with crape and jet and weepers there could hardly have been a stronger sense of death in the house.

Again he could not pin this down. Charles Porteous greeted him with quiet friendliness and made no parade of being a sorrowing man. He was tall, a little round-shouldered, his face bony and handsome and distinguished though very dark, with shadowed brown eyes and that strong growth of bristle which colours the face even after the cleanest of shaves. He wore his own hair simply dressed, and no lace: immaculate, though, and gentlemanly in his air – impossible, Fairfax thought, to imagine him raising his voice, or uttering guttural curse-words as Dr Stagg did.

'A great pleasure to welcome you, Mr Fairfax. Emma has talked of you. You are recovering from an illness, I think. I hope the road is smooth and swift.'

'Thank you. I am so well now as to feel something of an impostor.'

Charles Porteous smiled an attractive, tired smile. 'There is no being too careful of one's health. The air of Chelsea is very good. But an enforced lack of occupation can be trying. You are a tutor, I believe. You have my respect. I would have us all scholars, and not warriors. You have written?'

'I have earned my bread by my pen in the past, though in no very exalted fashion. I could never join this company,' Fairfax said, admiring the bookcases which filled one end of the drawing room. Latin and Greek authors, the English poets, philosophers and metaphysicians: a substantial collection, and obviously read.

'A great resource. I do not apply to it as often as I should, but what man does? Well, anyhow, we are People of the Book, as the Mohammedans say, and we are not many in these days of ours, and must cleave together. You are acquainted with our singular neighbour, I hear.'

It was Cordelia who at once leaped to Fairfax's mind, and for some reason he felt himself blushing: but of course, Porteous meant Wolfgang Mozart.

'Yes, quite by accident. A marvel, apparently: I confess I long to hear him play, for part of me doubts that he can be genuine.'

'I have not heard him play, but Emma has looked over his compositions, and knows enough of music to be – what would you say, Emma? Impressed?'

'Most forcibly impressed,' Emma Henlow said. 'And quite put to shame, when I think of the heavy weather I make of the simplest pieces.' There was a spinet in the room too, with sheet-music open on it. Everything, indeed, proclaimed taste: no burgher clumsiness here. And yet how ferociously respectable it was also! Fairfax had been in the houses of the aristocratic great, where monstrous portraits stared and there was a smell of dogs and milady cursed the poacher in robust Anglo-Saxon terms; he had been in the houses of merchants newly fattened with wealth, where the brand-new silverware shone so bright the cheerful merchant's wife could not help admiring her plump face in it. But he had never been in a house in which the cult of Politeness was so much observed. And remembering Tabitha Dance, he thought that he would not like to be a servant in such a household.

'You wrong yourself, my dear. You play admirably,' Charles Porteous said. 'And as for this wondrous child, I do not mean to denigrate his abilities, but it can surely do his moral character no good to be petted and fawned upon in this way. And to be continually going before the public, like a common actor or ballad-singer – it must teach a very ill lesson, that the applause of the rabble is to be preferred to the dignity of the gentleman.'

What a combination of pomposity and vulgarity, Fairfax thought. And yet Emma Henlow, no fool he was sure, listened attentively, and murmured agreement. Her face when she looked at her brother-in-law was serious, even solemn – not what Fairfax thought typical of her at all.

And after that Porteous stopped talking like a prig and became an agreeable, sensible man again. He asked after the curriculum of Fairfax's studies, and spoke intelligently of Bacon, a favourite of his, and scientific philosophy. Strange mixture or odd fish, Fairfax thought, but again could not pin down why – except that the man had no freshness about him. There was the staleness of a damped fire, and always a kind of distance, as if his host were entertaining him from behind a sheet of glass. He had even refrained from shaking hands when Fairfax came in – it was Emma who did that.

And here was another curiosity. Whilst Emma was in every visible respect the devoted handmaiden to the lord and master – asking if the new-trimmed candles hurt his eyes, running to fetch his snuffbox, and falling reverently silent when he spoke even if he interrupted her – Fairfax began to feel that what kept her here was power.

It was a subtle atmosphere, but once he had sensed it he

could not let it go. Porteous reigned here, but Emma ruled. When a servant came with a question about supper, it was she who was brisk about the business, whilst he sat with averted, dreaming eyes. And when the baby was brought in after his feed by the wet-nurse, Fairfax saw with what conscious authority Emma took the child, and presented him to his father to be kissed. Like an archbishop christening a prince, he thought, as she bore the little shawled bundle slowly and grandly across the room.

But the ritual faltered when Porteous put back the wrappings and looked into his son's face. He sighed, and was thin-lipped, his fingers lightly resting near the tiny round cheek.

'A little pale today, I think.'

'No, no,' Emma said. 'He has fed well, and does splendidly. It is only the light.'

'Hm. Yes, I suppose.' Porteous glanced at Fairfax. 'You know, of course, of our late loss. Arthur thrives, yet still after such an event one always fears – one hears doom and mortality in every colicky cry.'

'Very natural,' Fairfax said, and after a hesitation: 'I cannot begin to imagine the feelings . . . But you have a pretty boy, sir, and he looks hearty.'

'His looks are Catherine's,' Porteous said in his faintly tired way. 'And it is on that account that sometimes . . . sometimes the reminder is bitter. An irrational man might say that the child is, all unwittingly, his mother's murderer.'

'And an irrational man, thank heaven, is precisely what you are not, Charles,' Emma said, crisp and cool as ever. 'You will not withhold a kiss because of morbid thoughts, I know.'

Porteous shook his head, a little irritably it seemed, but he kissed the baby. Emma returned the child to the nurse with a satisfied look, and soon they went into supper; and Fairfax thought yes, it is power. In the house of her brother-in-law, a man bereft and enfeebled, she had a unique consequence. A wife could have had no more.

The meal was very good – a chine of mutton, veal collops, pies and tarts and a syllabub – and the wine had made Fairfax hungry. But he was too uncomfortable to enjoy it. Again he had the feeling that he shouldn't be here. Charles Porteous talked to him – fluently if not with animation – of books, of the London theatres, of events in the American colonies, and Emma Henlow helped him to food and pressed him to take more. And yet he felt like some needy but near relative who came unasked, and had to be entertained.

Porteous drank freely, but ate very little – even though Emma, with a devotedness that raised Fairfax's eyebrows, not only carved but cut up his meat herself so that he had only to fork it listlessly up to his mouth, one-handed, while the other picked fretfully at the snowy tablecloth. The portrait behind him, perhaps, cast a pall. The resemblance of the woman in the painting to Emma was so strong as to leave no doubt that this was the late Catherine Porteous. Hers was not the largest or most prominent picture in the well-appointed dining room, however. That honour belonged to the portrait of a gentleman above the mantelpiece: grand tie-wig, large black-browed face, and pouchy eyes that seemed to look down at the laden table with disapproval, as if reckoning the cost of the veal.

'My uncle,' Porteous said, following Fairfax's gaze. 'The name of Sir Andrew Porteous is familiar to you, no doubt.

There can be few respectable circles in which it is not.'

Some people had the sneezes or the fits, Fairfax thought: this man had attacks of pomposity.

'Indeed. It was mentioned in a certain connection today. Mr Gabriel Chilcott – the gentleman whose death I am charged with looking into – was an associate of his, I believe.'

'Very probably: my uncle has many associates, if few on an equality. I heard, of course, about that unfortunate business. A plaguey uncertain game this life of ours is.'

'I found the widow bearing up, though understandably fragile in her temper,' Miss Henlow said, with a glance of humour at Fairfax. 'But pray, my dear Charles, how did you find your uncle today? I was troubled by the last account of him.'

'No better, and a little worse, I fancy. His old gouty condition, the doctors say, but he is not so sure: there are flutterings about the heart, and I was concerned about leaving him this afternoon. But he was as gracious as always, and said I had a son to see to, and bid me not trouble about him – which is easier said than done.'

No telling, of course, but to Fairfax it sounded like a classic valetudinarian's trick. Keep your dependants on a string, make them dance whenever you fancy yourself ill. Emma, though, was solemn.

'You disturb me, Charles. The poor gentleman is all alone, and suffering . . . I do wonder the doctors cannot help him more.'

'Oh, one cannot expect much of that tribe of leeches,' Porteous said, with quite an ugly spasm crossing his face. 'Well, I shall go see him at Berkeley Square first thing in the morning: I confess I am a little uneasy myself . . . My

121

dear Emma, did not the chimney-sweep call today?' he added sharply, his eye falling on the cold hearth, where a trace of fallen soot disturbed the general neatness.

'He did not. And that, I fear, is because he is a shiftless rogue – all the neighbourhood says so – and does not keep his appointments. I said as much, Charles, and would have engaged another. But you would not have it, you recall.'

'Yes, yes, I recall.'

'It shows, my dear Charles, that you should be guided by me in these things.' She spoke lightly, but there was an edge in her tone: it reminded Fairfax of the squeak of a knife-blade on a plate. 'Is it not so, my dear? You will be guided by me, will you not, for your comfort and welfare?'

'I will, of course,' her brother-in-law said – sulky, yet submissive. This sudden, curious grating in the air between them made Fairfax even more uncomfortable, and yet he was fascinated too. As soon as Porteous began to talk of something else, Emma was all devout attention again: yet what steely firmness there had been! Fairfax found himself thinking of the eunuchs who took control in the palaces of the East, manipulating the power that had made them powerless.

'It does not do her justice, Mr Fairfax,' Porteous said, jolting him. He realized he had been gazing again at the portrait of Mrs Porteous. 'Mere paint cannot represent such fairness. You might say she was too fair for this world.'

'That is, I truly think, the only way of looking at it,' Emma said. 'Charles, you have eaten so little. Is it not to your liking?'

'Oh . . .' Porteous shrugged. 'Sustenance.'

'I wish you would take a little more. Try a morsel of this tart.'

He did, moodily enough. The thought crossed Fairfax's mind that Charles Porteous might resent the continued existence of his wife's sister, so like her and yet so abundantly healthy. And yet he was dependent on her ... An emotional see-saw, he thought: first one rose, then the other, but each was powerless alone.

As for a third party, one could only feel superfluous. At the end of the meal there was, to his relief, no suggestion that Emma leave them to a session of port, a custom he disliked at the best of times; and with some excuses about not keeping late hours on medical advice, he managed to get away pretty soon.

'You must come and see us again before you leave Chelsea, Mr Fairfax,' Charles Porteous said with shrivelled courtesy, not getting up. It was Emma Henlow who accompanied him to the door and, dismissing the maid, shook his hand and thanked him.

'It has done Charles good. You may not think so; but though he is so low-spirited, he is appreciative, as am I.'

The door closed: Fairfax's eyes strayed wistfully to next door. A light shone cosily in the Mozarts' quarters, but it was of the downstairs tenant he was thinking, and wishing mightily that he could just step freely in, and talk over the evening, and laugh ... Well, he had not that freedom, and after their charged encounter he was not sure how to face her anyhow. Not without having his heart pulled to pieces in a way he didn't feel equal to. Bed was the only place for him just now. Returning to Royal Hospital Row, and finding his landlord out, he retired straight away.

But perhaps because of the sleep he had had this afternoon, and the food and wine, he lay in a drowsy, twitchy discomfort for some time. It was well after midnight when he dozed, and then started awake at the sound of the front door. In the room below, Dr Stagg's parlour, he heard the young physician move about: there was a chinking of glass, and then a steady soft tapping of footsteps, back and forth, as if Stagg were pacing about. The rhythmic sound went on so long that Fairfax at last fell asleep to it, and dreamed of a shadowy animal prowling the confines of a cage.

Five

Taking his walk the next morning, a little late from oversleeping, Fairfax faced the fact that he was getting nowhere with his investigation – indeed, that it was for all practical purposes at an end.

Often he relied on a night's sleep to clear perplexities, and present him with fresh perspectives come daylight: the process was somewhat like digestion, he supposed. But today he had nothing, and no idea where to look. What Cordelia called his talent for ferreting out mysteries seemed to have deserted him.

But then what precisely *did* he suspect? he asked himself. What was the ferret supposed to come out clutching in its jaws? Well, he suspected Mrs Jane Chilcott. He suspected she was lying about the strange man Wolfgang had seen; and that, taken together with the damage to her carriage – leaving aside her husband's death – made him suspect she was involved in some intrigue or conspiracy. If she was not, then someone had still meant to harm her or her husband or both – and she was still lying about the man in her room.

Either way, Jane Chilcott was the key. But she was not going to open any doors for him, that was certain. He couldn't force her to tell the truth. There were others peripheral to the mystery, but try as he might he couldn't bring them any closer to the centre. That unfortunate Tabitha Dance had been at the Chilcott house yesterday, begging charity from a kindly servant – that was all. She had been at the Spread Eagle on the day of Mr Chilcott's death, but far gone in drink and wrapped up in a lover's quarrel with Jemmy Runquest. As for Runquest, he had played the saucy swaggerer with Mrs Chilcott, and predictably roused her husband's anger – but it had come to nothing, surely meant nothing to any of them. The rich uncle of Charles Porteous, Tabitha's former employer, had been a business associate of Mr Chilcott – but then City men were likely to know one another: a link without meaning. And Dr Stagg had omitted to mention being at the Spread Eagle earlier on the fatal morning – but then a large inn had so many functions in a small community that a man often had legitimate business there.

He was stuck. And what doubled his frustration was that no one would much care. Mr Yelverton the magistrate had been content for Fairfax to nose about on his behalf: he would be just as content if nothing came of it. As for proving that young Wolfgang was no liar or fantasist – well, that would be a satisfaction to Fairfax, because he liked the boy, and because he disliked the sturdy English assumption that anyone who was foreign and clever was untrustworthy. But the boy's father had made it clear he preferred Wolfgang kept out of it in any case; and soon they would surely return to London, and the acclaim of the public stage, and it would all be forgotten.

It's you, Fairfax thought as he strolled down to Ebury

Bridge, where he had first met Wolfgang: you're the only one with a stake in this. Pride and self-importance. He just had to show that he was right and everyone else was wrong. Well, this time he couldn't, and it ought to be a very smart lesson to his vanity. And perhaps it stung all the more, and made him feel like a sulky boy, because of Cordelia. Ah, yes, that was it, wasn't it? If she still could not be his, he wanted at least to impress her, to dazzle. To strut like a cockerel on a dunghill, he thought with a disgust that turned into amusement. You, my friend, are hung-over, liverish, crapulent. That is why you are painting the universe various shades of black. He had had more wine at that supper, and he could taste the bilious ghost of it.

And then Fairfax's queasy stomach was tried in a way he could never have guessed. A shout – a wailing, terrible shout – came from the far side of the timber bridge. Fairfax turned to see the figure of an old waterman, down by the canal-side, frantically waving his broad-brimmed hat. Something long and dark was on the grass beside him. The waterman cried out again, then dropped to his knees. He was still kneeling and trembling when Fairfax reached him.

Somehow Fairfax was not sick. But he couldn't look long: had to turn away and stare at the meadows, green and glorious under the summer sun, so that he was not seeing the sprawled limbs, not seeing the great oily stain on the grass, not seeing the smashed head with its long dark hair and single streak of grey, not seeing the dead body of Tabitha Dance.

The grave's a fine and private place, the poet famously said – but before the grave, death had no privacy, Fairfax thought. There were four people gathered about poor Tabitha now.

The waterman had been to fetch the parish constable and Dr Stagg, whose face was very pale as he straightened up from examining the body.

'She must have died very quickly from such a blow,' he said. 'That's all the comfort . . . Yes,' he added, as Fairfax pointed out a jagged stone the size of a large orange. He had spotted it very easily: it had been tossed down in the grass with no attempt at concealment. It was ghastly with blood and hair. 'Yes, there we have it, I fear. A blow, or blows. The attack was . . . most determined.'

'Murdered. The poor creature,' said the parish constable, a gaunt and melancholy man who still wore his chandler's apron. 'Not in daylight, sir? It fair chills me to think of it.'

'No. The flesh is stiff, and the blood congealed. She must have lain thus some hours at least.'

'Killed last night, then? That chills me too,' the constable said. He began to examine the grass round about, though Fairfax had already done that, and found nothing more. It was just a quiet stretch of grassy bank under the shadow of the bridge, starred with a few kingcups. Bees hummed: flies, too . . . There was no sign of a protracted struggle. She must either have innocently met her killer at this spot, or been followed hither.

'I thought 'twas a bundle of old clothes when I came along,' the waterman said. 'The poor maid! The cruellest sight I ever saw!'

'Cruel, but I'd not say "maid" when it comes to Tabitha Dance, I fear,' the constable said. 'Not to speak ill of her, but she had a name for – well, well, I'll not say it. No creature deserves such an end, mind.'

'There is more,' Stagg said, wiping his big face with his

handkerchief. 'She must be carried to some better place than this where I can examine her, and with a woman present.'

The constable scratched under his wig. 'Why, I can't think where, sir, excepting the place where she was living lately. 'Tis a sad pity, but that's all that suggests.'

'Where had she been living?' Fairfax said.

'Just an old hut, sir, down by the river turning. Used to be a shed belonging to the waterworks, I fancy – walls and a roof and no more, but 'twas all she could get. She was turfed out of her lodging a fortnight since, and had to make do. She was lodging with Goody Soper, you see.'

'An old widow,' Dr Stagg said at Fairfax's look. 'She is Jemmy Runquest's grandmother, and he lives there also.'

'I see.'

'Aye – her beau – an odd arrangement, and rather a shocking one too,' the constable said. 'And an awkward one, when they came to a-falling out, as they seemed to lately. 'Twas mentioned to me that she surely had no claim to be living in that hut, but I didn't meddle, not I: it was empty, and she had to live somewhere, poor wretch.'

'The hut it must be, then,' Stagg said in a hollow voice.

The waterman knew where there was a fence-hurdle that would do for carrying the body; and presently the sombre procession with its covered burden – Stagg drew the shawl she was wearing over her face – made its way down to the riverside, where a ramshackle timber hut stood amongst a jungle of nettles and cow parsley. Inside there were only a few scavenged sticks of furniture and a straw mattress, on which they laid her down. It was bleak, indeed, to think of this as her only home, and the only place that would receive her murdered body.

The constable went off, at Stagg's prompting, to notify the magistrate, and the waterman to fetch Goody Soper, whose cottage was at a short distance down-river by the white-lead works. Fairfax stood outside the hut with Stagg, taking deep breaths of sweet air.

'She will do as well as any to make a formal identification – I have never heard of the girl having any family,' Stagg said. 'And she can be with me when I examine her.'

'You fear a rape?'

'Perhaps, but . . . Well, I may break the confidence now: Tabitha was with child. There are two lives snuffed out.'

'Dear God . . .'

'So she came to tell me, at any rate. I made no examination, but the symptoms were convincing enough, and I do not doubt . . . Well, we shall see.'

'Goody Soper is all very well,' Fairfax said, swallowing bile. 'But I fancy her precious grandson is the one who must account for himself.'

'Runquest? Aye, it looks bad, I confess . . . but we must see.'

Hasty conclusions, Fairfax reproached himself. But the man was a two-fisted brute, the girl he wanted to shake off was pregnant – was it not obvious?

Or was it, in fact, too obvious?

Fairfax had observed before that old women who had got the title of Goody or Goodwoman were usually harsh harridans with very little that was pleasant, if not good, about them; and Goody Soper appeared true to type. She came sniffing and grumbling in a voice like a saw on wood, a lumpy old creature who carried a stick less for support, for she seemed robust enough, than to wave and poke and jab generally. Her hook-nosed face was half hidden by a great mob-cap, though it might have been better hidden entirely, Fairfax thought.

''Tis no concern of mine,' she kept saying. 'I'm sorry for her, but 'tisn't no concern of mine. I turned her out and wouldn't have her back, and no decent body would blame me, for she was a trollop when all's said and done. I knew she'd come to a bad end, and I'm sorry to be right, but 'tisn't no concern of mine.'

She consented to go into the hut with Dr Stagg, however; and when she came out was a little chastened. Not much, though.

'Well-a-day, a shocking thing. A woman of my time of life shouldn't have to see such things, indeed, 'tis too bad. You'd best look for a tinker or a gypsy – they're the ones for such murderous tricks, and there's any amount of 'em about these days. They'd be long gone by now, mind. Well, mayhap it's a blessing for the girl, for there's no gainsaying the condition she was in – ugh! A trollop, like I said, and there's the proof.'

Dr Stagg nodded at Fairfax bleakly.

'Heigh-ho,' the old woman said. ''Twould only have been another bastard on the charge of the parish, and Lord knows there's too many of them.'

'When did you last see her?' Fairfax said, trying to mask the disgust on his face.

'See her? Why, I can't recall. I turned her out, like I tell you, and wanted no more of her. She's been back to my door more than once, bothering my Jemmy, but I always sent her away, sharp.' The old woman emphasized the word with a jab of her stick.

'Last night?'

'No. Not last night. Never saw hide nor hair of her. Learnt her lesson, I should hope – forever plaguing my poor Jemmy—'

'And what about your poor Jemmy? Where is he now?' Fairfax couldn't keep the fury out of his tone. 'And where was he last night?'

Goody Soper's mouth fell open, then she shut it with a snap and glowered at him.

'I'll not say a word more. You'd run his neck into a noose, would you? Shame on you, whoever you are. Cess on you. I'll not speak a word unless the beak asks me.'

'A fine idea,' Fairfax said. 'I think it is time we went before Mr Yelverton, and you with us, Mrs Soper.'

It seemed hard to leave the murdered girl alone in her dingy dwelling, but there was nothing else for it. In a body they trooped over to the magistrate's house, Goody Soper complaining at every step, though she was as hale as an ox. Going to Mr Yelverton's would fulfil a double purpose, Fairfax thought, for Jemmy Runquest was probably there . . . and it had to be Runquest, surely. Innocent until proven guilty, he reminded himself. He was struggling to keep hold of reason, his touchstone: he felt shaken to the core. And also, somehow, ashamed. He had been gnawing in frustration, wishing for some new development . . . well, now he had his wish. And the irrational part of him moaned that he had made it happen.

Mr Yelverton received them, with very ill grace, in his library. The impedimenta of dead civilizations filled this room too, and the old waterman looked deeply troubled by the Egyptian horror that frowned over him while he gave his account of finding the body, and mighty glad to get away from it when he was dismissed.

'Of all things!' Mr Yelverton groaned, holding his face tenderly in both hands. 'Of all things to happen, at such a time . . . There must be an inquest, I suppose, and then she must be buried at the parish's expense, no doubt, unless the girl has family anywhere . . . You, my good woman—' He paused, looking at Goody Soper with a kind of fascinated revulsion, as if he had never seen anything like her: as if, indeed, she were a species of exotic creature that he was not at all sure about having indoors. 'You are not related to the deceased? I confess to being a little confused by this dreadful business . . .'

'The dead girl used to lodge with Mrs Soper, but was turned out by her,' Fairfax repeated patiently. 'Mrs Soper, sir, is the grandmother of your manservant, Runquest. And as he was known to be the sweetheart of the dead girl, there is surely—'

'Runquest? Don't speak of that wretch, I beg,' Mr Yelverton said, pettishly hitching his nerveless legs. 'He is no longer in my employ. I dismissed him first thing this morning, as soon as he arrived. It has quite disturbed me, and has thrown my plans utterly in disarray, but there was no help for it. The man had tried to impose upon me. I required excellent testimonials as to character and suitability for such a post, and these he had supplied – hm! Fraudulently, it turns out. I am a fastidious man, and took the trouble of writing to the former employer who gave him such a glowing character. It turns out there is no such person; no such address. His letter of reference was a sheer fakery. I confronted him with it this morning. There was nothing to say, of course, and I dismissed him directly. It is a great inconvenience to me, but—'

'Poor Jemmy! Lost a plum job!' Goody Soper cried. 'Oh, for shame, 'tis not fair – he's the best of grandsons, sir, and you'll not find a better man . . .'

'What – what does she say?' appealed Mr Yelverton, wincing, though the old woman spoke clearly enough.

'That Runquest is a good man,' Fairfax said. 'He did not live under your roof, sir?'

'No, no. A day-servant only. It seemed not worthwhile to lodge him here, as we were to set out for Italy so soon. Such inconvenience . . . ! You suspect him of this dreadful crime, Mr Fairfax?'

'I think he should give an account of himself, that's all. He was, or had been till lately, Tabitha's lover. I myself saw them quarrelling, apparently over his cooling towards her, and in that quarrel he struck her. Also . . .' He looked at Dr Stagg.

'The girl was with child,' the doctor said. 'She had come to me about it last evening, and my examination confirms it, I regret to say.'

'Abominable!' said Mr Yelverton, though whether he meant the crime or pregnancy in general it was hard to say. 'And did she mention the father, Dr Stagg, when she consulted you?'

'Yes and no . . . The fact is, she came to ask me if I would help her to the means of – of getting rid of it. She was without employ or accommodation, and on the parish, and altogether desperate. Of course I told her I could do nothing of the kind. In that case, she said, she would go before the magistrate and swear the father, and so compel him to look after her.'

'Indeed? That is not a legal proceeding until the child is born, you know,' said Mr Yelverton. 'Though I know that these – these girls will hold out this threat in order to bring their men to heel, as it were.'

'Yes . . . yes, so I thought,' Dr Stagg said, chewing his lip. 'Well, all I could do was urge her to be calm, and do nothing rash, and so she went away.'

'With her mind changed, would you say, sir?' the constable said, rubbing his chin. 'Or still the same?'

'The same,' Dr Stagg said after a moment.

'Dear me. And Runquest was her . . . paramour,' Mr Yelverton said. 'He stood to lose a great deal if the girl held him to his responsibility. An excellent position with me – which last night, of course, he still believed was his. Dear me . . .'

'The girl was a trollop!' croaked Goody Soper, flourishing her stick and nearly demolishing something ancient and bull-headed. 'That's what you need to think on, sir, before you come down on my poor Jemmy. Why, she had the blackest name in five miles. Anyone'll tell you so, and I'll go on oath whenever you want me, and say it. A filthy, loose-living trollop—'

'What does she say?' gasped Mr Yelverton. 'Does she mean to imply that the deceased was likely to have come by her condition in, ahem, any number of quarters?'

'Why, she had more men than you could shake a stick at,' the old woman snorted – though as she shook her stick at everybody, this was not a forceful figure. ''Twas on account of her whorish ways I turned her out. She led my

Jemmy astray, to begin with, and he's a good boy.'

'You do not deny, then,' Mr Yelverton said, addressing her with reluctance, 'that there was a – an intimate connection between your grandson and the girl?'

'Oh, she got him in her toils, true enough. But if she was in the straw, the brat could have been anybody's – that's what I say, and I'll take my oath on it. Too good for the likes of her, I told him. Don't get dragged down by her, I told him.'

'Well, that's as may be, Goody,' the constable said. 'But where's Jemmy now? And where was he last night? – that's the question.'

'He was at home with me last night, God bless him. He sat with me the whole even, from cockshut till bed – that's the sort he is. Sat up reading to me, and then turned in.'

'Reading to you?' the constable said, with obvious disbelief.

'Aye, don't I tell you? Then we turned in. And if he'd gone out, I would have heard him, being but a poor sleeper, on account of the screws in my joints. Why, a falling feather wakes *me*.'

'And when did he go out this morning?' the constable said, still dubious.

'Early – early as may be. Always an early riser, no slug-a-bed my Jemmy, honest and hard-working . . . And he came here, of course, to do his duties. So he thought, poor lamb. Give him another try, sir – take old Goody's advice, you'll never do better—'

'Out of the question,' Mr Yelverton said with a shudder. 'Well, and I suppose he has gone home to – to this person's abode now.'

'Mebbe. *I* wouldn't have been there to greet the poor lamb, on account of being fetched here. *That's* plain enough,' the old woman said, giving the floor such a thump with her stick that Mr Yelverton fairly jumped.

Don't get dragged down by her . . . Well, Fairfax thought, it certainly seemed that Jemmy Runquest had taken that advice to heart. The old woman would lie for him, of course, and say he had been with her all the time: plainly he could do no wrong in her eyes; Fairfax had noted before the partiality of strong-minded hags for brutish young men.

But was he being impartial himself? Did he *want* it to be Runquest, who was everything he was not – robust, self-confident, a virile and careless seducer?

Ridiculous. The evidence pointed to Runquest, and that was his only concern. Assuming, of course, that it was to be his concern at all. Mr Yelverton might want to take matters into his own hands now, with an indisputable and horrible crime on his doorstep. Fairfax hoped not. He wanted to see this through.

'Mr Fairfax . . .' The magistrate was doing his little writhe of appeal, and Fairfax saw he was to have his wish. 'You see how I am situated – and the interruption of my plans mean I have a thousand things to do. As you were so good as to undertake enquiries into that unfortunate business at the Spread Eagle, I feel sure you will oblige me, and the law of course, in pursuing this new matter. Our good constable, of course, will give you any assistance you require, as far as his . . . ahem' – Mr Yelverton gave the constable's apron a pained glance – 'his trade allows. But now, what think you, sirs? Here is a girl horribly murdered: a girl who was with child by a man who—' He held off a protest from Goody

Soper with a tremulous hand. 'Apparently with child by a man who was not eager to acknowledge her. She is attacked in the water-meadows and brutally struck down – last night, you would estimate, Dr Stagg, at a late hour? It is unlikely there would be witnesses at such a spot, at such a time. Indeed, one wonders what she could have been doing there in the first place.'

'She might have been returning by the river-path to her lodging,' Fairfax said. 'That would lie in her way; and she could easily have been followed thus.'

'Or she might have been coming or going to your place, Goody,' the constable said. 'That would take her that way, you know.'

'I tell you, we never saw hide nor hair!' shrieked Goody. 'And as for you, that cheese I had of you last week was full o' mites.'

'I see,' Mr Yelverton said, suppressing a shudder. 'Another reason suggests itself. It was a fine night, and the spot is in my remembrance a pleasant one – suitable for a rendezvous or tryst. All of which suggests, indeed, that Runquest must be found and questioned at once, and questioned very closely. He has a duplicitous nature – that I have just discovered to my own cost. By heaven, to think that I might have travelled with a murderer, in utter bodily dependence on him . . . !'

'Certainly he is at least a first suspect,' Fairfax said.

'You have others in mind?' Mr Yelverton said in surprise.

'I don't know . . .' He could think of no one else with sauch a plausible motive for murdering Tabitha Dance – at least, with what he knew of her. But what he knew of her was notably incomplete. And there were connections that had not been considered. She had been a visitor yesterday to the Chilcott house, she had been sacked by her last employer, Charles Porteous, in contentious circumstances. And then there was the mysterious man Wolfgang had seen at the Spread Eagle . . . and now that he thought of it, another mysterious man, the one Runquest had accused her of meeting in the stables earlier that same day. Fairfax had tended to see that as the exaggerated tit-for-tat of a lover's quarrel . . . now he had second thoughts. Suppose, indeed, it were the same man? Wolfgang would be able to identify him – that is, if he could ever be found.

And then Dr Stagg himself, his enigmatic landlord, had come in late last night: he remembered the restless pacing below his room . . .

Surely not. The most relevant memory, he told himself, was of that casual, brutal slap Runquest had given Tabitha.

'Well, sir, you will oblige me by seeking out Runquest, and examining him most minutely. I fancy the testimony of this – this person' – he waved a hand at Goody Soper, who actually growled at him like a dog – 'rather prevents me from making out a warrant for his arrest, as yet. But hold him to it, sir: be exacting: let him know that you have all the authority of the Commission of the Peace behind you. You may indeed mention to him that I am still debating whether to take further this matter of the fraud he has practised on me. I take that very ill, you know. There is absolutely nothing in the world worse than having carefully laid plans disrupted!'

Fairfax thought that what had happened to Tabitha was, just conceivably, rather worse.

Outside he parted with Dr Stagg, who said he would notify

the parish officers and arrange for a pauper funeral after the inquest. He looked grim and saddened, reasonably enough: also tired, like a man who had not slept all night.

Grumbling all the way, Goody Soper led Fairfax and the constable to her cottage, a trim enough little place, with its own vegetable garden and a view over the river. A tethered goat winked its slanted eyes at them from the patch of coarse grass before the porch.

'He's mebbe not here,' the old woman said, opening the door. 'He's mebbe gone a-looking for work, poor soul, now that old spavin-shanked mollie has turned him out. Shame on him, dirty ole wort.'

'Here, don't you talk of Mr Yelverton that way,' the constable said.

'I can talk in my own house, can't I? And what would he ever do for you? You're only a grocer who sells maggoty cheese. He wouldn't stand up for *you*, lug, and don't think he – Jemmy!'

Jemmy Runquest was in the kitchen-cum-parlour, standing shirtless at the deal table, where there was a ewer and basin. It was dim in there, and the whites of his eyes seemed to flash as he turned.

'What?' He shook his wet hands, picked up a piece of towelling. 'Damn it all, old 'un, what do you mean bringing this issue of folk into a man's home when he's washing?'

'I didn't want to. Jemmy, there's trouble, and I've had to go before the justice, and be questioned and treated frightful, and they made me bring 'em here. 'Tis trouble, Jemmy dear.'

'Trouble, is it?' he grunted, wiping his bear-like chest with the towel. 'Well, I've had enough of that today.'

'I heard, dearie – heard from his own lips, the splatty ole

toad. But don't fret, Jemmy, there's work aplenty for a fine man like you—'

'I wanted that job,' Runquest said curtly, throwing the towel down. 'Now what's this trouble?'

'You must prepare yourself, heart; and when these gentlemen speak to you, you must—'

'Thank you, Mrs Soper,' Fairfax said. 'It will be better if you go out of the room, if you please, and let us talk to your grandson alone.'

She started to protest, but Runquest silenced her. 'Go on, old 'un, hold your clack and shift out of here . . . Well?' he said when she had gone. 'What's to do?'

'Tabitha Dance is killed,' said the constable. 'Down by Ebury Bridge, last night. Someone stove her head in with a rock, poor creature.' Then, seeming to grow intimidated by the huge half-naked figure glowering over him, he looked to Fairfax.

'It's murder,' Fairfax said. 'And double murder, you might say. Tabitha was pregnant. Or did you know that, Jemmy?'

'Tabby killed . . . oh, that ain't right . . .' Though the beams were so low that Runquest had to stoop perpetually in here, his shoulders seemed to slump with genuine shock. Of course, Fairfax thought, a guilty man would have carefully prepared his response to the news. Runquest's eyes flashed again. 'Aye – I knew about that. Her being up the stick, I mean. What of it?'

'You've been seen quarrelling lately. Was it about the pregnancy?'

Slowly Runquest sat down. 'Yes . . . that kind of thing. She was badgering me about it. Only like I told her, 'twasn't no concern of mine . . . Dear God. She weren't twenty-three.'

'Where were you last night, Jemmy?'

'Here.' Runquest's great fist tightened on the table. 'Why, what's all this? You're reckoning to lay it in my dish, are you? Me – and Tabby – why, I should throw you through that window . . .'

'It would make no difference if you did. The justices will have Tabitha Dance's murderer, Jemmy, and you must know that you are under suspicion. Tabitha wanted you to claim the child, did she not? And that would have spoiled your future – the very desirable position you had with Mr Yelverton.'

'That's gone – finished,' Runquest said with great bitterness. 'He's turned me off. So no difference.'

'You didn't know that last night,' Fairfax said. 'Which brings me back to the question—'

'I was here, damn you – all evening and night. The old 'un'll back me. I sat up reading to her after supper.'

'So she said.'

Runquest's eyes narrowed. 'Oh, I see it. You fancy I'm no reader, eh? Matter of fact, I am. Mr Yelverton'd never have took me otherwise. You have to have your letters if you want a good place in service nowadays – not some slavey's job with a bed on the coals – and I've read more than a bit. I've been through *Pilgrim's Progress*, and *Philip Quarll*, and *The Distrest Mother*, and last night I was reading out of *Robinson Crusoe*. I'll show you the books if you like.'

He was angry, and defiantly flushed; and Fairfax felt a twinge of shame. Another hasty judgement, he thought, and a superficial one. There was more to Runquest than he supposed. Not that literacy precluded murderousness, God knew . . .

'No matter. And then you went to bed – when?'

'Don't know. Might have been eleven o' the clock or thereabouts. The old 'un went up afore, and I stayed for a smoke of a pipe and a sniff of air outside, and then I turned in.'

That was not something the old 'un had mentioned, Fairfax thought. Still, he had never doubted that Runquest could have had the opportunity to slip out and kill Tabitha. The question was, how he would have known to find her at that spot? Perhaps he knew when she was likely to come by on her way to the hut, and lain in wait. Or, as Mr Yelverton suggested, there might have been a tryst . . .

'When did you last see Tabitha?'

'Can't recall rightly . . .' Runquest ran a hand through his long glossy hair, frowning. 'At least – well, I did see her yesterday. 'Twas late in the afternoon, and she came by here. Oh, the old 'un didn't know about it: she was visiting one of her gossips. Just as well: she never did hold with Tabby overmuch, even when she was lodging here. Tabby came knocking, and started with the old tale, but I wasn't interested like I'd told her a dozen times, and so she went pretty soon. I . . . well, damn it, I'm shamed to think it, but I gave her two shilling, just to be rid of her. She'd been tippling, and I knew her thirst, and if she'd got money she'd go away and drink it, and so I gave her some.'

'The old tale . . . about the child she was expecting.'

'Aye . . . Damn my eyes, she was no saint. It could have been anybody's – that's all I'm saying, and that's what I said to her. We'd already fallen out, and 'twas all past – a fine lark, and it ran its course, and that was it.'

Late afternoon . . . and early evening she had come to Dr Stagg and, according to the physician, asked his help in aborting the baby. And, unusually, she had money on her, because Runquest had given her some: did she think it could buy her some purge or medicament that would do the trick? There were unscrupulous doctors who would procure such things, though he doubted Stagg was of the sort. Well, it all fitted so far. And so far, in fact, he believed Jemmy Runquest.

'And this morning? Mr Yelverton said he turned you out first thing. Where have you been since?' Fairfax's eye fell on a wooden wash-tub in which a piece of linen lay in cold soda-suds. White linen – but stained.

'Now someone killed poor ole Tabby last night, isn't that so?' Runquest said, the big fist tightening again. 'So what's this morning to do with it? Nothing, I'd say.'

'In that case, you won't mind answering,' Fairfax said. 'And also showing us that – I think it is your shirt – in the tub there.'

Runquest only glared, so the constable made a tentative move towards the tub. With a sudden furious lunge Runquest plucked the wet garment out of the suds and flung it in the constable's face.

'There. My shirt, right enough. I took it off for washing. Fly it from a flagpole for all I care.'

'It's bloody, Jemmy,' the constable said, stung out of his mildness a little. 'That's blood, else I'm mistook. How d'you account for that?'

Fairfax examined the shirt. It still had an odour of fresh sweat. On the breast were several pinkish splashes.

'Why, I don't believe I have to,' the big man said sulkily.

'Explain here, or direct to the magistrate,' Fairfax said. 'Choose.'

'Now look here. There's a law about a man incriminating himself, ain't there? Or there should be. And I'm not talking about Tabby. I'm sorry for her and all, and it never should have happened – but I ain't your man, do you hear? And it ain't fair if you're a-going to pin it to my tail on account of that shirt, because – well, if a man does a little poaching of a fine morning, when he finds himself out of work of a sudden, which I ain't saying I did, but if a man's made to say he does, then a man can be had up before the law for that too. And I know the law's not much kinder to poachers than to murderers. So I'll not say it. But I'll say this. If I'd killed poor Tabby last night, and got blood on my shirt from it, God forbid' – he gave a shudder that again seemed genuine – 'why, do you think I'd come home, and then go off to work for my master in the morning in the same shirt, and then only when I came home again take that shirt off and clean up, right in my gammer's kitchen? Wouldn't any sane man burn that shirt to ashes as soon as he could?'

The same thought had begun to dawn on Fairfax as he looked at Runquest's hand. There were clear traces of stains around the nails. Would he, indeed, be cleaning up the evidence only now? Why not before?

He caught the constable's hangdog eye. The man looked as if he wanted to go home.

'You said that the father of Tabitha's child could be anybody,' Fairfax said. 'Were you thinking of anyone in particular?'

'What's this?' Runquest said with a small, sour look of triumph. 'Trying to make me finger someone else now?'

'I was thinking of something you said, that day at the Spread Eagle. You remember I was there.'

With something of the old swagger Runquest said, 'I remember. A lucky day it was for you, when I decided not to flatten you.' But he seemed to regret this at once.

'Well. You and Tabitha were quarrelling, and you said you had seen her with a man in the stable-block earlier. Making up to him – that was the gist of it.'

'I remember. Poor ole Tabby. Trollopy in her ways: I suppose she couldn't help it. Just born whorish.' There was a kind of stony sneer on his face. How curious we men are, Fairfax thought. The willing girl was sought, celebrated, toasted – and despised for it.

'Who was the man? Did you know him?'

Runquest brushed a hand across his eyes, as if something tickled him. 'Nay. I don't know. Could have been anybody . . . That's what I mean about Tabby. 'Twas crack-brained in her to go fastening on me when she found she'd caught the belly-cold: I knew what she was like. Everyone did. Besides, she could have put the babe on the parish – or even found some other man to keep her: she was still toothsome enough.'

'Perhaps she loved you,' Fairfax said. He was surprised to see a great blush spread from Runquest's face right down his neck and on to his bare chest.

'Well, then, she was a fool,' he said in a stifled voice. 'Now see you here. I'm damned if I'll bear this any more. It's like the old 'un said – I was here; and less'n you've got something else up your sleeve to pin on me, then I've said all there is to say. I do beg your pardon if I ain't as polite as you'd like' – he grimaced a mock bow – 'only today's not been the best of days for me, and this is the last feather, this is.'

'Yes,' Fairfax said. 'A great pity about the job.'

'More than a pity. A bloody crime. Now I'm stuck here again . . . penned in like a damned sheep . . .' Runquest reached up and scratched viciously at his bare back, as if he would tear the very skin off. 'I'm fair sick of it. Ever since I was breeched I've done dull work that goes nowhere. The ostlering was all very well – but who wants to end up an old dunder-headed stable-boy, bent over with the screws from sleeping over stables? Or else it's day-labouring, or picking in the fields – all lifting and carrying and grubbing along and a pot of beer in the same ale-house every night. I could have seen the world – places and things that folk round here never dream of. A manservant's wages and consequence, and travelling into the bargain – oh, it ain't fair! I'm no saint, I don't pretend to be. I've had my bits of trouble in the past, and on that account I couldn't get anyone to give me a character, not for what Mr Yelverton wanted, and so I . . . well, 'twas fakery, but only because I wanted that job so. Do you think I like living here amongst a set of clods?'

A pity, Fairfax thought again: all other things being equal, he might have been tempted to ask Mr Yelverton to reconsider. But he still didn't trust Jemmy Runquest: couldn't help noticing that he felt much more sorry for himself than for poor butchered Tabitha. From what he had observed, it was egotism above all that characterized a person who killed. Nothing beyond the circle of the self, its wants and needs and concerns, was entirely real to them.

Was Runquest such a person? Well, he was at pains to emphasize that it was all over with Tabitha. She was past:

he was a man who carelessly threw women over. Whether he was also a man who killed them if they threatened him was the crucial question, and Fairfax couldn't answer it.

'Well. I shall report what you've said faithfully to the magistrate. The rest is up to him,' Fairfax said. The constable was making urgent can-we-go expressions at him, and he couldn't see what more they could do. Turning, he felt a soft pressure at the toe of his shoe, and found that a large lurcher dog lay on the floor close by him, paws by its nose, brow wrinkling. He drew in a sharp breath. The dog had been so still throughout that in the dim light he had not noticed it.

Runquest grinned like a child. 'He could have had your throat out if I'd said the word.'

'This matter of the bloodstains is most perplexing,' Mr Yelverton said. 'It has a very bad appearance. And yet I can well imagine in court any counsel worth his salt fixing on those very inconsistencies you mention. Why, indeed, would a guilty man take so long, and be so heedless, about dealing with such damning evidence? I confess I did not notice anything about Runquest's shirt this morning when I dismissed him. But a nice attention to the linen of my servants is scarcely my province . . . There is nothing to prove he did not do it. But more importantly, Mr Fairfax, there is nothing to prove he did.'

'I agree, sir. And my feeling about him is far from certain. But I am not convinced by his explanation of how he *did* come by the bloodstains, which is – suffice it to say it is curious.' Poaching. He was asked to believe that having been sacked by his master, Runquest went off and did a little poaching in daylight. Of course, he could have been in the habit of laying snares – there were parks and enclosures aplenty hereabouts – and checking them in the mornings. It was possible, he supposed . . .

'I wish I could have him arrested at once,' Mr Yelverton said. 'Nothing would be more satisfactory. Unfortunately, on this evidence, I do not think I can. Not yet. But he will bear watching, as the saying goes; and my hope is that someone will step forward with just the information we need to bring him down. The news of this frightful crime will soon spread: indeed, I shall see to it that notices are posted. People will put two and two together. It might indeed be helpful if there were a matter of a reward . . . but alas, even if I were to meet with my fellow justices before I leave, and propose it, I doubt the funds would be forthcoming for . . . well, for such a case.'

For a girl like Tabitha? thought Fairfax.

'You intend still to make your journey as planned, sir?'

'There may be a slight delay. But as soon as I can procure a replacement for Runquest, then certainly, I shall be off. There are remarkable discoveries being made at the site near Naples, Mr Fairfax.' Mr Yelverton writhed, his smile yellow and placating. 'And if there are discoveries to be made here – why, I am sure you are the man to make them. Your zeal for justice, I'm convinced, is unabated; and if it is not too tiresome for you functioning as the eyes and, alas, the legs of a man who shares that zeal but is rendered incapable by press of business as well as disability from pursuing it as he might . . .'

There was no need for the magistrate to butter him up. Fairfax was not about to forget the sight of Tabitha Dance face down in the summer grass. He would have begged to be allowed to pursue it: he would have done so anyway if refused.

As for discoveries, he had a feeling he would have to dig over the whole ground of Tabitha's life to unearth them. But he knew the place to start, and very soon he was rapping at the door of Mr Charles Porteous.

'Yes, sir, he's in, but not to be disturbed,' the maidservant said.

'It is a matter of some urgency. I will not keep him long.'

'I'm sorry, sir, but he's still abed and not to be woken. Miss Henlow said so.'

Still abed? It was well past noon . . . 'Then may I see Miss Henlow?'

'She's visiting next door, sir. Taking the foreign gentleman his posset.'

Well, he had not thought to see Cordelia so soon. And all unprepared as he was, he felt his spirit kindle when she answered the door to him. It was not just the firing of love. He felt something healing too, as in the sight of a dear home. It was such a good feeling that he pushed away, for now, the knowledge that it was a home from which he was barred and exiled.

'We have heard,' she said soberly. 'It is all round the neighbourhood – in various highly coloured versions. You were there?'

He nodded. 'The truth was grisly enough.'

'Dear God . . .' She pressed his hand briefly. 'Is anyone taken for it? That brute she loved must surely be suspected.'

'He is, but it is no more than suspicion. I've just come from Mr Yelverton, who feels he cannot commit him. There

150

must be more . . . Miss Henlow is upstairs?'

Cordelia's eyes widened. 'Yes, Lord, is *she* under suspicion?'

Emma Henlow? In theory, he thought, it was entirely possible. Any healthy adult could have wielded that rock. If Emma Henlow could be imagined doing such a thing, then it could only be for Charles Porteous' sake, he reflected, remembering that strange supper last night. But could devotion go that far? And for what reason?

'Of course, you cannot say,' she said, seeing his hesitation.

'I must examine everyone who had a connection to Tabitha,' he said, shrugging. 'Cordelia – I don't know if this was included in the various versions, but Tabitha was with child.'

She paled. 'This is too horrible . . . Then surely that beau of hers—'

'That's how it would seem. We must see.' He kept thinking of Jemmy Runquest's words: *could have been anybody*. A piece of coarse exaggeration, making Tabitha out to be all but a whore. But suppose there had been one other? Suppose Jemmy was not the father of her child?

His mind whirling, he followed Cordelia upstairs.

All was pleasant domesticity in the Mozarts' quarters. Leopold was drinking his posset, Frau Mozart was putting curl-papers into Nannerl's hair, and Wolfgang was at the desk mending a pen. Standing beside him, leafing through his music manuscript, was Emma Henlow, the light from the window behind her giving an angelic look to her fairness.

'Well, I am not a good sight-reader, but your *sinfonia* looks most magnificent,' she said, laying the papers down.

'And I am sure your missing piece will turn up, you know. Mr Fairfax, how do you do.'

'Oh, Herr Fairfax, this is shocking news, is it not?' Leopold Mozart said. He was dressed for the first time, though his neck was still swathed with flannel, and his eyes had lost the rheumy look. 'You know about it, of course, sir?'

'I know about it, and am charged with finding out more by the justice,' Fairfax said.

'God give you his aid,' Leopold said, 'for it is the most vile and . . . well, we shall say no more with the children here. But that poor young woman! Miss Henlow was just saying she used to be their servant, so you may imagine how shocked she is.'

'It gives me some uneasiness, indeed, to think that we were obliged to dismiss her,' Miss Henlow said in English, her voice so cool it seemed to moderate the sunshine streaming into the room. 'I fear that, unable to get another place, Tabitha fell into a poor and debauched way of living, which made her vulnerable to such a dreadful end. If she had still been with us . . . well, no matter. I fear I sound pious and moralizing, and that is not what I mean at all. Well, Mr Fairfax, when a person is murdered, I know the law seeks out who saw them last, and so forth. That *may* be me. Quite late last night – well past eleven o'clock, I would say: the servants had gone to bed and I was ready to go up – there comes of a sudden a rattling and hallooing outside; a voice I recognized, though disguised with drink. Looking out of the drawing-room window I saw Tabitha below, at the area steps. She was shouting up at the house, and shying mud at the windows – with no very great effect, because I fear she was prodigiously drunk. Insults, and reproaches for our treatment of her, and curses . . . it was not pretty, but it did not last long. I thought of opening the window and answering her, but deemed it best not to disturb the peace any more, and so I closed the curtains and resolved to take no notice, and it worked. She soon went away, with a few more curses, and presently I retired to bed.'

'I see. Yes, I thank you for the information, Miss Henlow . . . But pray, was Mr Porteous not disturbed by this?' Fairfax said.

'He surely would have been, but he was not at home. Shortly after you left us, Mr Fairfax, after our agreeable supper, Charles' uneasiness over his uncle's health got the better of him. He had his horse saddled, and rode into town there and then to see Sir Andrew. Between ourselves, though I was naturally anxious for the old gentleman, I urged him not to, and to leave it till the morning. Again between ourselves, I suspect Sir Andrew sometimes of playing a little on his infirmities, the better to secure his nephew's attachment, though his dutifulness cannot be in doubt. So Charles went, and was unable to return till very late – the small hours, indeed; and so he sleeps still. I may add that Sir Andrew was quite well when he left him – it was a trifling complaint.'

Again Emma Henlow left Fairfax with the feeling of there being nothing more to say. He turned to Leopold, and in German asked if he had been disturbed last night.

'No, I heard nothing. But Frau Mozart and I sleep at the back of the house, away from the noise of the street.'

'Wolfgangerl!' It was Nannerl, jumping away from her

mother's primping fingers. 'Where is that kitten we found? Let's get it and show Herr Fairfax. Come, come.'

She nudged him up from the desk. He went along willingly; but Fairfax was sure the boy had been about to say something.

'Well, you will wish to talk to Charles, at any rate,' Miss Henlow said. 'Will you not? Believe me, he will be as anxious as I to help when he hears the news. Tabitha was in some ways a trial, but no one could wish such an end on her. I shall go and rouse him. If you will wait a little while, Mr Fairfax, so that he may dress and drink a dish of tea . . .'

'Of course.' He bowed as she left, and caught a glint in Leopold's eye. 'Ah, Herr Fairfax, a most delightful young woman, is she not? I am sure your heart is not made of stone,' he chuckled.

'By no means.' Emma Henlow's beauty and charm, indeed, impressed him afresh each time he saw her. Clearly it did not occur to Leopold that when Fairfax looked at her, he looked at her in the light of a possible murderess.

Well, the beauty and charm were no disqualification; and as for whether she was morally capable of it, he had no answer, simply because he couldn't get beneath that smooth, poised surface.

What he balked at was the notion of Emma Henlow doing something so messy, desperate and uncivilized.

Wolfgang and Nannerl were back, but without any kitten. Large-eyed, Nannerl approached her father.

'Papa, may we tell Herr Fairfax something?'

'Of course, my dears. Why do you need to ask?'

'Well . . . we did not like to say with Fräulein Henlow by.

Because we perhaps should not have been up and listening and also it is – it is rude.'

'Hm. Not too rude, I hope.'

'Well, I don't know.' Nannerl turned her limpid blue eyes shyly to Fairfax. 'You see, I only know some little bits of English, and Wolfgangerl not any—'

'I know some words!'

'Well, but not many. And the woman was shouting in English but I couldn't understand all of it—'

'Wait, Nannerl. You mean last night? The young woman Miss Henlow spoke of?'

'Yes. We heard her. Wolfgangerl's bedroom window is at the front over the door—'

'And I woke up because she was shouting,' put in Wolfgang excitedly, 'and I peeped out of the window and saw her there, throwing things at the house next door. So I ran to Nannerl's room and said come quick and we went to my window and we listened and she was very drunk I think and also she was weeping—'

'Weeping?' Fairfax said.

'Yes – in between swearing,' Nannerl said. 'I know it was swearing because I have heard the words like *damn* and *bitch* . . . and I think there was a worse one because the woman said *whore* . . .' Nannerl blushed. 'That is a bad one, isn't it?'

'And the woman – Tabitha – shouted that?'

'Oh yes!' Wolfgang said. 'And *shite* too and I know what that is because it is nearly the same in German! And sometimes I say it when I—'

'Wolfgang,' said his father sternly.

'And this is what she kept shouting,' Nannerl said,

drawing a deep breath and struggling with the unfamiliar English words. '*You will not go away with, you will not go away with . . .*'

'*Get away with it*,' Wolfgang corrected her, singing the words like operatic recitative. 'And then she said *I will tell*.'

'Are you sure of this?' Fairfax said.

'Again you don't believe me,' Wolfgang said gloomily.

'No, no. I only need to be sure.' *You won't get away with it. I will tell.* The former might just be the drunken complaint of someone who felt unjustly dismissed. But *I will tell . . .*?

'Is it important, Herr Fairfax?' Leopold said, watching him narrowly. 'I am greatly concerned at this grievous crime, of course, and would gladly see it punished. But again I am uneasy at the thought of my children having to go before the law . . .'

'I see no prospect of that, Herr Mozart. But I am grateful for the information.'

It was intriguing, indeed: troubling also. Saying goodbye to the Mozarts, and taking a restrained farewell of Cordelia, he made his way to the house next door with a mind reeling in speculation.

He found Charles Porteous dressed but unwigged, a cap covering his head. Unshaven, he had a swarthy saturnine look as he sipped tea in his easy chair, a little table set out with gleaming silver at his elbow. But he was mild and courteous and, when Fairfax presented his apologies for disturbing him, all amenability.

'Not at all. Emma has just told me the news, and my first thought, after the fearful shock of it, was that the perpetrator of such a deed must be caught. Anything that I can do to help . . . Tabitha was, of course, lately our servant, and it is natural we should be applied to for information. Though I fear . . .' he dipped his lips delicately in tea, 'I fear I can offer little that will be of use.'

Fairfax glanced at Emma, who had seated herself close by.

'Miss Henlow tells me you rode out last night, after I supped here, to see your uncle in London, and returned very late. I wonder if you recall at what time you came back to Chelsea?'

'Oh, it would have been well past one o'clock in the morning, I think, when I reached home – perhaps nearer two. Emma?'

'I believe so, Charles.'

'I see – I was just wondering, as you were abroad so late, whether you saw anyone about, anyone in the vicinity of the canals particularly, anything at all that—'

'That could hardly be,' Porteous said, 'as I came out of London by the King's Road, and so passed nowhere near that spot.' He drank tea again with sharp, almost ferocious sips, his dark eyes fixed on Fairfax's.

'Yes, of course. A pity.'

'A very great pity. I have already thought that if I had only come by a different road, I might just have been on hand to disturb or scare off whoever did this . . . But there, at such a late hour I naturally took the broadest and most used road. Even so pleasantly removed as we are from the city, perils lurk at night for the unwary – as this dreadful event shows. For what it is worth, I believe the poor girl must have fallen victim to some vicious vagrant, who chanced upon her and took his horrible opportunity.'

'It may be so,' Fairfax said. 'But that would suggest a

robbery, and there were no signs of such – Tabitha had nothing worth stealing, I think.' The examination in the hut had revealed Tabitha to be without a penny, with nothing in fact but the clothes she wore. Runquest had given her a little money, but it seemed highly likely, as he had expected, that she had spent it on drink. 'Nor had she been molested, it appears.'

'My dear sir, it needs not any such motive in these sad days for an innocent creature to be set upon. Why, you must know that to walk abroad in many parts of London of a night is almost to invite a broken head – and that goes for a man in the prime of life. It was with such considerations that when I went to my uncle's last night I carried with me a pocket pistol. Even with such precautions, it was not a journey I relish. But I was in that condition of anxiety about my uncle's health that grows and feeds on itself, and as Emma was in agreement with me that it would be best if I went, I took the risk.'

A rather different account from that of his sister-in-law, who had said she discouraged him. Fairfax glanced at Emma, whose face was smooth and unruffled as porcelain. Perhaps Porteous simply interpreted everything she said as in agreement with him.

'Miss Henlow,' Fairfax said, 'if I might allude to what you told me – about Tabitha's making a disturbance outside the house last night. She was abusive, I gather – but what exactly was the substance of her complaint?'

'As I have told you, she was very drunk, and took the opportunity – having, I imagine, had her fill at the inn – to air her grievances against us.' Emma smiled and shrugged slightly.

'Those grievances being . . . ?'

'Come, Mr Fairfax, I think you are not obtuse. You know we were forced to dismiss her from our employ, and she took it very ill. And when one is inebriated, one takes things ill all over again, as it were. So I am told – believe me, I have not tried the experiment,' she said with a slightly impish look. 'So she cried her woes, and threatened our undoing generally. I'm sure you can picture the scene. I will only add that you know of those aspersions that were cast on me, and on the propriety of my establishment here with regard to my brother-in-law, which were the last straw for us when Tabitha worked here; and yes, she made abusive references to them. But I can assure you, Mr Fairfax, that I would not kill someone because they said nasty things about me.'

'Emma . . .' Her brother-in-law frowned.

'No, Charles, please: and you, Mr Fairfax, were about to protest too. But someone did kill poor Tabitha, and I myself do not think, Charles, that it was the casual act of a passing stranger. It is therefore very natural that the law looks for people who might have had a reason to do it. I was, quite probably, the last person to have anything to do with her, and in no very pleasant way. So I may as well say it now. These are after all direful matters we are talking about, and not who danced the *écossaise* at last week's ball.'

Fairfax found himself surprised into an admiration for her. Also, surprisingly again, he was reminded of Cordelia – the bright, dry quickness. Not a comparison that would please Cordelia, of course.

'That may be so, my dear,' Porteous said, 'but I am disturbed to think that in offering to help you, Mr Fairfax, my sister-in-law and myself are being considered in the light of suspicion. One hears of drunken weavers beating or starving their apprentices to death, but to suggest that we are in the habit of murdering our servants—'

'Or former servants,' Fairfax said, 'and I am far from suggesting anything, Mr Porteous. To understand Tabitha's death I have to understand her life, and any help you can give me in that . . . One hears her spoken of as a girl of easy virtue. It may be mere gossip, of course; but when she was in your employ, was that one of her failings? Did she have followers?'

'Oh . . .' Porteous looked weary. 'They always do. As well try to turn back the tide as stop it. But with Tabitha, yes, it went beyond the bounds . . . This was not a development we foresaw, you understand. I am exacting in the hire of my servants: they have a very good, respectable place, and I expect a good character in return. Tabitha seemed eminently suitable at first. Her weaknesses only became apparent later. Tippling. And yes, the men. There was that hulking fellow who was an ostler – Runquest; and besides that she always seemed to be conducting some flirtation or other.'

'I see. She was, as you may know, with child when she was killed. That is why—'

'Shocking. Shocking,' Porteous said abruptly, and bent to pick up the silver teapot and pour himself more tea. But something – grogginess from sleep, perhaps – made him trembling and clumsy, and the teapot fell from his hand and clattered to the floor. Hot tea ran on the Turkey rug and splashed his stockings.

'Charles! What are you thinking of?' Emma was swiftly on her knees beside him. 'You should let me serve you. That is why I am here – you are weary beyond anything after last night, and yet you still will not consent to be looked after . . . Are you scalded?'

'Nothing – nothing. Emma, don't fuss, I pray you, 'tis the merest spill . . . Mr Fairfax, ring that bell, if you will be so good, and we will have it cleared.'

Fairfax did as he was bid, getting up. 'I will inconvenience you no longer. All I would ask is that you consider that question generally – of who Tabitha might have known, and been entangled with—'

'Runquest,' Porteous said, looking with distaste at his stained stockings. 'That is the only name I know. I may add that I believe he treated her abominably. I remember her weeping over him.' For a moment his tone was musical, gentle. Then he shook himself a little – or shuddered? – and said briskly, 'I will of course put my mind to the problem, but I doubt to any result, sir. What happened to Tabitha is horrible to contemplate – but I mean to be merely truthful, not disrespectful, when I say that death has already touched this house, and that death concerns me more nearly. There is only so much room for grief in a man's heart.'

Well, he certainly had a way, like his sister-in-law, of making you feel there was nothing more to say.

Fairfax left the house, hearing from upstairs the faint sounds of the motherless baby crying. With something of the same thin, nagging persistence, that last phrase of Charles Porteous' echoed in his mind: *only so much room for grief in a man's heart.*

And what about love? Might not a man with a sickly wife, cocooned in the last stages of a difficult pregnancy, find room for a little tenderness towards a pretty servant girl with a willing nature?

Again, it was a commonplace of bawdy tales. Masters tumbling maids; his lordship slipping nightgowned into the giggling servant's bedchamber. But Charles Porteous was no rumbustious squire snapping his fingers in the face of politeness. He had a deeply respectable reputation, and everything depended on his keeping it.

I will tell . . .

Porteous had been out late last night. The story of going to attend on the old uncle's sickbed was unlikely and yet might well be true: it could be checked with Sir Andrew, if it came to that. Even then, there was the return journey to Chelsea at a late hour. Ample opportunity to kill Tabitha.

The heat of the summer day was at its fiercest, but Fairfax felt chilled by his own ideas. Pursuing them to their logical conclusion, he could not decide which was worse: the idea that Porteous would snuff out the life of a girl who threatened his position, or the idea that his devoted sister-in-law would know about it, approve it, and cover up for him.

Well, if it were true, he did not see how he would ever prove it, in the face of such unanimity. That was the worst idea of all.

Six

At the Spread Eagle he ate a meal, and listened: he hardly needed to ask questions, for the murder of Tabitha Dance was the talk of the inn. Everyone had a theory. Gypsies, tinkers, Irishmen, and even crazed veterans from the Royal Hospital were in turn placed in the dock, convicted, sentenced, and executed by the taproom talkers. Jemmy Runquest was hanged several times, but cut down by his defenders, who said there was no real harm in him. Morals were drawn as freely as the ale, mainly along the lines of bad women coming to bad ends. But useful facts were not so plentiful. That Tabitha had been drinking here last night was definitely established, likewise that she had departed about eleven, alone, spent out, and 'drunk as a fiddler's bitch', as the potman succinctly put it. But whether she had talked to anyone in particular or said anything in particular was a more debatable question. She was a common sight, and not much regarded. One toothless old man, steeped in gin, opined that she had been drinking with a black man who had given her a hatful of gold guineas; but when it was pointed out to him that he had been at his brother's funeral five miles away last evening, he regretfully conceded that he must have been thinking of something else.

At any rate, the episode of Mr Gabriel Chilcott was quite forgotten now, under the influence of this new and gruesome sensation. Fairfax had almost, but not quite, forgotten it: he realized he had a vague, elfin, weakly hope that somehow it might throw light on this mystery. The one substantial connection was the fact that Tabitha had been known at the Chilcott house, if only by the steward. Not much to justify the tramp across the fields to Kensington, perhaps, but he needed to work off the perplexed energy in his brain. And he had had some of his best inspirations when walking.

Perspiration, however, was his only result when he came in sight of Brockleigh, the imposing residence of the late Gabriel Chilcott. The rhythm of his footsteps had only beaten out repeated images of Tabitha lying pillowed in blood, occasionally interspersed with other images that haunted without telling him anything: Dr Stagg hovering silently outside his chamber door, Emma Henlow beautifully haloed by sun as she stood by Wolfgang's desk, Jemmy Runquest towelling his sinewy torso, Charles Porteous dropping the silver teapot from his long, elegant fingers, Mr Chilcott frozen in staring, horrified death. He was sick of seeing these things, he was half blind from sun and half swooning with heat, and when he plodded up the steps and rapped at the door all that was in his mind was to beg a glass of water at any price.

It was the ancient footman who answered the door, opening it with as much slow, gasping effort as if it were a great temple door of solid bronze. But before Fairfax could speak, the footman was elbowed aside, and the steward, Minter, thrust his lugubrious face out.

'What? Is it—? Is it—?' Recognizing Fairfax, his excitable tone dropped. 'Oh. Good day, sir. I thought – unless you bring news, sir? Do you? *Has* she been found?'

'I don't understand . . . Do you mean Tabitha Dance?'

'What? No, no. The mistress. Mrs Chilcott, you know, she . . . Oh, no matter. Forgive me. If you have come to call on the mistress, she isn't here.' Minter opened the door wide, shooing the footman away. 'And I don't mean that as a convention, you know. Saying she isn't in when she is. Because she isn't – Lord knows, she isn't!'

The steward put his trembling hands under his old drab wig, as if to flip it off like a lid, and groaned. There was a peculiar flush about his sallow face, and snuff all over his waistcoat.

'I had hoped to see Mrs Chilcott, indeed,' Fairfax said, 'but I would esteem it a favour if I might speak with you, Mr Minter. And if I might have a glass of water—'

'You shall have better than that. You shall have ale – or madeira – or brandy. Whatever you fancy.' The steward's eyes lit up, and he all but dragged Fairfax into the hall. Too surprised to speak, Fairfax could only suppose that Minter had been out in the sun too long.

'Thank you, you're very kind – water will do admirably—'

'Have something stronger! I'm going to. I already have, you know.'

Tugging at his sleeve, Minter led Fairfax across the blessedly cool tiled hall to a room behind the stairs. 'My pantry. I seldom entertain – in fact I never do – but why not, today? All else is topsy-turvy. I might fly away on a broomstick before the day is out. Who knows?'

The sedate, steadfast steward was drunk. In his little whitewashed room, which looked as if it had never seen anything nearer to debauchery than reckoning up the accounts by the light of two candles instead of one, there was an unstoppered jar of ale and a pint mug, which Minter seized and drank down, smiling at Fairfax with a kind of desperate merriment.

'Here's my comfort!' he said – but not convincingly. There were tears in his eyes. He groped about on the deal table, then held up a snuff-box. 'See? I have been trying out vices. Not my habit, but needs must, you know. Vices, they say, are a great resource in time of trouble. Everyone flies to 'em. They cheer a man when he's low. And if ever a man was low . . . !' The steward groaned again, then laughed hilariously, and half sobbed, and at last took a prodigious pinch of snuff that made him cough and sneeze as if his head would explode.

'Trouble, Mr Minter?' Fairfax said, once the old man was tolerably composed again.

'Call it that. Some folk might say la, and fie, and pish to it. But I – strike me down, I have offered you refreshment, sir, and given nothing. Take some of this, sir, I pray, it cools and – and yet it heats, too! Mortal curious, isn't it?'

Fairfax accepted a cup of the ale gratefully. The steward watched him drink it, with eager fascination.

'Cooled – and yet heated, sir? And the spirits, sir – are they raised? Mine are. Not as high as I'd like, mind, but . . .' Abruptly Minter slumped into a chair, running his finger along the cracks in the table. 'But there we are.'

'Mr Minter, you disturb me. Something is amiss. Is Mrs Chilcott taken ill . . . ?'

'My thought exactly! Sir, I thank you – that is exactly . . .' With tipsy earnestness the steward seemed about to seize Fairfax's hand and shake it; but then he sat back with his old apologetic look. 'She is missing, sir. A curious term, perhaps: one thinks of a little child going missing in that way, and the mistress – well, I hope I don't step outside my place when I say that there's not much that's childlike about her. But I don't know what else to call it.'

'Missing since when?'

'That's just it, sir. I ought to know precise, as this household has been in my charge for so many years, and being precise is always what I prided myself on. My poor master valued it. "I set my watch by you, you know, Minter," he used to say, "you'd better not run down!" That was quite in his vein, you know. Sharp as a cobbler's awl Mr Chilcott was – folk don't talk of that, only of his bad points, but we've all got those, haven't we? You'll back me up, I know, sir.'

'I have more bad points than a porcupine,' Fairfax said. 'But you were saying – Mrs Chilcott?'

'Oh yes. 'Twas last night, quite late, I believe, but I can't be sure. The pith o' the plant is, until poor Mr Chilcott met his end the keys of the house were carried by him and me – two sets. And at night I would lock up and see to everything, and that would be the end of it till morning. But yesterday the mistress, quite naturally I dare say, asked for Mr Chilcott's set of keys for herself. And last night, after I'd locked up at ten o' the clock and gone to bed, Mrs Chilcott must have used her keys and gone out. I never heard a thing, but I'm a heavy sleeper, and she's a light-footed lady: the kitchen maid thought she heard the door a-banging late, a

little before eleven perhaps. And when Mrs Chilcott's own
maid went to rouse her this morning, she found no sign of
her, and her bed not even slept in. There was a cloak missing,
and a pair of overshoes, the maid reckons, and the bolts were
drawn on the door; so all we can think is that last night she
took it into her head to go off on one of her walks – and
hasn't come back yet!' Minter lifted his pint pot, but looked
as if he had lost his taste for it.

'One of her walks? Is this her habit, then?'

'Not at that time of night, mebbe – but then all's changed
since poor master died. Nothing the same – I hardly know
where I am!' The old man blinked tears. 'Well, going on
long walks, quite alone, has always been Mrs Chilcott's
fancy, and not just of a morning like most ladies. Quite a
tireless walker she is. Nothing weakly about her, though she's
so slight. When master was alive, there wasn't much stirring
abroad, his health and his habits being what they were, and
I fancy the walks were what gave mistress a bit of ... well ...'

'Freedom?' said Fairfax.

Minter looked unhappy. 'Well, I was going to say a bit of
time to think, but – mebbe freedom. Oh, not that it was ever
a question of her not being able to do what she wanted. Only
master watched over her so very careful – cherishing, you'd
call it, like she was a tender young plant. I know he'd want
me to do the same – fine mess I've made! That's why I'm
disgracing myself like this,' he said with sudden disgust,
slamming down the mug. 'Well, not just because of that.
Because of everything. Master gone – *that* I can't get used
to. We're meant to be burying him tomorrow. I've a thousand
things I need to ask the mistress – and now she's gone too.
Where or why, the Lord knows! 'Tis not for me to know her

mind. I'd not ask, and she'd not tell. We don't have that understanding, not like I did with Mr Chilcott. Most of the time I feel as if she don't even see me – just looks through me like I'm a ghost. It's not the same – nothing's the same any more . . . ! But I'm troubled for her, of course I am. Gone all night, a lone unprotected woman – what am I to do?'

'You have no conception of where she might have gone?'

'None. With master being the way he was, they didn't have what you might call a circle of acquaintance. I've took the liberty of sending the coachman out with the carriage, and the stable-lad afoot, to go about and see if they can find word of her. I don't know what else to do. Betty – that's the cook-maid, been here as long as I have – she says not to fret, as 'tis not as if . . . well, 'tis not as if Mrs Chilcott isn't in her right mind, or anything of that shape. If I was to go before a justice and report the matter, he might say do I reckon the lady was distracted with grief on account of her loss, and liable to do something rash. And that I can't say yes to, not in truth. I don't mean any reflection, sir, believe me.'

Fairfax nodded. 'You mean that Mrs Chilcott was bearing up with the fortitude of a Christian and the dignity of a gentlewoman.'

'All of that, sir. I don't mean to suggest that she didn't care. Only that 'twas more a wise than a wild wedding. Mr Chilcott had been pushing hard at business all his life, and now that he was settled, and could afford the best of everything, he looked about him for a wife on the same principles. And the mistress – Miss Matheson, as she was – had been brought up very genteel, and is quite the perfect lady as you know, only her father had died without leaving her much of a portion, and so she – well, she had to make the best bargain she could. There, 'tis how the world wags, you know, sir, and many marriages are worse made, and I think they rubbed along pretty well all in all . . . I believe 'twas the matter of her brother that made things uneasy. But there, that's not my affair.'

'Mrs Chilcott has a brother?'

'I shouldn't talk of it,' Minter said, with the air of a man who is going to. 'But there, past cure past care as they say. Young Mr Matheson was very like his sister: quite the gentleman, and mighty educated; but more brains than means, I fear. I think he was intended for a law profession, but hadn't took to it, and was at a loose end and needy, and so the master took him on as a secretary. Mr Chilcott still kept quite a few business interests warm, and then there was his musical library that he was a-building, and so there was work enough for a clever young man, though nothing over-burdensome. It was done to please the mistress, of course – that was Mr Chilcott all over, and I honoured him for it, though the young man was a little high-handed, I found, and I was never easy with him. This was a year ago, or a little more. But the arrangement didn't last long. That young man betrayed my master's trust. He forged some business papers, so as to profit by them – a fine return for kindness! Foolish as well as vicious, for Mr Chilcott had a hawk's eye for detail, and very soon smoked him out; and so that was the end of him. I reckon Mrs Chilcott pleaded her brother's cause, but he had to go – anyone could see that – and so he went, in disgrace, haughty to the last, and we have seen naught of him since.'

'Do you think Mrs Chilcott might have gone to her brother?'

'That would depend if she knew where to find him, sir, and that I doubt. Not that the master strictly forbade any communication, as you might say, but I think 'twas discouraged, and besides, the young rip took himself off from here in such a passion, as if he would shake our very dust off his shoes . . . Shocking ingratitude! I've been with my poor late master for nigh on thirty years, ever since he started with a little common brew-house in Southwark, and that shows you, I reckon, what he was like to work for . . . Hey-day!'

An interesting sidelight on the Chilcott household – but of more direct concern just now was this strange absence of Mrs Jane Chilcott.

'Well, it is all very perplexing to you, Mr Minter, I can see. I had hoped to speak to you on another matter, and I fear it is yet more unpleasant, but it is urgent. Tabitha Dance – the young woman you were kind to yesterday – is dead. She was found murdered at Chelsea this morning.'

Minter stared, his lips moving soundlessly. At last he shook his head with a great sigh.

'Well, that's three.'

'I beg your pardon?'

'Ill news comes in threes, they say, sir – and I can only hope that's the end of it. Poor Tabitha! I can scarcely credit . . . Betty always said she would come to a bad end, but that's just Betty's way, you know, and she'll be as shocked as I. For my part, I never thought Tabitha was as bad as they said, not at heart—'

'You knew her well then? I am charged with investigating

this crime, Mr Minter, and I must ask that you speak with frankness.'

'Oh, yes, I knew her. Tabitha was formerly a housemaid here, sir. It would be some six or eight months since. I didn't care to speak of it t'other day, sir, with the mistress by, and so much a-doing. The fact is, she'd not take kindly to me handing out charity from the kitchen, and true enough 'tis not mine to give, but Tabitha was in such a poor way that I couldn't help myself.'

'Tabitha used to be employed here? That I didn't know.'

'She didn't last long. She was a smart, brisk piece, but she didn't come up to Mr Chilcott's standards. She drank – I'm very much afraid she drank . . .' The steward looked with vague uneasiness at the mug in his hand, but went on quickly, 'And then there were men. Mr Chilcott caught her at last, entertaining a man in the kitchen. Yes: she did.' His look was profoundly solemn.

'A very tall, burly man, by any chance – name of Runquest?'

'That sounds like him. But just the fact of its being a man, you see – well, there's few masters who'll put up with that, and mine was particular, and so that was the end for poor Tabitha. She was dismissed without a character. My heart misgave me for what would become of her – I had a soft spot for her – oh, Lord, only in a fatherly way: she was always jolly with me and made me smile. No real harm in her, I thought. Well, she had a second chance, it seems, and lost it again. So she told me yesterday. I never expected to see her; she came a-knocking, quite out of the blue, wanting to know if she might have her old place back. She'd heard about poor master, and so she thought that with him gone she might have more luck, I dare say – tsk, a forward piece! But then she was poor, and quite desperate – I could see that. And so I gave her what I could, food and a few coppers, and hustled her gone, for there was no question she would ever be took back here. And now she's killed, poor wretch! What a world! How came it about, sir? She hadn't – oh Lord, she hadn't taken to selling herself?'

'Nothing is certain yet; but I tend to agree with you, Mr Minter, that she was not so black as she was painted.'

'Nothing is certain,' the steward echoed mournfully, looking into his mug. 'And I should not drink any more of this – but who knows what is to come, in this sad world?'

'Do you fear for your place here, now that your old master is gone?' Fairfax asked him.

'I really don't know, sir. I would gladly serve; and I am fretted half to death thinking where mistress might be. Yet I know well that she doesn't care about my fretting, as the master would have . . . She's a mystery to me, sir – quite a mystery.'

'Yes . . . That was all Tabitha said to you yesterday? That she hoped she might get work here again?'

'That was all, pretty much. She wasn't the bright starling that I remembered, but then poverty's a terrible grinder of the spirits . . . God speed you find the person who could do such a thing, sir. She was young – young, and human!'

An eloquent enough reason. Fairfax thanked the steward for his hospitality and made ready to leave.

'You're not going, sir?'

'Alas, I must. But I hope you have news of your mistress soon, and I'd urge you not to worry unduly. She—'

'I can't help it! I'm sorry, sir. It's just been a relief to speak with someone. 'Tis so solitary here. Master, God rest him, wasn't one for company, and so no one ever calls here. I believe you are the only gentleman to pass the gate in an age – no, I tell a lie, there was the gentleman on Monday, but then *he* never even came up to the house.'

On his way to the door, Fairfax paused. 'What gentleman was that?'

'I've no name for him. It was the gardener he spoke to, in the drive. He asked if the Chilcotts were at home – which for once they weren't, of course, that morning. They'd gone off in the carriage to Chelsea, to see the musical boy, not half an hour before – so the gardener told the gentleman. Little knowing it would be poor master's last journey . . . ! Well, the gentleman said just thank'ee, and turned about and rode off on his mare, and never came back.'

'Odd. The gardener didn't recognize him?'

'No, sir. A youngish, well-dressed gentleman, on a fine grey mare, the gardener said, and that's all. You'll think me fanciful, no doubt – but I can't help thinking, with what happened to poor master that day, that the name of that gentleman was Death! Scripture says he rides a pale horse, doesn't it?' Minter waved a hand apologetically, opening the front door for Fairfax. 'A fancy. Good day to you, sir. I think I shall go and be ill now.'

Though Fairfax's tired feet protested at every step of the trudge back to Chelsea, his mind was too busy to heed them. Probably a good proportion of what he was thinking was nonsense, but no matter: it was better than that blind frustration.

That Tabitha had a solid connection to the Chilcotts was

encouraging, for one thing. It appeared to confirm his intuition that the death of Mr Chilcott at the Spread Eagle was more than a meaningless stroke of mortality. Only *appeared* to, of course. He was still prepared to find that there was no link between them at all. But at least he felt that he was chasing something solid, and not a cloud of random entities.

The story of the ne'er-do-well brother was telling too. The icy Jane Chilcott was touched by the messiness of common humanity after all. And as for the elusive stranger who had been in her room at the Spread Eagle – who could he be but that disgraced brother?

Someone else, of course. That was still possible. But the brother was fixed in Fairfax's mind. Could it be that he had arranged to meet his sister there – that between them they had plotted her husband's death, with the broken carriage wheel as the means? The trouble with that theory was that she was surely to go home in that same carriage . . . unless they had planned some way of ensuring Mr Chilcott went home alone. As it happened, it had been unnecessary. Mr Chilcott, coming upon them, had collapsed – the seizure brought on by surprise at seeing the brother there, perhaps? Somehow that didn't account for the sheer horror on the dead man's face. But it was a possibility.

And then Tabitha. Mrs Chilcott's midnight wanderings had made it entirely possible for her to have made her way over to Chelsea, and killed her former maid. What he still lacked was a reason for her to have done so. Think . . . Tabitha had not lived two days after Mr Chilcott's death – which suggested a compelling reason to get rid of her. Had she seen something, known something, guessed something . . . ?

Yet she had not acted, those last two days, like a woman in possession of a powerful secret – at least not as far as the Chilcotts were concerned. Unless it were something she had been unaware of possessing.

Very vague. A fancy, as the old steward would say. And that brought him to the well-dressed stranger, calling on the morning of Mr Chilcott's death. If it had been the brother, he would surely have been known by the gardener, Mr Chilcott's male servants being of the ancient retainer type. A well-dressed man on a grey mare. Fairfax sighed involuntarily. In the genteel outskirts of London, such a figure would hardly be a rarity.

She's a mystery to me – quite a mystery, the old steward had said. Fairfax had a hidden conviction that Minter had spoken more truly than he knew. If anyone possessed the key to this whole affair, then it was surely Mrs Chilcott. But the first thing was to find her, and though he had no high expectations of the Chilcotts' coachman and stable-boy (a mere stripling of fifty, no doubt), he did not know where to look either.

For the moment, though, he needed a wash and a clean shirt: his addiction to bathing was a peculiar quirk to many of his contemporaries, who with their twice-yearly ablutions would have found him sweet enough, but Robert Fairfax had never reconciled himself to the 'honest stink' even when it came from himself. Coming into Royal Hospital Row, he saw Dr Stagg just dismounting at his door – and reminded himself that Dr Stagg's horse was a roan. He had seen it before, of course; but his interest in horseflesh was such that his landlord might have ridden a unicorn without him noticing.

'The inquest is set for tomorrow,' Stagg said without preamble. 'Also I have notified the parish officers that I will bear the cost of a casket and a church plot.'

'That is a generous gesture, Dr Stagg.'

The physician shrugged. 'There was enough indignity in the poor creature's passing. I would not see her thrown to her rest in a pauper's funeral to add to it.' Stagg tethered his horse to a post and then opened his front door. 'But then you are busy on her behalf too, are you not? You look fatigued. I suppose there is no news?'

'Nothing firm. I am a little weary, indeed, but it will wash away.'

'My errand too. I have just come from a patient.'

Stagg threw off his coat, and Fairfax saw flecks of blood on his wrist-bands and around his fingernails.

'I hope nothing serious.'

'No.' Stagg stumped towards the kitchen. 'I'll have the maid bring you up some water, Mr Fairfax.'

'Thank you. Oh – Dr Stagg – can you think of any gentleman hereabouts who rides a grey mare? A young gentleman.'

'There's Charles Porteous,' Stagg said, pausing. 'Has a fine grey. Cost him a pretty penny, I believe.'

Porteous. That was the very name that had occurred to him . . . but of course, this confirmed nothing. And what had Porteous to do with the Chilcotts anyway?

'Ah. Well, I have, of course, spoken to Mr Porteous, and Miss Henlow, as Tabitha was in their service. Indeed Miss Henlow, it seems, was perhaps the last person to see Tabitha—'

'You surely cannot suspect Miss Henlow,' Stagg said

sharply, silencing him. 'That is . . . Oh, I understand you must be thorough. But surely that fellow Runquest is the likely man, if he could only be pinned down. Everything points to it. And speculations are . . . well, forgive me, I am a man of science, and perhaps I am a little enslaved to fact.' He was gone before Fairfax could speak.

Man of science . . . Fairfax had a good deal of respect for Dr Stagg, but that, he thought going upstairs, was mere flummery. There were those outpourings of prayer he had heard; and there was also that revealing response to the mention of Emma Henlow. Plainly Stagg was still enslaved, not to fact, but to that beautiful, imperturbable woman. Fairfax was far from inviting confidences – indeed, he would rather have had several teeth pulled than spend an evening with someone who, heavy-eyed and solemn, proposed to Tell Him the Whole Story – but still he thought Dr Stagg might have been more honest. Stagg was surely full of romantic, tragical, and turbulent feeling, rather than science.

Whereas you, of course, are perfect, Fairfax reproached himself as he washed and changed his shirt in his chamber. What about him and Cordelia? He only had to think of her name to turn into a man of sorrows. The heart-troubles of others were always counterfeit, and one's own always authentic.

Then as he dressed he recalled Charles Porteous' words about the room in a man's heart, and began applying them to Dr Stagg. Before he knew where he was, he had reached a horrible supposition.

Suppose Tabitha had come to see Stagg about her pregnancy last evening not just to consult him as a physician, but to confront him as the father of the unborn child?

At once Fairfax turned sick with guilt. He was living under the roof of this man – a man of uncommon integrity as a physician and, given what he had just said about the funeral, of generous feeling too. But once the idea was planted, it flourished and he could not stop it. If Stagg *had* strayed with Tabitha, then he had much to lose should she advertise the fact. There was his reputation – and if he still cherished hopes of winning Miss Henlow, he had all the more reason to guard it.

Reason enough to kill?

Or how about this, Fairfax said to himself, unstoppably: what if Stagg was not the father of Tabitha's child, but knew who was? And had killed Tabitha to protect that person – or rather that person's sister-in-law, who would share the downfall?

I must have sunstroke, he thought. Surely Frederick Stagg could not be so desperately in thrall to Emma Henlow that he would go to such lengths . . . and for what reward, after all? Could he hope then to tell her what he had done for her, and expect her all at once to love him, rather than recoil in horror? Unless, of course, Emma was involved in some way – had even, perhaps, pressed him to help them . . .

Fairfax would have discounted all of this as sheer fantasy – if it were not for the fact that Stagg was so damned odd. There was a furtive, covert *something* about the man. Downstairs the front door banged, and from his chamber window Fairfax saw Stagg remount his horse and go off at a trot up the dusty street. He was going in the direction of Five Fields Row. To see Emma . . . ? For a moment Fairfax debated following him. But it was quite likely that he was simply going to make his daily call on Leopold Mozart, later than usual: after all, the grim business of Tabitha this morning had disrupted his schedule.

Well, there was nothing now to prevent Fairfax from having a look around Stagg's quarters, and seeing if he could find anything with a tale to tell. Nothing to prevent him except common decency, of course: could he justify prying into his landlord's privacy, simply on a faint suspicion?

'Yes, I can,' he muttered to himself, going into Stagg's bedchamber. After all, Stagg knew that he was investigating Tabitha's murder: if he had left him alone in the house with incriminating evidence, then he could hardly cry 'unfair' if Fairfax found it . . . The doctor's bedchamber was spartan, no hangings on the bed nor rug on the floor. A Bible lay open on the table by the bed, but Fairfax could find no significance in the text, which was a particularly murky passage of Chronicles, full of seizing and smiting. In complete contrast, he found between the leaves in the middle a single pressed flower. A pink, he thought, though he had a townish vagueness about the flowers of the field. Certainly a treasured memento. He had little doubt about who had worn that flower. Replacing the Bible as it had lain, he went to the bureau in the corner, and found it unlocked. There were medicines in small glass bottles inside, some labelled: antimony, calcined magnesia, paregoric, cinchona – the common apothecary's stock. He picked up, and hastily put down, a brass object that he realized was a clyster-pipe for enemas. Tarnished brass scales, an old cracked leech-glass, a mortar and pestle cracked likewise, even a tea-cup with some medicinal dregs in it – all rather contrary to Dr Stagg's tidy habits, which made Fairfax suspect this must be old, disused apparatus, from his prentice days perhaps. In fact now that he thought about it, there was another bureau downstairs that he had seen Stagg use. Closing this one, he went softly down, making sure there were no servants about, and entered the front parlour that Stagg used as his consulting room.

No: this bureau, as he had half expected, was locked. There was a desk, however, with papers on it. Medical notes, it seemed; but he was leafing through them when a loud rapping at the front door made his heart jolt in his chest.

He had left the door ajar: a servant coming through from the kitchen to answer the knock would see him in here, prying in Stagg's consulting room . . . After a second's indecision he leapt out into the hall and flung open the front door himself, just in time: a moment later the maid appeared behind him from the kitchen.

'Not to worry, Mary – I've answered it,' he called out with loud insouciance, and then, even before he had seen who was on the doorstep: 'I'm sorry, Dr Stagg is from home—'

'That's pretty well,' said Jemmy Runquest, whose hulking figure quite blocked out the light. 'Because it's you I want to speak to, sir, if you'll be so good.'

Doubly surprised – it was the first time Runquest had *sirred* him – Fairfax beckoned him in, nodding the maid away. He took the giant man into the back parlour, where Runquest stared about him, breathing hard and rubbing his lower lip tentatively. Fairfax caught the smell of spirits.

'Well, and what can I do for you?'

''Tis more what you can do for me,' Runquest said, with his old truculent look; then he sat down, a little unsteadily, and frowned at the floor. 'Now look here – you know I didn't do for poor old Tabby, don't you? I'm no saint. I've said it before and I know it. But I'm not a man to go knocking a wench dead because she's going to bring him down, nor for any other reason. Why, that's chicken-hearted – and no one's ever called me that!'

Whereas hitting a woman in the face, Fairfax thought, is all right.

'Now I've been thinking about it,' Runquest went on, 'and I dare say 'tis fair enough that the law came to me first, me and Tabby having our history, as you might say. But I was able to give an account of myself; and I notice no one's come knocking on my door to carry me off to gaol, nor bothered me at all, and that makes me suppose that you don't believe I did it.'

Fairfax wagged his head noncommittally. 'Enquiries are still being made.'

Runquest gave him a narrow, shrewd look. 'Well. You have to say that. But man to man, sir, I don't believe *you* believe I did it. You're no fool. What you see is an innocent man – and a man, as you well know, who's just lost the chance of his life. I'll be honest, sir, I could have wept when Mr Yelverton turned me off – and I haven't shed a tear since I was a babe in arms. That'll give you some notion.'

'I can see it was a very good position, and losing it must have been a bitter blow. But that had nothing to do with this business: it was simply that your character reference didn't stand up to scrutiny.'

'Exactly. That's why I want another. So I can look about me for – well, I doubt I'll find anything as good as that job, but something in that line. Not mucking out stables all day and staring into an alehouse mug at the end of it. So there's my request, sir. You're a scholar and a gentleman, I reckon. If you'll write me a testimonial, why then – then I'll be grateful, and I can't say fairer than that.'

Fairfax found himself gaping. How was he going to put this . . . ? 'Why,' he said, putting it plainly, 'should I do that?'

Runquest blew out a great breath, and his eyes were hard. 'Don't you believe in scripture? Helping a fellow creature in trouble, and all that?'

'But lies and fraud are hardly approved of in scripture.'

'Depends what you mean. Now if you was to write that I was a professed cook or a carpenter, that wouldn't be honest. But what I want is something to prove – well, what I am. I *was* fit for that job with Mr Yelverton. Strong as an ox, right enough; but no ox up here.' He tapped his head. 'I can read and write perfectly well, and reckon up accounts, and take care of a gentleman's clothes and wigs, and I'll wager in foreign parts I'd have picked up the language, and been equal to customs-houses and coach-routes and all the rest of it. Not like your common straw-mouth who's lost if he walks out of his parish. Now look here . . .' Runquest jumped up and took a book from Dr Stagg's bookcase, and opening it in the middle began to read out loud. '"A man's heart is infinitely deceitful, unknown to itself, not certain in its own acts, praying one way and desiring another, wandering and imperfect, loose and various, worshipping God and entertaining sin, following what it hates and running from what it flatters, loving to be tempted and betrayed, petulant like a wanton girl, running from, that it might invite the fondness and enrage the appetite of the foolish young man or the evil temptation that follows it . . ." Now this isn't a book I know, though I'd like to,' Runquest said, looking at the spine. 'Jeremy Taylor, *Holy Dying*. Very true words, and expressed very forceful. Now that proves something, doesn't it?'

Again Fairfax felt his misjudgment of the man, though without any liking. 'I don't doubt that you—'

'And this,' Runquest said excitedly, seizing on the chess-board. 'I can play a good game of chess too. Come – I'll show you. We'll have a game. I'll be white.' He began setting out the pieces, occasionally bashing one over in his almost childlike agitation.

'Very well, if you wish.' The smell of spirits was strong, and Fairfax surmised that Jemmy Runquest was in a condition suitable to being plied, coaxed and perhaps opened up. A little more drink would help, plus patience on his own part. Runquest responded eagerly to his offer of a glass of brandy; and only as Fairfax sat down opposite him at the chess-board did it occur to him that he might be entirely wrong in his estimate. This was a violent man: not, he thought, a killer, but that was far from certain. If he exposed a nerve, discovered more than he had bargained for, there was nothing to stop the big man breaking him in two right in this room.

Well, he would have to take the chance. But he watered his own brandy, so as to stay alert.

Runquest noticed. 'Why, man, you've half drowned it!' he said with a harsh laugh.

'A weak head,' Fairfax said, making his first move. 'Tell me, how comes it that Mr Yelverton was unsatisfied with your references?' He knew, of course, but counted on Runquest not realizing that.

'Huh. Mr Yelverton doesn't know what he's missing,' Runquest said, downing his brandy at a gulp. 'He'll not find another man like me to do the job – not in fifty mile.'

'Is there no chance, then, that you might persuade him to reconsider?' Fairfax said, refilling Runquest's glass.

'Why, don't I tell you, he'll have naught to do with me now!' Runquest said, firing up. 'Don't you think I'd have tried, if 'twere any manner of use? The fact is, he caught me out, and that's the end of it. The God-cursed gall of it is, it need never have happened, not if that bastard had known his trade.'

'Which bastard? There are a lot of them in the world, you know.'

Runquest showed his teeth. 'True enough. But this was a swindling bastard, and I hate those most of all. Now here's a question. Suppose you were a screever – you know the coves I mean?'

'I know them.' At the lowest point of his fortunes he had even considered becoming one, so Runquest's hypothesis was not unthinkable.

'Now as a screever, the goods you deal in aren't necessarily honest, so to speak. Sometimes you'll write letters for poor benighted wretches who can't write for themselves, but you know and I know that what you chiefly deal in is fakery. You write fake testimonials, letters of recommendation, and suchlike, for a fee. You know all the proper phrases and ways of address, and you can write copperplate or law-hand as required, and can give the whole thing a professional look that'll deceive the eye of the cunningest beadle or bailiff. In a way, I suppose, you're an artist.'

'I suppose I am – or he is, rather.'

'Ah, but now think on this. You're a tradesman too, taking money for what you sell; and though what you sell may be dishonest, the one thing it shouldn't be is shoddy. Right enough? The fellow who lays out good money for that article expects it to be up to scratch, and do what it's meant to do, just as a broom's meant to sweep, and is no good else. See? Your move.'

Fairfax played a cautious pawn. Runquest was a neck-or-nothing chessman, his queen and both bishops already in play.

'So. You paid a screever for a fake reference, but he let you down.'

'Paid a pretty penny. And look at me now. So when I say I feel hard done by, you'll understand what I mean. 'Twasn't my fault: I'd a right to expect that screever would do the job. But instead 'twas a gammy one! The bastard signed with the name of a man who never was, at an address that never existed – so I finds out this morning, anyway, when Mr Yelverton tackles me with it. Strike me, you'd think he'd have the sense to give it a touch of the real. That's the usual way – that's what I'd do. Give the address of somebody lately dead, mebbe, or who's away a lot – then if your employer has heard of 'em, or does check it, which most of 'em don't, damn it, and damn Yelverton for being the sort who does – why, then it's still got that likelihood about it, d'you see? But if it's Squire Nobody of Nowhere Hall then it must be fake. See?'

'I see.' Fairfax took his queen's bishop. Runquest glared, breathing inflammable fumes.

'Bloody Tabitha's fault, anyhow,' he grunted. 'Bloody

Tabitha. Oh – I don't mean the pun.'

Fairfax tried to mask his disgust. 'How Tabitha's fault?'

'Oh, she was the one who put me on to the screever. I know the very man, says she, when I told her I wanted a character so I could apply to Mr Yelverton. This was before we – well, before we weren't friends any more.'

'How did Tabitha know this screever?'

Runquest raised his great head from studying the board. 'Why, she'd used him herself, of course. I don't see how a poor slut like her could get a place at a respectable house without 'un, do you?' He laughed metallically: then his face darkened. 'Oh, you'll not do better than him, says she, an excellent fellow, says she. I should have known then . . .'

'How do you mean?' Fairfax asked, casually, refilling Runquest's glass.

'I mean what I say. He was another of her fancies. Why else would she simper about him so?'

'Oh . . . but you can't be sure of that.'

'Can't I? Can't I now? Then who was that she was a-making up to in the stables at the Spread Eagle that morning, eh?'

Fairfax set down his glass. 'The man you saw her with in the stables – he was the screever?'

'I'd swear to it. I'd – well, I'd not stake my life. She had him so snugged up in the corner that there was no getting a good view of him anyway.' Runquest turned his head as if about to spit, then apparently thought better of it. 'But I'll swear that was him. She denied it, of course, when I put it to her. No, no, Jemmy, says she, you're mistook . . . And so did he. Much good it did him, for I weren't concerned about that. 'Twas swindling me I wouldn't stand for.' Runquest swigged brandy and grinned like a dog. 'He knows that now.'

'Do you mean you've seen this screever since?'

'Mebbe I have. He swindled me, don't forget; and no one gets away with swindling Jemmy Runquest. But if he squeals about it . . .' Taking Fairfax's pawn, Runquest squeezed it a moment in his great fist, as if he would crush the ivory into powder. 'Why, he deserved what he got: that's all.'

Fairfax remembered Runquest this morning, bare-chested and baleful and defiant, fresh blood staining his shirt.

'Jemmy, where can I find this man?'

'Any number of places,' Runquest said, with a mock yawn. 'Like I say, I've mebbe seen him – mebbe not. I'm not going to incriminate myself, sir, and that doesn't mean I've done anything. Only that I've got to be careful.'

He studied the chess-board, pouting. Drink was making him mulish.

Fairfax got up and fetched pen and ink and paper.

'Now,' he said, mending the pen, 'as I am about to be a screever, I had better be sure that I at least am an honest one. I am, I suppose, a gentleman, whatever that means: my father was a judge of the Court of Common Pleas, with an estate in Suffolk. He was, however, disgraced, and that is why I am without fortune, and must earn my own bread. But I have a bachelor's degree from Oxford; my past pupils have included relatives of the aristocracy, whose names I may invoke, likewise those of the London justices Mr Fielding and Mr Welch, whom I have aided in the past. So if you think I will do as a character reference, then I shall write your testimonial: the choice is yours.'

Runquest blinked at him, licking his lips. ''Tis very good of you, sir. I'll not say no.'

'But first you will oblige me with the name of this screever.'

For a second Runquest looked stubborn, as if out of sheer habit. Then he sighed. 'Bayley's his name, Giles Bayley. Youngish fellow, white as a lily – whiter than you, sir.'

'Hm. And where can I find him?'

'That depends. He has regular haunts, you see – that's how he gets his business. He goes to such-and-such a tavern or coffee-house on such-and-such a day, and sits there with a mug and his pen and ink; and if you want him, you step up and name your business. That's how his sort go on as a rule. Betwixt here and Westminster he's got a dozen haunts, along the river mostly. But I do know where he lives.' Runquest looked significantly at the brandy bottle.

'Well?' Fairfax refilled his glass.

'Obliged to you, sir . . . Now when I say I know where he lives, that don't tie me to anything, you know. It doesn't mean to say I've been there lately. I know – Tabitha knew it, damn her, and that should have warned me—'

'Where?'

Runquest belched, an oddly discreet sound. ''Tis in Petty France. A poor, moiling sort of place, name of Cherry Yard. They might well call it a yard, for it's hardly a yard across. God send I never end up in such a place . . . And now, sir, a bargain's a bargain.' He tapped the inkstand.

Fairfax nodded and swiftly wrote a testimonial to Jemmy Runquest's character. It was a piece of cold-blooded fiction; but it had got him the information he wanted. And if Runquest did turn out to be the murderer they sought, he would get hold of it and tear it up. Still, he was glad to have it done.

'There.' He sanded the letter and handed it over. 'Now, if you'll forgive me, I must be going—'

'You'll back this up, sir?' Runquest said, reading the letter with shining eyes. 'If I get a post, but they want it confirming, you'll back it up?'

'I will,' Fairfax said, with an inward grimace.

'Well, then I call it handsome,' Runquest said, stowing the letter carefully away. 'Oh – there's our game to finish, sir.'

'So there is.' Fairfax studied the board a moment, then played his queen. 'Checkmate.'

Runquest stared in surprise at the board, then gave a slow, sardonic, unpleasant smile. For a moment Fairfax wished he hadn't done that: he recognized, almost like an odour in the air, that hint of menace familiar from taverns and inn-yards, familiar too from Oxford club-rooms and St James's gaming-houses; the menace of a man who, jaunty and life-loving and hail-fellow-well-met though he might be, had anger in his blood, and would fight upon any occasion, almost as if only fighting made him feel real.

And then, as was the way with such men, Runquest suddenly relaxed and became expansive. 'Well, I wasn't paying attention. We must have another game.'

'Yes, some time soon,' Fairfax said. 'But now I have business, and—'

'Oh, I know. You're the law's man, and the law never sleeps. Well, I wish you luck, sir. I think you know I didn't kill Tabby, because you're a man of reason. And being such, you'll ask yourself: why would a man like me need to kill a woman like that? Because, before God, sir, they're easy enough to get rid of.' Jemmy Runquest, staggering a little with drink, placed his hat on his head with stately deliberation, as if he were crowning himself. 'Cold, mebbe, but true.'

Cold but true. Fairfax sat for some minutes after Runquest had gone, staring at the chess-pieces arranged in their elegant pattern of conquest. Runquest was right, of course, in his brutal way. Women were easily got rid of. They fell and were ruined, they were turned out of doors, they were worn out or snuffed out by childbirth. Only on the super-refined symbolism of the chess-board was the queen triumphant.

And yet how difficult men were to get rid of. He was thinking of Cordelia Linton and her absent husband. No out-and-out bruiser like Runquest – but still, from what he remembered and from what he had been told of him, a man capable of great selfishness and cruelty towards his wife. And yet still the chains bound her to him, and she could not be rid of him. The chains were in her very name: the chains were – he had seen them – in her eyes.

He shrugged the sombre thought off, put his mind to what he had learned from Runquest. This man, this screever, Giles Bayley: if Runquest was to be believed, and Fairfax saw no reason not to believe him in this regard at least, then Bayley had been at the Spread Eagle that fateful day. He had been seen with Tabitha earlier – and later? Was he the mysterious man who had been in Mrs Chilcott's room? It might be. He seemed to know Tabitha well – had supplied her with a false character reference. For her job at the Porteous house? Certainly Charles Porteous had spoken as a man who did not take on domestic servants without a good character.

Connections, coincidences . . . The rudiments of a pattern were emerging. But as in a game of chess against a superlative player, the pattern seemed to make no particular sense.

In chess, of course, the pattern only became clear when it was too late: the moves coalesced, the trap was sprung, and you were checkmated. But if Fairfax could make sense of this pattern, he would be the victor: he would have Tabitha's murderer. And whoever that person was, he or she must have a powerful tincture of evil in their nature. Murderers always felt that there were pressing, even good reasons for what they did – but still the evil was there. A worthwhile victory, then: no game.

Whoever that person was . . . Fairfax recited the names aloud, sure that one of them was that of Tabitha Dance's murderer; and as he did so he took a chess-piece and set it before him, one for each.

'Jemmy Runquest.' A black pawn seemed right: for in spite of the brawny size and the bravado, he cut a small figure in the world, poor and struggling for work, destined for obscurity.

'Emma Henlow.' The white queen: apt for that glowing fairness, that self-possessed, well-bred assurance. And the house where she lived was certainly her domain.

'Charles Porteous.' What else but the white knight? He rode a grey mare, and was as thoroughly courteous as any knight of old – on the surface at least.

'Mrs Jane Chilcott.' The black queen. The imperious regality went without saying: her colouring was dark and so, perhaps, were her secrets.

'Dr Stagg.' The black knight, for he was another rider,

and one who rode to succour the distressed.

'Giles Bayley.' Here he hesitated, for though he had a name, an occupation, a physical sketch, still he did not know this man. After a moment he took the black king and placed it in the middle of the others. Dark, unknown, but surely paramount to the solution of this whole mystery. All that remained was to find him.

Putting the chess-set away, Fairfax had an unpleasant realization. He was not the only player, after all. Of those six people, five at least knew perfectly well that he was investigating Tabitha's murder. Which meant that they were watching his moves as avidly as he was watching theirs. Which meant that the killer who had taken Tabitha's life might decide, if he got too close, to take his, and sweep him from the board.

Seven

He did not relish walking into London, even as far as Petty
France, which was an insalubrious quarter on the near side
of Westminster. Luckily he found a sedan chair outside
Ranelagh Gardens: the chairmen had just brought thither a
lady singer who was to regale the crowds at the fashionable
resort tonight with operatic excerpts, and had come early to
rehearse.

'Judging by what she weighs,' one of the chairmen said,
rubbing his biceps ruefully, 'she ought to give value for
money. Queer, ain't it, how the Almighty always puts the
sweetest voices in the fattest bodies . . . Where to, sir?'

'Westminster – as quick as you can manage, after that.'

'Be there in a pig's whisper, sir. Why, you don't look no
more than a small bit fallen off her. I mean that respectful.
Hup, Tom!'

Even after a few days of seclusion in Chelsea, it felt
strange to be entering the great city again: smelling (and
tasting and feeling) its miasma of coal-smoke, seeing its
fabulous profusion of brick and tile, sensing its wealth
and vitality and sorrowing over how cheaply, for all its
brilliance, it held humanity. For every lacquered carriage

awaiting the entrance of a gentleman tricked out in braid, silk, powder and pomade, five gaunt faces stared, like starveling sparrows in the presence of a peacock. For every boastful edifice florid with pilasters and statuary, there was a seething alley or court that looked like a segment of hellish night even under the summer afternoon sun. As for the stink of cesspits and middens, it struck him so forcibly that he began to understand the sweetness of that Chelsea air to which his doctor had recommended him; and that it was particularly noisome in Westminster, about the seats of government, was an irony he noted without being able to enjoy it, as he was too busy muffling his nose in his handkerchief and wondering how he had ever been able to walk about this city without being sick.

At Petty France he paid the chairman and took stock of his surroundings, breathing in little conservative gasps. Here, and about the Sanctuaries of the Abbey, and the aptly named Thieving Lane, there was a squalor that his mind could only label medieval, though he knew that in medieval or even later times the district had been rather handsome than otherwise. It was age itself that had degraded it. While the new squares had risen up spacious and symmetrical to the west, here the poor and the criminal had crowded into lopsided and cater-cornered antiquity. Down the middle of the cobbled streets ran a turgid stream of ordure, like some ghastly urban brook. Every dweller here seemed to have undergone some species of enchantment – for the dogs looked like rats, the children looked like gnomes, and the young mothers looked like raddled hags; whilst such men as were to be seen, lolling at corners, hunkered in groups around a game of taws or dice, or sleeping off a dose of gin in doorways and on area-steps, had something fiery-faced and yellow-eyed about them that could only suggest demons.

And yet every district in old London had an enclave like this: it was no more supernatural than an unpaid bill. Picking his way through the refuse, Fairfax began to understand Jemmy Runquest a little better. This was what lay in wait for the labourer or servant who went astray, who had bad luck, or who simply grew old or infirm. Impatient ambition was comprehensible simply as a desire to put as much distance as possible between yourself and places like this.

Fairfax had noticed before that some of the most purgatorial places in London had the prettiest names – he had held his nose through many a Paradise Alley and Eden Court – and Cherry Yard, suggesting fruitful rusticity, was notable for being such a dry, airless, stony spot that not even a sprig of moss grew between the cracks in the cobbles. Otherwise it probably counted as an eligible address as far as this district went. The little enclosure of half-timbered buildings was only peeling rather than falling down, and the lines of washing that criss-crossed its meagre square of sky were recognizable as garments rather than rags. From one of the open windows came the forlorn sound of someone practising scales on a kit-fiddle; from another came a massed twittering of caged songbirds. Fairfax felt a curious ache of familiarity. He had not lived here, but in his younger years, following the wreck of his fortune, he had lived in places like this. A Grub Street scribbler, his coat at the pawn shop, his head full of dreams of literary glory, he had laboured away at his penny-a-page and looked wistfully out into dingy courts like this at his neighbours, the arthritic dancing-masters, bird-sellers, washerwomen, petticoat-quilters, actors, and general strugglers, who looked back at him from their windows like so many prisoners in a gaol of disappointed hope.

It was of one such, a lank young man leaning in a doorway with a long clay pipe at his lips, that Fairfax asked the question where he might find Mr Bayley.

'Know him, do you?'

'Yes.'

'Ah. Friend of his? Well, don't matter. He lives up there – second pair back. I just hope you're friendlier than the other one.' The young man sighed, chewing his pipe. 'I wisht I had some tobacco to put in this.'

The other one? Fairfax thought: but he had an idea who was meant. Indeed, all the way here he had been mentally kneading at some pretty firm notions about this Giles Bayley – and that was why, when the young man had asked if he knew him, he had replied yes.

For he believed he did, in a way. Giles Bayley, the screever, had been seen at the Spread Eagle by Jemmy Runquest early on the morning of Mr Chilcott's death there. Little Wolfgang had seen a pale, thin young man coming out of Mrs Chilcott's room later. Mrs Chilcott, according to her steward, had a ne'er-do-well brother who had been caught forging documents and been sent packing for it. He was willing to bet that Giles Bayley and the brother were one and the same. Matheson was Mrs Chilcott's maiden name, but it was quite probable that her brother, an educated scapegrace reduced to screeving for a living, would use an assumed name to carry on his disreputable trade.

And then, climbing the dim, worm-eaten stairs of the tenement, Fairfax felt like slapping his own back in self-congratulation. Up above him was a hurrying female figure, and as she whisked on to the landing there was a rustle of hooped silk, and a whiff of scent very different from the prevailing odours in this place; and one glimpse of that fine-boned face beneath the capuchin hood was all he needed.

The mystery of Mrs Jane Chilcott's whereabouts, at any rate, was solved. Her wanderings had brought her to Cherry Yard, and to the man who called himself Giles Bayley.

Treading softly, Fairfax followed in Mrs Chilcott's fluttering wake. A door at the end of the narrow passage stood slightly ajar: she nudged it open, and he saw that her arms were full of wrapped packages. He took advantage of the moment, and slipped quietly into the room after her.

'There, my darling, I promised you I would not be long,' Mrs Chilcott was saying. 'I have brought things to cheer and comfort you – as well as bringing myself, of course.' Her back to him, she deposited the parcels on a rickety table, and then swept over to a man who sat in a chair by the bare hearth, and kissed him passionately on the lips.

Fairfax stopped dead: it was as if he had walked into an invisible wall. His mind performed a dizzy reversal of conclusions. He must be wrong, then, about Giles Bayley.

Or he might be right . . . And thinking of that, he

remembered the horror-struck face of Mr Chilcott at the foot of the inn stairs.

'And how do you feel now, my love?' Mrs Chilcott went on, kneeling at the man's feet and taking his hands in hers. The man did not answer. His eyes were fixed rigidly on Fairfax.

'Who the devil are you?' he said in a pinched tone.

Mrs Chilcott whipped round. Her nostrils widened in her best servant-cowing fashion.

'My name—'

'His name is immaterial,' Mrs Chilcott said, cutting Fairfax off. 'This, Giles, is the person who was bothering me with impertinent questions. Sir, I do not know how you come here, but you intrude. You intrude unthinkably.'

'That's clear enough,' Fairfax said. 'As it happens, I did not come here seeking you, Mrs Chilcott, though I am pleased to have found you. And there are others who will be relieved to know you are safe and well. Your curious disappearance caused some anxiety at home.'

'I am mistress in my own house, and may do as I please. I shall return at my pleasure. Tell them that.'

'With respect, Mrs Chilcott, I am not your messenger. And, I repeat, I came here on another errand. I seek Mr Giles Bayley, and I believe I have found him.'

'Well, what do you want with me? I am not well, sir, whoever you are; I do not like this disturbance,' the man said pettishly. *Not well*, Fairfax thought, was a politic way of putting it. This man had recently taken a severe beating. One eye was puffed and purple, and his lower lip was split: he had visibly winced at Mrs Chilcott's kiss. But the lineaments of a handsome young man were visible through the bruises – albeit a pale, refined, high-browed, hawkish sort of handsomeness, very much at odds with the bleak shabbiness of the room, which was relieved only by a few books and a couple of cheap prints plastered to the cracked wainscot. At odds too with the shabbiness of Giles Bayley's dress – though whilst the room could never have been anything but a dingy dwelling, Bayley's mulberry velvet coat and red-heeled shoes were the clothes of a gentleman, worn beyond repair.

'I apologize for it. But the matter is urgent. And it involves, I fear, Mrs Chilcott, more questions.'

'Don't stir, my dear,' Mrs Chilcott said to the young man, who showed signs of rising impatiently. 'There will be no trouble . . . By what right, Mr Fairfax, do you come here with your talk of questions? Is it not enough—'

'By right of the law. Or rather, the desire of the law to catch a murderer. Mr Bayley, a woman was killed at Chelsea last night – a woman known to you, I believe. Her name was Tabitha Dance.'

'Tabitha . . . ?' Mrs Chilcott said. 'Why, she used to be our servant.'

'So I have discovered. Someone struck her down most brutally, by Ebury Bridge late last night, and I am charged with discovering who. Naturally that has entailed finding out who Tabitha had to do with. So there is convenience for me at least in finding you both here. You both knew her: you will both, I am sure, wish to give an account of yourselves for last night.'

'Absurd,' Bayley said. 'A woman I hardly knew, in a place far from my haunt . . .'

'Your – illness makes you forgetful, perhaps, Mr Bayley,'

Fairfax said. 'You were at that place quite recent. A man named Jemmy Runquest, who identified you to me, saw you at the Spread Eagle in Chelsea on Monday morning. He is one of your customers – an unsatisfied one, I gather. I believe he has been to see you earlier today, and expressed his dissatisfaction very forcibly.'

Giles Bayley stirred sufferingly, hesitated, then said, 'Yes. That was Runquest right enough.' He added, with a glint of humour that Fairfax thought admirable in the circumstances, 'He made me feel quite ill.'

'Well,' Fairfax said. 'I wish he were other than he is, for your sake. But the fact remains he saw you at the Spread Eagle that day, in the stables, in company with Tabitha Dance. She, it seems, had been a customer of yours in the past, and she had recommended you.'

'Very well: business has taken me to the environs of Chelsea on occasion, and the woman you name did avail herself of my professional services once. But really, I don't see . . . I am sorry indeed for her dreadful fate, but I know nothing of it. And as for Jane here, I shall take it much amiss, sir, if you think to put her to the question. Lamentably humble as this place is to which unfortunate circumstances confine me, it is my home, and I will not see the honour of a lady impugned in it – least of all this lady.'

'Well, perhaps you will oblige me, then, by answering a simple question. The – intimate acquaintance between you is plain, and a man very much of your description was seen leaving Mrs Chilcott's room at the Spread Eagle that day – and so I would like to know what you were doing there.'

Bayley looked very fine and stormy and indignant – but

he was restrained by Mrs Chilcott, who squeezed his hand and then put her finger gently to his lips.

'No, my dear,' she said in a soft, cooing voice that Fairfax, at least, had never supposed her capable of, 'what does it signify? 'Tis as I said earlier – we have nothing to fear. Our time for concealment is past.'

She kissed him urgently, again ignoring his wince – and Fairfax's. *Her brother?* he thought; and said uncontrollably, 'Some things are better concealed. Forgive me, but—'

'What is it, Mr Fairfax?' Mrs Chilcott said. 'Can there be offence in a true and tender passion? Or is it the fact that my husband is dead but two days that brings out the conventional moralist in you?'

'Madam, I hardly know what to say. I had better mention that I have been learning about your – your family, and an episode in which one of them was employed by your husband, and dismissed. And I could not help but come to the conclusion—'

'This is the gentleman,' Mrs Chilcott said, standing with queenly pride beside Bayley's chair.

'But I am not her brother,' said Bayley, whose taste for the grand gesture seemed less developed than Mrs Chilcott's, and who waved a weary hand as he went on: 'You have been putting together wrong conclusions, Mr Fairfax, and though I cannot see that it has any bearing on this grim matter you speak of, I will supply you with the right ones.'

'We shall be open from now, in any case, my love,' Mrs Chilcott said fervently, 'and so it is only beginning early.'

'Quite so, Jane, quite so . . . Well, Mr Fairfax, you have had the tale, no doubt from some rascally servant or other. The true one is this: I did indeed come to be Mr Chilcott's secretary, at Jane's urging, for I was in sore need just then: he was a man of wealth and I a man of talent, and it was a – a good arrangement. I was introduced to Mr Chilcott as Jane's brother, a deception easily enough accomplished, as her parents are long dead, and she and Mr Chilcott being but recently married, and in a union that was – well, it was not a love-match.'

'Never,' whispered Mrs Chilcott.

'And as such, those intimate confidences, those eager outpourings of lovers who would know everything about one another, had no place. And so it was easy enough for Jane to say she had a brother, recently returned from abroad, and that he – he was worthy of a responsible position. This subterfuge concealed the true relation between us, which was—'

'A bond unbreakable by all save death,' said Mrs Chilcott in a rapid, glowing whisper.

'Pure, I was going to say, my love,' Bayley said, patting her hand. 'Pure, in as much as the subterfuge did not extend to – to going behind Mr Chilcott's back in his own house, in short. The fact is, the attachment between myself and Jane – Jane Matheson, as she was – was formed before her marriage. We fell deeply in love: but cruel circumstance was against us. I was a lawyer's clerk – a position not entirely suitable to my birth or education, but parental improvidence had left me without that independence which should have been my portion. Jane was residing with an aunt, and though of good family likewise, and accustomed to moving in the highest circles, was possessed of only a small inheritance. Sordid material bars, then, lay across our path to felicity. The difficulties were so perplexing that I think we quarrelled somewhat; and at last I went overseas to try my luck in the colonial planting line, with no firm undertaking or engagement between us. Well, the colonies did not answer – I found the climate and the coarseness equally insupportable – and I returned to these shores, with but one thought and aim in mind . . . and found Jane newly married to Mr Gabriel Chilcott.'

'I believed you gone for ever,' Mrs Chilcott said dolefully. 'Upon my soul I did. And my happiness gone with it. My aunt had died and I was alone: and so I took the – the easy road.'

'Well, I sought Jane out – I had to: I was in such a ferment. One glance was enough to vouchsafe that time, misunderstanding and separation had not quenched that mutual flame—'

'Say, fanned it!' Mrs Chilcott said ardently.

'True indeed – but what were we to do? Fate had interposed itself between us again, this time most finally. And so we came to the expedient of my becoming Mr Chilcott's secretary, under the name of Giles Matheson, her brother. An unbearable proximity, you might think, Mr Fairfax: but when a man worships a goddess as I did and do, then just to be close to her shrine is enough for his soul – even if he may not draw back the veil.'

'I see,' Fairfax said. 'And then Mr Chilcott discovered you in a forgery, and dismissed you.'

Jolted down from his romantic heights, Bayley reddened. 'It was an unfortunate episode,' he said, 'and as you cannot know the exact details of the case, I will pass over the crude construction you have put on it. Yes,

I was dismissed. I considered myself ill-used, and its being at the hands of a man who lived daily in enjoyment of that bliss which I was denied – a man coarse, obtuse, utterly unfit to drink from the sacred vessel – well, that made it galling beyond endurance. I took my leave hasty and heated. I regret to say that in shaking the dust of Brockleigh from my feet, I rather included Jane in the general renunciation. She had defended me, tried to save me, of course: but I was so unworthy as to feel that her loyalty lay with him, in the end, and I was simply making a fool of myself. So we parted again.'

Fairfax jumped as a strange, hyena-like laughter broke out from the room next door, followed by a series of odd rhythmic thumps. Giles Bayley sighed and said, 'Ignore it, sir. My neighbour is, I regret to say, a drunkard, and in between debauches he suffers delirious horrors which cause him to racket about in that manner. His being the possessor of a wooden leg makes the noise that much more insistent, though, if one has a mordant turn of humour, occasionally amusing.' As he spoke the neighbour seemed to take a spectacular crashing tumble including several chairs.

'And so, all that time,' Fairfax said, trying to collect his scattered thoughts, 'Mr Chilcott believed you were his wife's brother?'

'Just so. We were fortunate in having some little resemblance to one another. You know, sir, the idea set forth in the *Symposium* of Plato – that each of us is but half the whole being, which was split in two before our coming into the world? I always think Jane and I would make the perfect illustration to that amiable fancy.'

Well, he would, thought Fairfax. Mrs Chilcott protested that Giles had talked enough, and would tire himself, and going to the table unwrapped her packages. Coming up with the heart-shaped sugar cakes known as sweethearts, she proceeded to feed them to Bayley with much coy insistence. Lovers, Fairfax reflected: so much of the art and literature of the world was devoted to them, and yet how stupid they were when you really looked at them.

'And so,' he said, 'after your dismissal, you turned to your – your current profession.'

'I was hard pressed, sir,' Bayley said, frowning and dabbing sugar from his cheek, 'and sometimes a man is driven to desperate expedients. Yes, I was reduced to such, and to living in a dwelling like this. The fact is, I'm cursed with an imitative talent. With a pen in my hand I can be anybody. It was partly this which caused my downfall with Mr Chilcott. I felt that a business decision he had made was unwise, and took the liberty of making a correction with a feigned signature . . . well, enough of that. Suffice it to say that the screeving line, as the cant phrase has it, is very much a come-down for a man like me; but I must live, sir. All I can say in its defence, and mine, is that there is a good deal of art and invention in it – though employed to deplorable ends.'

'Believe me, Mr Bayley, I am the last person to stand in judgement on that. All that concerns me is the matter of how you and Mrs Chilcott met up again. Am I right in supposing it was at the Spread Eagle, on Monday?'

'It was – but there was no underhand arrangement. It was entirely by chance. I pursue my trade in such hostelries, along the river from here, and decided on Monday to go a little further afield. And I had taken up my station in the taproom when—'

'I saw him,' Mrs Chilcott said. 'I arrived with my husband, and passing through to the staircase I saw, through the taproom door – I saw the man whose image was forever fixed in my wounded heart. He did not see me – think of that, my love! Me passing by, and you not knowing I was there! – and so I went upstairs, feeling as if I should swoon at any moment. My husband had bespoke a room, where I composed myself to wait whilst he went off on his absurd hunt for the musical boy. But composed was the last thing I could be, knowing that Giles – my only true love – was downstairs. And so I went down, and I beckoned to him at the taproom door . . .'

'I shall never forget it,' Bayley said, kissing her fingers, 'when I looked up, and saw you there! Well, I followed, after a discreet moment, my head and heart in a whirl; and there in that common inn-room our mutual flame flared again to a new brightness and – well, in short, all the ill-starred division there had been between us just fell away. There was no resisting such a passion. The embrace was illicit – I know it. But after such prodigies of patience and continence as we had shown, it was surely not surprising. It was just a piece of supreme ill-luck that Mr Chilcott should return sooner than expected, and—'

'Walk in on you and Mrs Chilcott kissing as if your life depended on it,' Fairfax burst out: it would have been funny if it were not so tragic, and vice versa. 'To have caught his wife *in flagrante* like that would have been shocking in any event: but with the man he believed was her brother . . .' He shook his head.

'I would have explained,' Mrs Chilcott said, with some of her former primness. 'As soon as I saw the door open and my husband standing there, I had an inward resolve: let there be no more pretending. Come what may, let us be truthful now. But Mr Chilcott was always of such a hasty, inflammable temper, really the most unreflecting creature, and he *would* stand and stare and gasp—'

'He is hardly to be blamed for being unreflecting, at such a moment,' Fairfax said, a little sharply.

'I dare say, sir.' Mrs Chilcott looked at him as if he were about fifty feet below her, say at the bottom of a well. 'But it is quite wrong to speak of blame at all, in this connection. I cannot emphasize that enough. It was pure mischance, and I – we – cannot be held accountable for my husband's collapse. You must understand that, sir.'

'I understand. If it gets out, people *will* say that, of course. But you need not fear my indiscretion. I am just grateful to have one mystery cleared up. A pity, Mrs Chilcott, that you would insist on denying that little Wolfgang saw a man leaving your room – as he undoubtedly did.'

'Yes, I – in the circumstances I thought I had better make myself scarce,' Bayley said, a trifle shamefaced.

'I could not be open about such a matter then, sir,' Mrs Chilcott said. 'The constructions that would be put upon it – it was simply too much. I had enough to contend with, being suddenly a widow, and everything turned upside down. And very well, I felt guilt too: tormentingly so. There. Enough? Or would you have me cut off my hair and stand in the stocks?'

Fairfax shrugged impatiently. 'I care only for the truth, and for that I thank you . . . What I still cannot account for is the damage to the wheel of your carriage on that day.' He looked at Bayley, but the man returned the look neutrally; and really, Fairfax couldn't see any way to link them. Plainly Bayley did adore Mrs Chilcott: why endanger her life? Unless he had had a plan to detain her somehow at the inn, sending Mr Chilcott off alone in the carriage. But that made no sort of sense.

'What happened was regrettable in many ways, Mr Fairfax,' Bayley said as if reading his thoughts, 'but it was simply in the stars. Fortune delivered this lady from the bondage of that marriage, and by that same fortune' – he clasped her hand – 'we are here together now. But it was high time, I think, that fortune *did* smile on us.'

Fairfax didn't know what to say to that. Through the wall came a series of bizarre thumps and whoops, as if the wooden-legged man were executing a frenzied jig. 'And what of last night, Mrs Chilcott?'

'Last night, sir, I put an end to suffering. I had spent every moment since my husband's death in a paralysing agony of feeling. At about eleven o'clock last night, the paralysis broke . . . I am twenty-nine years old, Mr Fairfax: I have only one life; and I have tasted regret for so long that I sicken at it. Giles is the one I want, the one I am meant for. And so I walked out of the house and came looking for him. He had spoken only briefly of where he was living, when we met at the Spread Eagle: it took me a good deal of questing to find him here. But that was no bar. I knew my love, and I sought my love out: and I can do this because I am free. You can call it hard and bold-faced, if you like, sir, so soon after my widowing: I don't care for your opinion, or the world's. I am free now.'

And rich now, thought Fairfax; and could not help wondering if Bayley read the thought in his face.

'Here I am, and have remained since I found him this morning – and found him so cruelly used!' she added, caressing him. 'My dear, will you let me put on a little more of that salve?'

'I am well enough, my love. I suppose,' he said with a rueful look at Fairfax, 'this is my just reward for careless work.'

'I know Runquest was mighty displeased,' Fairfax said. 'And I think I know, now, where the drops of blood on his shirt came from.'

'Drops? I was a damned fountain when he'd finished with me. 'Twas unfortunate that he knew where to find me at home, and could – deal with me undisturbed. At least there are no bones broke . . . The fact is, I must have been a little tired and liverish when I wrote the testimonial for Runquest. Normally I take a pride in making these things as likely as possible, but instead I just conjured up a fictitious gentleman – something like Sir Bertram Ffoulkes, Bart., I believe . . . Well, it was difficult: the man was such a thorough brute that no real gentleman would ever have given him a character reference.'

Fairfax stirred uneasily, having done just that. 'And Tabitha Dance – you had previously supplied a screeve for her.'

'A much better one, though I say it myself. Yes, when she was dismissed by – by your late unlamented husband, my dear . . .' Bayley and Mrs Chilcott exchanged a rather nasty smile: but then lovers, needing only each other, were very often nasty, Fairfax thought.

'She sought me out as a screever, and said she had been turned out without a character by her last employer, Mr Gabriel Chilcott of Brockleigh House. Well, of course I happened to know that old party rather well; and as she had actually worked there, I composed her a glowing testimonial full of characteristically pompous phrases, such as he would have used, and signed it as from Gabriel Chilcott. I was careful, though, not to directly imitate his all too imitable script – he wrote a foul hand – as that might raise the question of actual forgery, and I had already been – well, let's say I was mighty wary of that. So I used my standard hand, and sealed it up, and off she went with it, highly pleased, and procured I believe a very decent position.'

'Yes,' Fairfax said, 'in the household of Mr Porteous . . . But that was not your only connection with Tabitha Dance, surely. That incident in the stables at the Spread Eagle . . . ?'

'Yes, well, that was a triviality, though rather unpleasant,' Bayley said, with a faintly nervous glance at Mrs Chilcott. 'She came in soon after I arrived – I shudder to say I believe she had been drinking even at that hour – and recognizing me, proceeded to pour out her troubles, namely that she had no work and no money. I was sorry to hear she had lost her job again, especially when I had taken such care to assist her, but it was hardly my concern. Well, the upshot was she wanted another screeve; she needed a character again, as her former employers would not give her one. But I cannot, of course, offer my professional services for nothing. Well, she said she would get money, and urged me to meet her at the rear of the building, where she . . . she proposed paying for a screeve in kind, as it were.'

'Abandoned wretch!' hissed Mrs Chilcott.

'It was not pretty,' Bayley said temperately, 'but then the poor creature was desperate, I believe, and of course disguised with liquor. Well, naturally I would have nothing to do with any such transaction, though she was, ahem, physically insistent. I was actually pinned against the wall for a short time.'

'Revolting hussy!' groaned Mrs Chilcott. Platonic halves they might be, but the half that was Bayley, who had a wry glint in his eye, had obviously got all the sense of humour.

'It was more embarrassing than distressing,' Bayley said, 'but I managed to extricate myself, and went back inside, and that was the end of it.'

So that was what Runquest saw, Fairfax thought. A sorry tale all in all, and nobody came out of it well. But nobody came out of it murderous either; and the mystery of the carriage wheel remained.

'Just a little salve, my dear,' Mrs Chilcott said, bending over Bayley, as if the mention of Tabitha had inclined her to re-stake her claim. 'It is an excellent remedy, you know, and you are too uncomplaining under pain, indeed you are . . .'

'Your injuries have been attended to by a doctor, I hope,' Fairfax said.

'Yes, thank heaven – by great good fortune it was that young man who attended my husband's death,' Mrs Chilcott said. Fairfax saw Bayley's foot inch out and press hers, too late.

'Dr Stagg? Dr Stagg has been here?'

'That is the gentleman's name. A very serviceable physician,' Bayley said austerely.

'I know. But it was remarkable chance that brought him

to your door, far from his home, at just this time.'

Bayley grimaced. 'It was not chance. Dr Stagg came to see me on a different matter – a business matter; and was good enough to treat my hurts while he was here. That is all.'

'A business matter . . . ?' Fairfax was so astonished that he could only parrot it. 'You mean – screeving, for Dr Stagg?'

'Sir, I have been frank with you, far more than I need, because I wish to establish my good faith, and most of all that of this lady,' Bayley said. 'And as for the solving of this horrid crime, I wish you heartily well. But my connection with Dr Stagg is a different matter. You will surely understand that in my line of work, confidentiality is vital.'

'But consider, my dear,' Mrs Chilcott said, 'things have changed. You can be done with this work now. And as for what happened at the Spread Eagle – that is no secret now. Do not forget, Giles, we are beginning afresh, you and I.'

'Well, I suppose it is so. It is no very edifying tale . . . but then as you say, Jane, there is no threat now. Nor any need to retain these people's favour, by God . . .' Bayley sat up, looking jaunty at that. 'Well, sir, it was the usual thing, where you have a gentleman or lady customer, literate and not in need. Letters. I'm sure you understand.'

'I'm afraid not,' Fairfax said, his wits still dulled by surprise.

'Letters the gentleman would prefer not to have in his own writing,' Bayley explained patiently. 'Letters which go anonymously to their recipient. Letters full of the usual phrases – knowing the secret, threatening exposure, hinting at disgrace, and so on. Poisoned-pen is the piquant phrase

I have heard used to describe such things. Surprising the number of people who have a taste for them: one of the lesser-known vices. I don't like them: I adopt my standard hand for them, and dash them off as quick as may be, and I never know, of course, for whom they are meant, as that would destroy the whole point. But I confess, when Dr Stagg sought me out with such a request, last Saturday, my curiosity was pricked. Here was this very upright and respectable young man, dabbling in some sort of extortion . . . it was so curious that having performed my first commission for him here, I took the liberty of following him some way, secretly, until he called at a druggist's shop, where he was plainly known; and by dint of patient enquiries there, found out who he was, and whence he came. And my idle curiosity was such as to bring me, on Monday, to the Spread Eagle at Chelsea, where I took up my pitch in some hopes of – well, discovering a little more about the gentleman, and—'

'And threatening him with exposure in turn?' Fairfax said.

'Dear life, you have a monstrous black-and-white way of looking at things, Mr Fairfax. It was a puzzle, and that was what led me on. Well, as it happened, the doctor saw me at the Spread Eagle before I saw him. He came in early on some errand, and must have spotted me there, and realized that I – well, that his anonymity was no longer secure. What happened after you know: my reunion with my sweeting, and my having to absent myself rather hastily. Unfortunately, Dr Stagg got to hear the foreign boy's account of a man fleeing the scene, and put two and two together. And so the next day he sought me out here again, and put it to me that I had been at the Spread Eagle, and said that the whole matter was being investigated . . . Well, at that juncture, you know, I preferred to be left out of it: it was a ticklish business, and there was this lady's good name to consider. And so it became rather like one of those games of arm-wrestling that boys play: now the doctor had the advantage of me, and was pushing the other way. But he did not push too hard, you know. All he wanted was another specimen of my professional services – another of those vulgar letters, in short. Your secret is mine, do not sleep easy, all the usual Gothic rigmarole. And of course, he wanted guaranteed discretion, which I was hardly in a position to refuse; and so we agreed to it, all very gentlemanly. I decided it was more prudent to keep my curiosity within bounds.'

'And . . . his visit today?'

'For a third letter. Yes, of the same sort. The Biblical quotation about sin finding you out was a feature – dear me, it so often is. I was going to say that my making you privy to this information is an exceptional licence, and urge you to keep it entirely to yourself . . . but of course, I need not trouble about these things any more.' A dreamy smile crossed his face as he gazed at Mrs Chilcott. 'This dreary, grubbing, and unsavoury life of mine is no more – my angel wills it!'

'You flatter her with the angelic address,' Mrs Chilcott said, blushing like a girl, 'but she does will it indeed. Ask away, Mr Fairfax, anything more that may occur to you – we have no secrets under heaven, and no fears this side of the grave: but make haste, for we shall be gone from here soon. Yes, Giles,' she said, kneeling down by his chair. 'I mean it. Today. Why should we wait? The world may condemn, but who gives a fig for the world? I may do as I please.' The man next door gave an extra loud yelp and fell, judging by the noise of clanging irons, right into the fireplace. Mrs Chilcott put fretful fingers to her forehead and was again for a moment the frosty lady with the glare of Medusa. 'It will be a mercy to take you out of this frightful place, my dear.'

'You are in earnest, Jane? Today?'

'Today – now. As soon as you can pack a bag, you shall come to Brockleigh and be with me. I am mistress of the house, and may have a guest if I choose, at least until—'

'Until the banns are called!' Bayley said, gripping her hand.

Curiously, Fairfax did not feel in the way throughout the incoherent embracings that followed. Indeed, looking at the couple, he felt that he had made them even happier by his being here – by being a witness to their highly theatrical love.

Not that it was insincere on either side: he was pretty sure of that, though sure also that Giles Bayley, deep inside, could hardly believe his luck. Shabby-genteel young men with a history of bad habits and missed opportunities were very seldom granted such a chance as this, and Bayley had the grace to look grateful.

'Indeed, my dear, never mind the bag,' Mrs Chilcott said. 'You shall have new clothes. We shall get a hackney to Kensington at once. We've lost too much time, I think.' Suddenly she gave Fairfax a very straight look. 'I am not a bad woman, sir. My life with Mr Chilcott was not lacking in material comfort – but it was hard. Hard and joyless. He was not a bad man, but he was a harsh, thoughtless, and domineering one. Being in such a marriage is not like starvation or illness; but still it is grindingly horrible.'

Fairfax inclined his head. The image of Cordelia came to him, a bright, still shape amongst the myriad splintered thoughts flickering through his brain.

'I wish you well, and I thank you both for your time and your frankness,' he said. 'May I call you a hackney on my way?'

'Oh, if you would be so good,' Mrs Chilcott said absently, occupied with wrapping up the sweethearts. Lovers, he thought again: they took it for granted that you would do things for them.

Late afternoon was melting into tender dusk above the chimney-stacks when he came out of Petty France. He found a hackney down by the Abbey, and having sent it off he stood for some time in a sombre dream, his eyes taking in the noble proportions and the ranks of soaring buttresses, as if to beguile his thoughts into a similar harmony.

Instead they were more like the graceless lines of St Stephen's Chapel close by – the old barn of a building where the parliament of the realm met. Well, appropriate perhaps. One was a lofty edifice of the spirit: the other a place where human beings, contentious and factious and all too fallible, gathered to thrash out the intractable complications of human life. Suitable, then, for the crowd of ugly ideas that his interview with Giles Bayley and Mrs Chilcott had given him.

He was surprised to find how sorrowful he felt. Dr Stagg a blackmailer! He had tried to think of some other explanation for a man purchasing anonymous threatening letters from a screever – but no amount of ingenuity could produce one.

He had to accept this new view of Dr Stagg. He might have to accept an even worse one . . . But the thought of that capable and compassionate physician, that awkward but decent-seeming young man, dealing in such things as poisoned-pen letters was already repulsive enough. Why it saddened him so he couldn't say – it was not as if he had become firm friends with Stagg, or even reached a point of mutual understanding. Perhaps he simply wanted someone to come out of this business with clean hands.

Well, Stagg was buying those letters to send to someone, and Fairfax had a clear suspicion as to who it was. And the secret they threatened to reveal, the source of the power that Stagg was gloating over . . . ? It was surely to do with Tabitha. The secret of who had made her pregnant?

Or did Stagg know the identity of her killer? Was that the secret? And yet Bayley had said Stagg had bought three such letters from him, the first on Saturday, long before Tabitha was killed. No: that wouldn't wash. Whatever he was up to, Stagg had begun it before Tabitha's murder. Could it be then that Tabitha herself had somehow discovered his scheme, and tried to use it against him? Fairfax remembered her calling at Stagg's house early on the evening of her murder – to consult him about her pregnancy, Stagg said. Or to threaten him? A threat he had ended by killing her that night?

And yet that still left the person to whom Stagg was sending the letters, and Fairfax's suspicion about that person was growing on him like the creeping chill of fever. For who, of all the people involved in this tortuous case, was most vulnerable to blackmail? Who could not afford to lose their appearance of utter integrity and respectability? Who had lately dismissed a maidservant who had turned out to be pregnant and had loudly protested that she would swear the father?

He knew who. And Stagg must know too. It was Stagg who must give him some answers, whether he liked it or not. For all his disappointment in the doctor, Fairfax was in no mood to pussyfoot about him. Stagg, after all, had been playing a duplicitous role all along: he had known or guessed about Bayley being the stranger that little Wolfgang had seen at the Spread Eagle, but had kept it to himself. Remembering the way Stagg had hovered outside his chamber door, Fairfax wondered if the doctor had had it in mind to speak out and come clean. Things would have been easier if he had. Fairfax could have cleared up and put to one side the whole matter of Mr Chilcott's death, which was after all mere accident, though of a grimly ironic kind.

And yet, and yet . . . it *wasn't* cleared up, because of the carriage wheel. And because of that, it wasn't separate either. Somehow there was a connection: there must be. But he was damned if he could see it. The interference with the Chilcotts' carriage seemed a random element, a loose card in the pack.

First chess, now cards, Fairfax admonished himself: must everything be a game? But he was not feeling frivolous, as he contemplated his return to Chelsea. He was in deadly earnest, and had too a sense of dark foreboding, like the quiver of coming thunder in still summer air.

Ferry-men were touting for business down by Parliament Stairs. Fairfax decided he would take a boat back up-river to Chelsea. When he gave his direction, the ferry-man remarked as he sculled the boat out into the mid-stream: 'Lot of company going out that way tonight, I fancy, sir. Grand concert at Ranelagh, with fireworks and all.'

The words awoke in Fairfax an acute wish – a vision – a dream: it involved him and Cordelia strolling through the artificial groves of Ranelagh, admiring the coloured lanterns and pagodas, and going into the Rotunda to hear the music in a sweet, suspended haze of contentment. He allowed himself to dwell on the dream for the rest of the journey. Unlikely ever to grasp the substance, he could at least touch the shadow.

He disembarked below the Royal Hospital with the sky the red of a dying furnace and the first night-blooms of darkness appearing amongst the flame-tipped trees. At Royal Hospital Row he hesitated before entering Dr Stagg's house: how would the doctor react to being confronted in this way? Fairfax found himself rather warier than he had been of the drunken and touchy Jemmy Runquest, simply because Stagg was such an unknown quantity.

But Stagg was not there. Rode out a few minutes since, the maid told him. 'Don't know where, sir. Always in and out, he is, like a dog at the fair. Said he wouldn't be long, so the foreign gentleman, mebbe.'

Perhaps so: Fairfax bent his steps to Five Fields Row, willingly enough, for he was still a little caught up in that dream, and it would hearten him just to see Cordelia again. More than that, he could think of no one better to share the perplexities of this case with. Her mind was at once sceptical and imaginative – as well as blessedly unshockable. And the thoughts still germinating in his mind looked set for a growth that was not only shocking but monstrous.

Candles had just been lit, he saw, in the drawing room of the Porteous house. The fever-chill of suspicion tingled the back of his neck again. And yet while it remained suspicion only, he could not barge into that house of mourning and start throwing accusations around.

Next door, it was the Mozarts' manservant, Potivin, who answered his knock. Potivin smelt as if he had been sampling Leopold's favourite cider, and cheerfully greeted Fairfax in German, French and English before inviting him to walk up.

'Is Dr Stagg here, by any chance?'

'Doctor, no. We are all well, and happy, and Herr Mozart most of all, God be praised,' Potivin said, adding proudly in high-pitched and mechanical English, 'Very-well-I-thank-you-I-hope-I-find-you-the-same.'

'That is very well said. Really I was hoping to speak to Mrs Linton . . .'

'Up, up, sir – she is upstairs too. Come, come. We are all convivial and having tea,' Potivin said, tripping on the stairs.

Frau Mozart, Nannerl, and Cordelia were at any rate gathered around the tea-table. Leopold was seated at the desk, with sheet music spread out before him, and little Wolfgang looking over his shoulder, or rather his elbow. The boy seemed to be in a curious state of pleased agitation, curling one leg round the other, licking his lips, and clutching at his father's sleeve: Leopold's first words explained it.

'Ah, Herr Fairfax – please, join the ladies for tea, and forgive me while I finish this. I am looking over the completed manuscript of Wolfgang's *sinfonia* for orchestra in E flat.' Leopold's eyes glinted with pride. 'The missing page turned up, of course. Be at ease, sir, while I continue to admire. And *correct*,' he added with a mock-tap on Wolfgang's nose.

'My dear Mr Fairfax, have you been haymaking?' Cordelia said. 'You look quite brown, quite the Robinson Crusoe indeed, not of course that a lady should make personal remarks over the tea-table like that, what am I thinking of . . . Feel free to observe that my own complexion is like neat's leather, as indeed it is, and without the excuse of labour under the hot sun. Tea?'

The rattling manner always came out when she was nervous. He took a moment to feel pleased that his sudden appearance made her react that way. 'Thank you. Well, labour I cannot claim to, except the labour of going hither and thither and back again.'

'Have you found him, sir?' Frau Mozart asked. 'This dreadful murderer? I swear I shall not feel safe in my own bed till he is caught.'

'Oh, I can assure you, ma'am, there is no call to be uneasy. As for catching him . . . well, we will do so. He won't get away with it. I'll answer for that. Tell me, has Dr Stagg been here this evening?'

'He came this afternoon to see my husband – do you observe, sir, he has taken off the wrapping of his neck? I was a little fearful that it was too soon. But the doctor gives such a good account of him, and he feels so much better, that all of a sudden he said he needed this no longer, and off it came.'

'I am glad to see so thorough a recovery. This means, I dare say, that you will soon be returning to London?'

'Yes. I shall miss it here: it has been so peaceful – at

least, until this dreadful crime. And I shall miss our good Mrs Linton, indeed I shall.' Frau Mozart squeezed Cordelia's hand. 'But we must be in town, so that Wolfgang and Nannerl can go before the public.'

'Oh, I shall miss you too!' Nannerl said to Cordelia, with sudden animation; and then, like any thirteen-year-old, she grew embarrassed, and took herself off languidly to the window.

'Yes . . . yes, of course,' Fairfax said absently. His restless mind was putting together thoughts like paper chains. Blackmail. Dr Stagg. Tabitha. Tabitha finding out that Dr Stagg was blackmailing someone, and putting pressure on him in turn . . . But how would she find out? From Giles Bayley? He knew her, but there was no reason at all for him to let her know such a thing. And besides, if she had discovered this secret that Stagg was making use of, why not make direct use of it herself? Why go to Stagg?

And besides, he had come to the conclusion that the secret must actually be *about* Tabitha. The identity of her child's father, no less. And if Stagg possessed that secret, then killing Tabitha made absolutely no sense. Putting it coldly, it was better to have her alive, to bear witness. The paper chains fell apart.

All except one. And that one, indeed, he had been holding all the way back from Westminster, if not before. He suspected that the father of Tabitha's child was Charles Porteous. Stagg had discovered that – he surmised – and had been delivering those taunting letters on the strength of it. Suppose Porteous had decided not to deal with the blackmailer, but with the whole source of the trouble – the woman who was threatening to disgrace him by revealing him as the father of her child?

It fitted. It was enough – wasn't it? Porteous had removed the main threat – Tabitha – by killing her. The blackmailer remained. Indeed, Stagg had procured another letter from Bayley today, after Tabitha's death. Apparently it included the phrase *be sure your sin will find you out*. Had Stagg drawn his own conclusions from Tabitha's murder, and decided to increase the pressure? Signal to Porteous that he not only knew his sordid little secret, he also knew the worst one – that he was a murderer? Well, that would surely place Stagg in some danger himself – but of course the letters were anonymous. Unsigned, surely hand-delivered, and written in Giles Bayley's 'standard hand', as he called it, so that no familiar handwriting could be identified.

It all fitted.

And yet it wasn't enough.

That damned carriage wheel remained unaccounted for. Charles Porteous making an attempt, even such a clumsy and tentative one, on the life of Mr and Mrs Chilcott simply didn't add up. There was no reason for it. Again the paper chains fell apart.

The voice of Wolfgang Mozart, raised in shrill protest, penetrated Fairfax's thoughts.

'What, Papa? Show me. You're joking with me. I don't believe it—'

'See for yourself,' Leopold said, pointing at a line in the music manuscript. 'There. You really mean this E natural in the triplet? Here – I'll show you.' Jumping up and darting over to the harpsichord, Leopold played a few little skipping figures, with a searingly wrong note at the end. 'So, you don't believe it, eh? And yet you have written it twice.

Wolfgang, Wolfgang, such a horrible *bêtise* as that – why, you were beyond such mistakes when you were five years old.' Leopold shook his head sagely. 'It is as I always say, my son, *concentration* – concentration is what you must add to your natural gifts, application, thoroughness—'

'I did not write that, Papa.' Wolfgang's cheeks were pink. He snatched up the paper and waved it at his sister. 'Nannerl, you made my copies. It must be you, you copied it wrong.'

His sister, who had been shyly waving to someone in the street below, came away from the window with a wry smile. 'Oh, of course, it must be me, it is always Nannerl's fault,' she said. She took the music-paper from Wolfgang and rolling it up, batted him on the head with it, then opened it out and studied it. 'Well, *I* can see those mistakes, and I would not have copied them: I would have quietly corrected them, dear brother. I think, indeed, that this is not my copy. The clef is too spidery – see?' She thrust the paper back at her brother. 'It must be your original, Wolfgang.'

'But I tell you it is not,' Wolfgang said, almost on the verge of tears. 'I do not write the clef so either – and I would never make such a—'

'My God,' Fairfax cried, leaping to his feet so swiftly he almost upset the tea-table. 'Show me.'

Wolfgang looked startled to see Herr Fairfax standing over him, peremptorily holding out his hand; but he gave him the music-sheet timidly, murmuring: 'It is in the third and fourth bar, Herr Fairfax.'

Fairfax stared at the neatly written music, which seemed indeed to dance before his dazed eyes. He turned the paper over, and studied the blank side.

'There is nothing on that side,' Wolfgang said, helpfully. 'Sometimes, you see, the ink comes through, especially with ties on the notes, and—'

'You did not write this sheet, Wolfgangerl,' Fairfax said, his breath tight. 'Nor you, Nannerl. Tell me . . .' He turned to Leopold, who was looking at him as if he were mad. 'When Mr Chilcott called here, on Monday, and sent up a note introducing himself – what became of the note?'

Leopold frowned, but typically gave the question serious thought. 'I have no notion. Certainly I had no special wish to keep it, and I have not seen it about. My dear?'

'Oh, you know I would never throw anything away,' his wife said.

'Wolfgang – did you not say something about running out of paper that day, when you were working at the desk?' Fairfax said.

'Well, I often run out of paper,' the boy said, 'when my ideas are coming fast, and sometimes I will scribble on odd bits that are lying around . . .'

'Even on the walls sometimes,' his father said. 'But sir, I don't understand. Do you suggest that Wolfgang used the back of the note to write upon?'

'Exactly so. Well, Wolfgang – do you think you might have done that?'

The boy stuck his tongue in his cheek. 'I didn't think it would matter. It was on the desk, and so . . . was that note important, Herr Fairfax? I didn't know—'

'It's all right. Writing music on it didn't matter at all, Wolfgang,' Fairfax said. 'Indeed, I'm thankful that you did . . .'

'And yet I can't have done,' Wolfgang said in perplexity,

leafing through his manuscript. 'Because – see? – it isn't here now.'

'No . . . it is not here now.' Fairfax found himself in a trance of thought. He did not know how long he stood so: but when he awoke to a consciousness of the baffled faces of the Mozarts and Cordelia ranged round him, he felt as if he had been a long time away, in dark places. 'Sir, that E natural is not Wolfgang's or Nannerl's mistake, be assured of that. But I can say no more just yet . . . I'm sorry, Frau Mozart, I must miss the tea. I shall have to go at once. Mrs Linton – might I ask for the return of that book I lent you?'

Cordelia stared at him, blinked. 'The – oh! Yes, of course, the book – I will get it, Mr Fairfax, if you will step down to my apartments . . .'

Downstairs, in her parlour, Cordelia went to a cabinet and produced a bottle of brandy.

'I think tea is too mild a beverage for you, Mr Fairfax, just now – you look as mad as Ajax,' she said, pouring him a glass. 'Have you hit upon something, and are you going to tell me it? If on the other hand you are about to have a fit, please don't do it on the rug, for I've just beaten it.'

Fairfax swallowed the brandy in one gulp. 'I do feel a little mad,' he said, 'but don't be uneasy. The idea itself is so . . . Cordelia, why would anyone steal a commonplace note?'

'Lover's keepsake, perhaps?'

'Hm. But this is a note penned by Mr Gabriel Chilcott, bear in mind.'

'Well, that makes it rather unlikely . . . Because its contents were important in some way, then.'

'But this was merely a note of introduction, with little matter in it.'

'So it was. Well, then, to use it in some way, though why, I can't conceive.' She shrugged. 'Do I have to pay a forfeit after three guesses?'

'Forgive me, I'm thinking aloud. But you are almost there when you mention the *contents* . . . because it is precisely the contents that are unimportant.'

'An interesting way of saying I'm wrong,' she said, raising an eyebrow. 'Mr Fairfax, you do have the advantage of me, you know. You have been deedily pursuing your investigations all day, whilst I have remained here, turning bedsteads and bottling pickles, so it is hardly fair to expect—'

'It's not the season for bottling pickles.'

'Pickling bottles then. You know what I mean, sir. Have you found Tabitha's murderer? And is this matter of the note something to do with it? Or are you clutching at straws? – and I did not mean that expression as rudely as it came out.'

'Yes, yes, and perhaps yes. Sorry – I don't mean to be enigmatic. I have something, but it may yet turn out to be fool's gold . . . Cordelia, where is the back door of the Porteous house?'

'At the back, curiously enough, like the back door of this one. I have never found that fact overwhelmingly sinister, but of course if you—'

'Hush. It is a servants' entrance, yes? Leading to the kitchens and offices and such? Excellent. I want to go in there. The back way only, mind. So that the master and mistress of the house are unaware of it. Could you manage that? Conjure up a pretext for knocking at the back door?'

'I could, I suppose. I might disguise myself as the coal-man, or the knife-grinder—'

'No good. Think harder.'

'Then I could ask the cook-maid for the loan of something. I know her pretty well. But I will not, unless you tell me what you intend.'

He drew a deep breath. 'I want to count the next door house's tea-cups.'

Cordelia narrowed her eyes at him. 'Is this new slang for something saucy? I'm very behind-hand with these things, I know—'

'Truly, I have my reasons. Now do you think it can be done?'

A small devilish smile touched her lips. 'Well, if it cannot, it will be fun to try. Come.'

She led the way to the hall, but he stopped her.

'Can we not go the back way? I don't even want to risk being spotted at the front of the house.'

'Very well.' She took him down the passage, through a kitchen, and out to a yard with a long lawn and shrubbery beyond. A brick wall separated the yard from a similar one next door. 'There is this to get over. Not,' she added before he could speak, 'that that it is any difficulty to *me*.' She hitched up her skirts, and was over the wall in a moment, lithe as a monkey. Her eyes peeped at him above the top of the wall, and he could tell by them that she was grinning. He scrambled after her, pretending not to mind that he was much longer about it.

'Well, here we are, and there is the door,' she said, 'and that just leaves the question of how I am to explain your presence. Have you escorted me to protect me against marauding alley-cats, perhaps – ferocious pigeons . . . ?'

'What would be best,' he said, 'is if you were somehow to get the cook-maid, and any other servants, out of the kitchen, while I lurk here—'

'I have *always* wanted to do something that involved lurking,' she said, eyes alight.

'And then while you are gone, I can slip in and—'

'And count the tea-cups, of course. It shall be done, Mr Fairfax. Trust me.'

She knocked at the back door, whilst he crouched behind the water-butt.

'Oh, Sally – forgive me for troubling you, but I'm quite at my wits' end to get a piece of huckaback towelling. Not a scrap in the house, and there's poor Monsieur Potivin suffering with a wen, and needs a poultice. Could I trouble you . . . ?'

Still talking, Cordelia went in, leaving the back door ajar. Fairfax waited a minute, then tiptoed forward and peeped in. The kitchen was empty, though a joint was boiling and a pudding steaming on the range, and a heap of French beans and carrots was on the table next to a basin. Dinner was being prepared, then: he must be quick. He could hear Cordelia's voice, pitched deliberately loud, somewhere down the passage leading past the stairs: there must be a linen-closet that way, then. Excellent, so long as the china-closet was not there also . . . He flung open a door, found himself in a cool pantry with bacon flitches about his ears, opened a cupboard and found it full of silver . . . At last he found the cupboard containing crockery. Now, it should all be here, he thought: the Mozarts, new to English ways, might drink tea at this hour, but in a thoroughly conventional household like Charles Porteous' there would be no tea-drinking in the early evening – the cups would only be set forth after dinner . . . He lifted a fragile stack of saucers to count the tea-cups ranged behind them, and very nearly dropped the whole lot on the stone-flagged floor. It did not take much imagination to work out what sort of apocalyptic noise *that* would have made . . . Trembling, he counted, counted again to be sure, then replaced the saucers as gently as he could. They stuck to his perspiring fingers and inclined tipsily towards him. The best he could do was to nudge them upright with his nose, slide them on to the shelf, and quickly close the cupboard door. No incriminating crash came from within; and Cordelia's voice was still audible down the passage. He let out his pent breath.

And let in the monstrous notion that he had held at bay simply because it was so monstrous.

Twelve saucers, eleven cups.

Well, in one respect at least he had done Charles Porteous an injustice. Porteous was not the father of Tabitha Dance's child – not if his theory was right.

Twelve saucers, eleven cups.

As he stepped away from the cupboard, he remembered Porteous this morning, unwigged and weary, with the little tea-table set out beside him, and the way the silver teapot had slid from his fingers and clattered to the floor.

Weary . . . but not *that* weary.

Fairfax had a sensation of cogs and wheels fitting smoothly into place. At last. Yes, wheels. The business of the carriage wheel had remained so stubbornly odd, refusing to dovetail with everything else his mind had constructed . . . and now he saw it.

Porteous had refrained from shaking hands with him when he came to supper here. Porteous had had his meat cut up for him by Emma. Porteous had struggled to hold a not very large teapot. Porteous had surely hurt his right hand, hurt it in some way as to strain it, make it gripless: sprained the wrist, perhaps.

Fairfax remembered his own perplexity at the thought of damaging a carriage wheel. A crowbar or jack was easily enough procured in a stable-block, but a gentlemanly, scholarly type was likely to – well, to hurt himself using it. A type like himself, or Charles Porteous.

The voices were returning. He slipped out quickly, scrambled over the wall again, and waited for Cordelia.

She reappeared quite soon, tossing the roll of towelling over to him before vaulting over as deftly as before. She looked pleased with herself.

'The strength of an Amazon,' she said, 'and the wit of a – well, somebody else mythological who was clever. There don't seem to *be* any clever mythological women, in truth, which is rather revealing. Sally the cook-maid has a great tenderness for the Mozarts' servant, and so I knew that invoking his name would do the trick. I must remember to tell Potivin to pretend a wen . . . Well, sir? Are you satisfied with your tea-cup-counting? I think, you know, as a pastime it will never rival cards or dice, but I'm prepared to be proved wrong. Say hush, Cordelia.'

'Hush, Cordelia. And thank you, a thousand times. Come inside.'

In her parlour she sat down and looked at him expectantly. He realized he hardly knew where to begin.

'The note,' he said. 'The note is the key. You might say,

indeed, that the *note* of E natural in Wolfgang's symphony is the key, because it is in the wrong key . . . But enough of that.'

'Thank heaven,' she said.

'The note was in Mr Gabriel Chilcott's handwriting. And it was the *handwriting* that the person who took it was interested in. Once they had taken it, they saw that the reverse had been used by Wolfgang for a page of composition, and of course that would be missed. But they wanted to keep hold of that specimen of handwriting; and so they copied out the music on to a fresh sheet, and returned that to Wolfgang's desk – not noticing that there was an error in their copying, a wrong note which would affront the ear of someone like Leopold, or indeed the boy, who would never make such a mistake.'

'The handwriting,' Cordelia said slowly. 'Then this someone wanted to – well, compare it with some other specimen of handwriting?'

'Exactly. Or rather two specimens, I think . . . Today I met a man named Giles Bayley. He is a screever – a producer of documents, in a not very respectable way. It turns out he has been producing documents for my landlord – for Dr Stagg. Anonymous letters of the poisoned-pen kind. Dr Stagg is blackmailing someone.'

'Mercy!' Cordelia breathed. 'But he is so thoroughly . . . well, no matter: I fear I am about to hear worse.'

'Stagg employed a screever for the purpose, for a very good reason: the handwriting of the letters will not be his own. A person's handwriting can be almost as distinctive as their face: it can be recognized, and Stagg prudently chose not to run that risk. But Bayley, the man he employed, is also busy in the fake-testimonials line. One of his customers was Jemmy Runquest, who was not happy with the results. But another, who did better by his services, was Tabitha Dance.'

Her eyes wide, Cordelia poured him another glass of brandy; and then, shaking her head, a slightly larger one for herself.

'Tabitha used to be employed by Mr Chilcott as a maid, until she was turned off without a character. Needing a new place, she went to Bayley to purchase a false testimonial. As it happens, Bayley had been employed by Mr Chilcott too, and dismissed on a charge of forgery, though he had escaped prosecution. With that in mind, he did not go so far as to imitate Mr Chilcott's actual script on the letter he composed for Tabitha, contenting himself with reproducing the old gentleman's rather pompous style, and generally giving the thing an air of authority. All Tabitha had to hope, when she applied to her new employers bearing her glowing letter of reference, was that they would take it at face value and not write to Mr Chilcott for corroboration. And so it must have been, for her new employers took her on as a maid, in a very respectable position.'

'The Porteouses.'

'Just so: Mr and Mrs Porteous, as the lady was still living then. And so, the letter of reference was put away, I dare say, knowing their precise habits, in a drawer or bureau or something, and not thought of again . . . until earlier this week, when an anonymous threatening letter arrived.'

'You mean Charles Porteous is the one that Dr Stagg is blackmailing?'

'I'd swear to it. Here is this letter pushed through the

door, full of threat and danger, and no hint as to where it came from. Or is there? Is there not something familiar about the handwriting? Mr Bayley used what he calls his "standard hand" on both occasions. But Porteous is not to know that a screever has been at work. He digs out Tabitha's letter of reference: he compares it with the anonymous letter. The handwriting is the same – surely! And the letter of reference, of course, came from Mr Gabriel Chilcott. So, therefore, did the anonymous letter. The blackmailer, thinks Porteous, has unwittingly given himself away. And it is Mr Chilcott of Brockleigh – not a man personally known to him, but one with a vindictive, quarrelsome reputation. And worst of all, an associate of his uncle, Sir Andrew Porteous, on whose righteous approval Charles desperately depends.'

'Ingeniously horrible,' she said, 'or horribly ingenious, but – well, Mr Chilcott's death was a natural one, surely?'

'Yes, more or less,' Fairfax said, remembering Mrs Chilcott and Bayley locked in an embrace. 'Chance, and Mr Chilcott's troublesome heart, struck him down on Monday. But I believe his life was in danger, nonetheless. On Monday morning, according to the steward, a man on a grey mare came to Brockleigh House, asking after the Chilcotts – though he did not actually go up to the house; and when he heard that they had just departed in their carriage for Chelsea, he went off again. He went, I believe, in pursuit – may even have caught up with the carriage, and followed behind it. The carriage turned into the Spread Eagle yard. Its pursuer did not, not at once. To make himself less conspicuous, he tethered his horse outside – where I, coming along shortly after, very nearly walked into it. And then he must have slipped into the inn-yard and . . . well, what was he to do? It was daylight in a busy inn, and he perhaps lacked the courage or skill, or was simply too prudent, to make a direct attempt on Mr Chilcott's life. But he did what he could. He tampered with the wheel of their carriage, in hopes that it might overturn on their way back. It might work: it was a blow struck, at any rate. He was not to know that on his return to the inn, Gabriel Chilcott would be felled by a mortal seizure anyway.'

'And in the meantime, Mr Chilcott had been here – with the Mozarts,' Cordelia said, gazing into her brandy. 'First presenting that note. And also here was . . .' She looked up, her face solemn. 'Emma Henlow.'

He nodded. 'There never was a brother- and sister-in-law so mutually devoted. I fancy she is his great stay and confidante – and of course she may even have opened the first letter herself, or come across it: that house is so much her domain. In any case, it must have been Miss Henlow who took the note from the Mozarts' desk, that very morning: she was hovering about Wolfgang, I recall, and looking through his music, and it would have been the work of a moment to fold up the note, tuck it into her purse or pocket, and so away. That she did so is in itself the surest indication that she is her brother-in-law's accomplice in this matter, to some degree at least. She must have known that this man Chilcott was suspected as the blackmailer – that her brother-in-law had been comparing the anonymous letter with Tabitha's old reference. Something must have made her decide to take that note, so they could compare it – for further confirmation? Or did she even then have a suspicion that it was not so simple? Whichever way, she saw that that note was valuable, as an incontestable record of Chilcott's handwriting. The man had been there, actually in the room with her. So she spirited it away – and, I would guess, when she noticed that Wolfgang had written on the back, copied out what he had written and slipped the copy back in amongst his papers on one of her visits.'

Unnoticed, summer darkness had settled on the contours of the room like soft phosphorescent dust. Cordelia stirred, finding tinder and flint and lighting candles. She waved away a plump moth that came in blundering quest of the flames. The illumination revealed the flush still on her cheek from her late excitement, though it was the beautiful gravity of her expression that struck him like the pain of an old wound.

'Very well,' she said. 'I can put together what you have told me about Dr Stagg with this matter of the note. It is very plausible in itself. And yet fate took Mr Chilcott conveniently from the world, so the threat, whatever it might be, was gone . . . Then how came it that Tabitha was killed?'

'Mr Chilcott was gone – but the evidence of the note would show that he was not the blackmailer. His own handwriting was not the same as that on the threatening letter and on Tabitha's reference – Bayley's work. And then came another letter. On Tuesday Stagg went to see Bayley, and procured a second specimen. Bayley, I can reveal to you, was the man who had been in Mrs Chilcott's room at the Spread Eagle – yes, Wolfgang was not mistaken. He was, is, an old lover of Mrs Chilcott's, and now that she is a free woman they are not wasting any time . . . Well.' He shook his head. 'I am not so sure of myself as to blame them . . . In any case, Stagg had surmised the truth about Bayley's relation with Mrs Chilcott. Bayley in turn had found out the identity of this respectable young man who was employing him to write scurrilous letters, and no doubt hoped to use it to his advantage. It was a stalemate; but Bayley still needed money, and was happy enough to oblige. And so some time on Tuesday – very probably when he came here for his daily visit to Herr Mozart – Stagg must have delivered his second letter to next door. Now imagine Charles Porteous' consternation. Here is confirmation of what Emma's theft of the note had suggested. The blackmailer was not Gabriel Chilcott, who was in his shroud awaiting burial.'

'And he had actually tried to cause the wreck of the Chilcotts' carriage,' Cordelia said. 'And if it had worked, he would have killed an innocent man – innocent woman perhaps also – all in vain. My God, how desperate he must have been.'

'And more desperate yet, when the second letter came. It could not be from Chilcott: the only clue he had to its origin was the fact that it was in the same hand as Tabitha's reference. And so, I think he must have come to a new conclusion – that Tabitha, who was not a girl without education or intelligence, had faked her testimonial herself. And that the letters, and the threat, came from her alone.'

'What you are telling me,' Cordelia said, lighting another candle as if even the soft fringes of darkness were too oppressive, 'is almost beyond comprehension. That the gentleman who lives next door is – the murderer of Tabitha Dance. A man who could go out and beat to death a young pregnant woman . . .'

'And there you have what I *thought* at first, was his reason when my suspicions began to form. Her pregnancy.'

'You mean . . . Charles Porteous as the father?'

He nodded. 'Tabitha was comely. Had a reputation –

239

possibly undeserved. And she was under his roof, at a time when his wife was going through a long, sickly time of it with her own pregnancy. Yes, that too is very plausible. And now I no longer believe it. Certainly if he were the father of her child, it would be a monstrous bad lookout for him, especially if, as she threatened to do, she swore the father. How would he explain that to his uncle, the puritanical and exacting Sir Andrew Porteous? But that business of the carriage wheel did not fit. Supposing he suspected that this Mr Chilcott had somehow learned of his delinquency with the maid, and sent the first letter in reference to it: well, it is possible that Tabitha might have confided such a thing to her old employer, perhaps seeking his help, though not likely. But looking at it coldly, in such a situation would not the pregnant girl herself present the real threat – the obstacle to be removed, the one thing that must be done away with? Why try clumsily to do away with Chilcott first?'

'That is the rational way of looking at it. But we are not talking of rational acts, are we?'

'True. And it may be as I have just described – Porteous killing Tabitha because she was bearing his child. The question we cannot answer, except by deduction, is what the secret was that Stagg's letters referred to.'

'You do not know exactly what was in the letters?'

He shook his head. 'Only that Bayley, from sordid experience, did not find them difficult to write, for they spoke in ominous terms of a secret being known, of threats of exposure, of vengeance coming, and so forth. The sender of such letters generally exults in his power, I think: that, more than the extortion that may be involved, is the source of satisfaction. But I have an idea of the secret . . . one I can scarcely bear to entertain . . .'

'I have an idea too,' Cordelia said. 'And I hesitate because it concerns a person I am admittedly prejudiced against. Also it is – not a ladylike idea. But then this is no polite chit-chat, is it? This is . . . life and death. So I will say it: you suspected Charles Porteous of finding consolation, during his wife's pregnancy, with the housemaid – yes? What I suspect is that he found consolation instead with his wife's sister. With Emma Henlow.'

Fairfax nodded, aware of his blood drumming in his veins. 'We are on the same track.'

'An appalling – well, perhaps not crime, yet appalling nonetheless. Making love to her sister while his wife lay sickly with their child under the same roof . . . Think of it. And who better to discover such a thing than Tabitha, the maid? We know she was sacked for making gossip about the relation of Emma to her brother-in-law: and we know that the night she was killed, she had raised a hullabaloo outside the Porteous house, saying they wouldn't get away with it. And if Porteous supposed the letters came from her also . . . Think of it.'

'Yes. I am thinking of it, indeed. I'm thinking of Porteous going out late that night – supposedly to call on his uncle: certainly with ample opportunity to murder Tabitha. I'm thinking of him killing her, and then going back home, and believing himself finally free. And Emma? Troubled and frightened of exposure too, and eagerly setting her wits to discover the identity of the blackmailer, and help her adored Charles escape the quandary into which their illicit passion had led them. And, yes –

protecting him, as ever. Did she know, when he came back late that night: did she know, when Tabitha's body was found the next morning? And did she simply not speak of it – bury it, hide it away, as so much of their lives must have been a matter of hiding away? It is grim to think of. And yet easy enough to do. We have all closed our eyes to something we don't wish to know, so as to keep hold of what we love. We can all will ourselves blind. It's easy enough.'

'Yes,' said Cordelia faintly, 'it's easy enough.'

The moth was back. Fairfax caught it in his cupped hands and took it to the window to release it. 'So. I'm thinking of all this, and very likely it seems, and very horrible. And yet . . . and yet I hope that is the worst of it.'

'What? But what more . . . ?'

He hesitated, breathing in the sweet evening air. 'Well, suppose it were as we have said; and after Tabitha was dead, Porteous considered himself free. But of course he is not. The sender of the letters is Dr Stagg; and Dr Stagg, I know, procured another one today, his third, and I would guess has already delivered it. In which case Porteous is confounded with the knowledge that Tabitha did not write them: that her murder was in vain: that his blackmailer is still at large. And that brings us back to the point we have hardly touched upon.' He turned to her. 'What does Stagg *know*? I would ask him, and came here looking for him; but he is not to be found. But I have a dreadful suspicion, now, of what that secret is that Stagg possesses. A secret that he as a doctor was uniquely placed to discover. One can only hope . . . well, that Porteous has not come to the same conclusion, and realized that the sender of the letters is Frederick Stagg. If he has . . .'

'Then Dr Stagg is now in danger.'

'Perhaps . . .' A terrible disquiet was moving in him. 'And yet – if it never occurred to Porteous to suspect Stagg before, it may not now. All along Porteous was on the wrong trail. He will surely be desperate, if he has received a third letter . . . a man desperate enough to kill again . . . My God.' He started to the door.

'Where are you going?'

'I must speak to Nannerl again . . .'

Upstairs the Mozarts looked startled, and even a little alarmed, as Herr Fairfax burst into the room.

'Sir, you come upon us like a devil in a pantomime,' Leopold said frowning. 'It is lucky my nerves have recovered their strength, or—'

'Forgive me, Herr Mozart. Nannerl, who were you waving to from the window, a little while ago? Please – it is very important.'

'Why, it was – it was only Herr Porteous next door,' the girl said timidly. 'He was going off on his beautiful grey horse, and so I waved, but he didn't see me I think, because he was in a great hurry . . .'

'Thank you.'

He was out again, almost colliding with Cordelia on the landing.

'Mr Fairfax, if you are resolved upon breaking my neck, please tell me what this is all about first—'

'Danger. You were right. But not Dr Stagg, I think. Someone else, someone utterly unsuspecting. Charles Porteous has just ridden off, I believe to that person – and she may be his next victim.'

'Sally told me he had gone out, and told her to wait dinner
. . . *She?*'

'Mrs Chilcott.'

'Now I am at a loss.'

'I'll explain . . . but I must get to Kensington as quick as
may be. Porteous is on horseback—'

'The Spread Eagle. They hire saddle-horses. We can ride
after him. Come.' She whisked down the stairs.

'We . . . ?'

'Yes, Mr Fairfax. Tempting as it is to remain here
twiddling my thumbs, tantalized and half mad with fearful
frustration, I have overcome the temptation, and I am going
with you.'

He was glad of it: he feared for her, but knew there was
no overcoming her determination; and there was no time to
speak of what he felt.

Hurrying down the dark street to the inn, they saw the
first fireworks go up into the sky over Ranelagh Gardens
with brilliant spatterings of silver and gold. The inn-yard
was busy: some of the company visiting Ranelagh had
stabled their carriages and chairs here, and a post-chaise had
just come in and was changing horses. Fairfax feared there
might be no mounts available, but they were in luck. The
sharp-faced landlady was obliging, if steep in her price, and
presently they were trotting out towards the King's Road.
Fairfax's only dubiety now was that he hated riding and was
unconquerably awkward at it, though the mare seemed a
manageable enough beast. He noticed that Cordelia, though
she protested she never rode, sat much more easily than he.
But it was not a time to fret about such things. If they could
just get to Brockleigh House in time, he would swear an

eternal devotion to horseflesh . . .

'Why?' Cordelia said, as soon as they were breathing steadily enough to speak. 'Why Mrs Chilcott?'

'I tried to follow Porteous' train of thought. Initially he suspected Mr Chilcott, because the writing was the same as on his letter of reference. Then he suspected Tabitha, supposing she wrote her reference herself. Then, after Tabitha's death, comes another letter. His mind goes back to the Chilcotts – *both* of them. Have you – did you never write a letter in your husband's name?'

'Once or twice,' she said constrainedly. 'With business he could not be troubled with . . . more than once or twice, in truth.'

'Exactly. And they were after all husband and wife: could it not be that they were in the scheme together? And I recalled something else, something that suggests there have been suspicions towards Mrs Chilcott all along. When Emma Henlow went to call on her, the day after Mr Chilcott's death, to condole with her on her bereavement . . . she kept insisting that she would be happy to undertake any commission for the widow. If Mrs Chilcott would just write down whatever she needed done—'

'And then she would have a sample of Mrs Chilcott's handwriting! Dear God . . .'

'Mrs Chilcott is sure to be home by now. I know she will have her lover, Bayley, with her . . . And yet a man as desperate as Porteous might do anything. With such a secret to conceal . . .'

'You have not told me all,' she said, and after a moment: 'I am no lent lily, Mr Fairfax. I would not be here with you otherwise. I can hear it.'

A hare skittered across their path, and Fairfax's mare side-stepped nervously. He tightened the reins a little and said dully: 'You may wish you had not . . . The secret had to be something Stagg as a doctor would know. Stagg attended Mrs Porteous in her last illness: when, after a difficult pregnancy and delivery, she seemed to rally only to fall victim to the puerperal fever. I believe she did not. I believe she was hastened to her end – by her husband. Stagg suspected it – knew for certain even – but for his own reasons did not expose it, choosing to blackmail Porteous with his knowledge instead. There is a dirty tea-cup in a bureau in Dr Stagg's bedroom, with an odd faint smell about it. It is the missing tea-cup from the service in Porteous' kitchen. I think Porteous gave his wife poison with it as she lay recovering from the birth of their son, and so got rid of her; and Stagg, her physician, suspected it and took away the cup to keep hold of as evidence, as the trophy with which to torment Porteous. The secret that led Porteous to murder was – murder, no less.'

Cordelia was silent for some moments. When she spoke her voice was thick with distress.

'I have dined at that man's table,' she said. 'I have shaken that man's hand . . .'

'Yes. I also – though he refrained from shaking my hand, which was—'

He let out a groan as the realization hit him: he felt as if he had been punched in the heart. As his hands slackened on the reins, the mare slowed to a trot.

'Mr Fairfax . . . !' Cordelia's voice came to him as if from down a long tunnel. 'Robert – Robert, what is it? Are you sick? I should have known, you were meant to be convalescing and instead you have been flying about—'

'Sick,' he gasped. 'Yes, sick. Not ill, though, not ill. I'm sorry, Cordelia. I am not ill but a fool . . .' He took deep breaths while the starlit fields steadied themselves around him. 'I am wrong. His hand – he had hurt his hand. He could not even hold the weight of a silver teapot. How could he have struck such a blow with a heavy rock . . . ? I am a fool, Cordelia, a perfect fool. Charles Porteous did not kill Tabitha.'

'What? Then who . . . ?'

He urged his mount forward. 'We must go faster. Mrs Chilcott's danger is greater than I supposed . . .'

Eight

The gravel of the carriage-drive leading up to Brockleigh House was churned with numerous hoofprints. The hackney that had brought Mrs Chilcott and her lover home, Fairfax thought: and others? Was Porteous here?

'See – the grey,' Cordelia said, nimbly dismounting, and pointing to a pretty mare loosely tethered to an acacia that grew to one side of the house. Her coat shone ghostly white in the gloom – and then something moved, part blotting out the elegant shape. Leading his own mount thither, Fairfax saw another horse tethered by the grey: a roan that he recognized as Dr Stagg's.

'Stagg is here . . .' He looped the reins of his mount over a low branch. Stagg . . . but no third visitor. But then that visitor would have been formally received, no doubt, the visitor's horse led by a servant to the stable, the visitor invited in . . .

Suddenly the horses were stamping and whinnying in alarm at a noise, a loud, single, brilliantly sharp noise that rang from the house.

A gunshot.

As in a dream, climbing the short flight of steps to the

front door seemed to take an effortful age, and Cordelia beside him appeared to be moving no faster. At last he reached the door, which was still ajar: pushed it open, blinked in the brightly lit hall of the Chilcott mansion.

A series of strange tableaux.

First, a windblown Dr Stagg standing in the hall, in the act of thrusting his hat and riding-crop at Minter, the steward: both of them frozen, paralysed, heads turned to the left in the direction of the drawing room. Then, Dr Stagg running to the drawing-room door, and Minter simply letting the hat and crop fall to the floor and closing his eyes and placing his gnarled hands over his ears, if he would shut out everything, for ever more.

And then, as Fairfax and Cordelia followed Stagg, the most grotesque tableau of all.

In the drawing room, Mrs Chilcott and Giles Bayley were sitting side by side on the sofa, their linked hands raised, their eyes staring, as if in some fairy-tale enchantment. In the middle of the room Charles Porteous stood with bowed head, a pistol in his drooping left hand. On the far side, by the polished harpsichord that nobody played, Emma Henlow lay on the floor in a pool of blood, supporting herself on her elbows, staring down as if in sheer astonishment at the red stain blossoming across her skirts. Dr Stagg had just fallen to his knees beside her, with the expression of a man who sees something terribly fragile and priceless dropping from his hands, irretrievably.

One more element: and as soon as Fairfax saw it his heart seemed to rise drumming to his throat. A decanter of wine, and glasses, set out on a little table at Mrs Chilcott's elbow.

His throat seared him as he cried out: 'That wine – have you drunk it, Mrs Chilcott?'

She gave a start, as if woken from the enchantment, and blinked in bewilderment. 'The wine . . . ?'

'Have you drunk any of it, for God's sake?'

'No . . . No, we were just sat down to it with Miss Henlow – she came calling, you know, because she was concerned about me and – we had just sat down and – that man burst in and – and . . .'

She began to tremble uncontrollably. Beside her Giles Bayley gripped her hand and signalled to Fairfax with his eyes, fractionally nodding his head at Charles Porteous, who was quietly weeping. *Do something – seize him, stop him . . .*

But Fairfax doubted that it would be necessary. Porteous looked like a man whose fury, whose very spirit, was spent and gone.

'Don't touch the wine,' Fairfax said. He walked past Porteous and picked up the decanter, sniffed it. No unusual odour, but that meant nothing: Stagg would be able to tell for certain.

'This damnable hand of mine,' Porteous murmured, lifting his right hand and letting it fall. 'Since I sprained it I cannot make a good grip, and that is why – that is why I did not do a proper job, my darling. With my right hand it would have been swift – I would have sent you on quickly, with no pain. You see, I would still not see you in pain, Emma . . . but oh God, how could you have done it? How?'

His sister-in-law did not look at him. Her eyes were fixed on that spreading mantle of blood. She was very white, shaking, her cheeks sunken: but there was alertness in her eyes – sense, even, that steady good sense that characterized her. Or had always seemed to.

'Lift up my skirts, Dr Stagg, if you please,' Emma Henlow said in a tight voice. 'The ball has gone into – into the thigh, I think . . .'

Stagg did so, though with none of that superb calm he usually showed when dealing with patients. This was different. He could hardly control his hands. But at last he exposed the wound, at the top of her right thigh above the stocking: an ugly abomination against the white skin. Shreds of scorched fabric looked to have been carried into the wound. Blood poured.

'It must be bound tight, else . . .' Stagg swallowed and looked faint.

'Else I shall bleed to death.' Emma Henlow showed her teeth. 'Then be quick, sir.'

Again Stagg hesitated. 'I might probe for the ball . . . yet I fear to do that, close upon the shock, and my instruments . . .' He gave himself a shake, and gripping her petticoats began tearing off long strips. 'The haemorrhage must be stopped, that is the main thing . . .'

While Stagg worked, binding her thigh tightly with strips of cambric, Fairfax moved stealthily closer to Porteous. The man looked beat, but you could never tell . . . Glancing across the room, he saw how it had been: Emma had been seated in the armchair near the sofa, had jumped up when her brother-in-law came in with the pistol, had got almost as far as the window when he brought her down . . .

A sudden movement from Porteous: Fairfax tensed. But all the young man did was look listlessly at the pistol in his left hand, drop it, and sit down heavily in the middle of the floor. He put his hands to his head, squeezing his temples and cooing in grief.

'You have discovered the truth, then, sir,' Fairfax said softly. 'Did you find it out, or did she tell you at last?'

Porteous shook his head emptily, his breath whistling in his throat.

'That is – a little easier. I thank you, Dr Stagg,' Emma said. She made a shaky attempt to push herself up, but he stayed her with a brusque hand.

'You will make it worse – you are half swooning. You must rest easy a while yet.' Stagg fetched a cushion and placed it under her shoulders, then took out a brandy-flask. 'A little of this on your lips – a little only, mind.'

'Fortunate you were here, Dr Stagg,' Fairfax said softly. 'You came to the same conclusions I did, I presume? And came here to – what, try and undo at least some of what you had done?'

Stagg sat back on his haunches. He had the face of a man completely alone and unobserved, at leisure, pondering.

'Sir,' Mrs Chilcott said, recovering something of her old command, 'we must surely send for a constable – send to the magistrate. This man has—'

'This man,' Porteous said loudly, his voice cracking, 'has concluded a piece of private business, ma'am, and regrets that he has had to do it in this way. So – publicly. It should never have been. It should never have happened.'

'He has also possibly saved your life, Mrs Chilcott,' Fairfax said. 'Emma Henlow came here to kill you. You too, Mr Bayley, might have fallen victim, if you were in the way. Miss Henlow was desperate, and beyond finesse. Have you poisoned the wine, Emma? Or were you still awaiting the favourable moment?'

'You are mad, sir!' Mrs Chilcott shrieked. 'Miss Henlow has shown only the kindest—'

'It seems mad, I grant you,' Fairfax said. He still kept at a watchful distance from Porteous: he saw that Cordelia had positioned herself so as to block the way to the door. Brave, brave, and he must not let it happen . . . 'You surely cannot conceive why Miss Henlow should want to kill you, Mrs Chilcott. What possible reason could she have? Simply, ma'am, that she was being blackmailed. Someone knew of her monstrous secret, and was taunting her with it in anonymous letters. At first she thought it was your husband, ma'am. She recognized the handwriting on the first letter: it seemed exactly like that on Tabitha Dance's letter of reference from Mr Chilcott. Who, of course, had never written her one: both were your professional work, Mr Bayley. You must have discussed that first letter with your brother-in-law, Emma. There would have been no direction on it: no "Mr Porteous" or "Miss Henlow". Dr Stagg had to protect himself when employing a screever to write such letters: he could not give the game away to this wretch he was using as a tool, though as it turned out Mr Bayley did discover his identity, and would have pried into the business if he could. And so between you, brother- and sister-in-law, you looked at the first letter, with its references to your secret shame and dire warnings of exposure, and trembled. The insidious thing about such letters is their applicability. The most blameless among us, receiving an anonymous communication that says *I know your secret*, would have a horrible guilty feeling about the heart, I am sure. How much more, Emma, you and your brother-in-law! Who were lovers – and had been, I surmise, whilst poor Mrs Porteous was in her difficult confinement.'

'Don't speak of her,' Porteous grunted. 'Don't . . . I loved Catherine, I dearly loved her. But between Emma and me something happened – so irresistible, such a passion, I cannot account for it except to say it was like possession from something outside ourselves . . .'

'It was not.' Emma Henlow, who had closed her eyes, opened them and looked at him sharply. Piercing blue, unclouded even by pain. 'It was not outside ourselves, Charles. You know it. It was us: our choice.'

He could not meet her gaze, and hung his head.

'And so you at least, Charles, concluded that this was what the letter referred to: your illicit affair with your sister-in-law, begun while your wife lay pregnant under the same roof – no more nor less. And Emma went along with it, keeping her own counsel. Was it you, Emma, who made the comparison with the handwriting on Tabitha's reference? I would think so. The question was, how did Gabriel Chilcott, a man known only to you by name and reputation, come to know your secret? Well, there *had* been gossip: Tabitha herself had dealt in it, and been sacked for it; and Mr Chilcott was known as a busybody, often at odds with his neighbours. And he was besides Tabitha's former employer. Most alarmingly, he was an associate of your uncle, Charles, on whom you relied for your living. That was enough for you: Chilcott was the man, and the thing must be dealt with at once, nipped in the bud . . . And Emma, meanwhile – Emma kept her own counsel.'

She turned those blue eyes full on him, and for the first

time Fairfax felt afraid of her: of what she was.

'You thought it could well be Mr Chilcott,' he went on, 'but as an intelligent woman, kept an open mind. You thought also that the letter might well be referring to your affair with your brother-in-law; but you had to consider the worse alternative. That the sender of the letter knew of, and was taunting you with, your deeper secret – yours alone.'

'Shouldn't have done it – shouldn't have,' mourned Charles Porteous, almost petulantly, as if regretting a bad play at cards.

'Charles, at any rate, was all for swift action,' Fairfax went on. 'Early on Monday morning he rode here, to Brockleigh, to . . . what, Charles? What did you intend? Surely not to march in here and shoot Mr Chilcott dead? Or just to see how the land lay?'

'I don't know – something. Confront this man we were dealing with . . . show him we would not be – be *threatened* so monstrously. I wasn't thinking straight, I was so damned affronted and—'

'And scared?' Fairfax said. 'And so, having learned that you had just missed the Chilcotts – that they were gone to Chelsea – you went after their carriage, until it put up at the Spread Eagle. And there you slipped into the coach-house, and made a botched sort of attempt to do away with the threat once and for all. You tampered with the wheel of the carriage, injuring your hand in the process, as this was not at all the sort of activity you are used to.'

''Tis the wrist, I believe,' Porteous said with a curious calm detachment. 'I could not, of course, consult this fellow about it, as he might ask how I came by such a hurt.' He nodded at Stagg, uttered a brief laugh.

Mrs Chilcott stirred. 'You mean – you mean this is the man who tried to . . .'

'Yes, Mrs Chilcott, I fear Charles Porteous would gladly have seen your husband and yourself tipped into a ditch with broken necks,' Fairfax said. 'You have killed no one, Charles, and yet you have played with death, and danced willingly to its tune. And the odd thing is, I'm willing to bet Emma did not approve your precipitate action that day at all. And meanwhile, she was actually meeting Gabriel Chilcott in the flesh, at the Mozarts' lodging. Great self-possession you showed then, Emma – unlike your panicky brother-in-law; and when Mr Chilcott's note lay unregarded on the Mozarts' desk, you got hold of it and took it away, and compared it with the anonymous letter. The writing was not the same. You were right, it seemed, to have those reservations. Unfortunately young Wolfgang had used the reverse of the note for his work; but it must have seemed a simple matter to copy out those bars of music on to a fresh sheet, and place it among his papers on your next visit. Alas, your copying was imperfect . . . You must have been angry, Emma, learning of Charles's clumsy attempts to resolve the situation. For you were always the one in control, were you not? I recall your telling him, when I supped with you, that he should be guided by you. A sharp reproach, but justified, perhaps.'

'Look here,' Porteous said, 'that business with the carriage – you are wrong, I didn't mean to kill, I didn't mean . . . I just wanted to strike back a little. I wanted to *protect* . . . protect what Emma and I had, because it was precious and also *good*. You must understand that. Yes, we were wrong to begin it when poor Catherine was still alive, but now that she was gone it was nobody else's business. The love

257

between Emma and me – the *bond*, the unspeakable harmony and rightness of it – well, it had to be secret, yes, but it was good in itself and it was that I wanted to protect from this unconscionable prying and meddling . . .' He began suddenly to weep, with loud, barking sobs. 'That was what I believed, Emma. That was why I went along as I did. I thought I was shielding *us* . . . not what you did. Not what you did to your sister – to my *wife* . . .'

Porteous' voice shrilled, and he coiled himself as if to jump to his feet; then, just as Fairfax was about to seize him, he slumped back, burying his face in his hands.

'My wife . . .' he kept saying, his voice hollow and smothered, like a cry from a dungeon, 'my wife . . .'

'Yes. You laid that letter to your heart, as the Methody preachers would say, and the ones that followed. But the text was aimed at your sister-in-law, and spoke of a sin far greater than adulterous and clandestine passion. The person who wrote those letters – or rather, prudently dictated them – knew of that sin. He was perhaps better placed than anyone to discover, Emma, what you did to your own sister – and yet it seems you never suspected him. Out of regard for him, perhaps – or contempt for him?'

The blue eyes shone at him. Dr Stagg wound and wound a thread of cambric around his finger, his big shoulders hunched.

'Dr Stagg, you of course attended Mrs Porteous in her last hours?' Fairfax said.

Stagg nodded, and at last spoke, so low and husky he could hardly be heard. 'Yes . . . yes, I was there, and . . . It had been a difficult delivery. Mrs Porteous was very weak, and sorely stricken. I feared the onset of childbed fever. But on the second day after the birth, she seemed to rally. I saw no signs of puerperal infection, and had good hopes of her full recovery. On the third morning, I came to see her and – and she was on the threshold of death. There was nothing I could do: I could only watch her slip away. It was so unexpected – so *wrong*. I don't know how the shadow fell across my mind – the suspicion that someone had given her something. Had hurried her out of life.' He looked up sharply. 'And there you were, Miss Henlow – devotedly nursing your sister, always at her bedside. I looked at you, and I think I knew then . . . How?' He chuckled harshly. 'How does a man know when he is in love? When he looks into a woman's face, and is pierced, almost horribly, as if she knew every last secret corner and nook in his heart. As I was when I first fell in love with you, an age ago now it seems . . . Well, call it intuition; informed guesswork – for had you not taken a great interest in my work, once upon a time, and gained a good practical knowledge of medicine? But it might have been no more than that, if you had been more careful. But though you had taken away the tea-cup with which you had fed your sister poison, you had not washed it clean. It was there in the kitchen: I went down there, to speak to the servants about Mrs Porteous' laying-out, and I found it. The residue and the odour told their tale. Some arsenical preparation, I think. I kept that tea-cup. As you have no doubt discovered, Mr Fairfax . . . Did you not know, Emma? Of course not. If it had been anyone else . . . but I was just a blind spot in your vision. I was so . . . *unimportant* to you.'

She had closed her eyes again, but they could be seen moving rapidly beneath the pure, translucent skin of her eyelids, like those of a nightmare-rid sleeper; and her breath was coming fast and shallow.

'You knew that she had murdered her sister, weak and helpless in childbed,' Fairfax said. 'And your testimony as a physician could surely have convicted her. And yet, Dr Stagg, you kept it to yourself. You hid it.'

'Oh, yes. Certainly. Wrong, I know. Unlawful? That's your concern. I don't care really. I hid it. Because of who she was,' Dr Stagg said in a dreary monotone. 'Because it was Emma, whom I loved, and who would not love me. I never understood why she would not – and why my love did not even *trouble* her. Oh, I am making no great claims for myself. I know I was aiming too high. But it was as if she couldn't even see me . . . and then I knew. Her heart was taken – as absolutely taken, I think, as few women's ever are; and by her brother-in-law. So taken she killed her sister so they might be together. And knowing that . . . well, it was a kind of intimacy. In a sense I knew her better than anyone. I could not stake a claim to her with love. But with my knowledge I . . . I possessed her. You can be crude about it, Mr Fairfax, and call it the vengefulness of a spurned lover, exulting in his power. Perhaps there was an element of that. I cared nothing for extorting money, as some might do; and I certainly did not think I could win her by such means. But it was the only power, you see, I could ever wield over Emma Henlow; and it would be something to know that she suffered, and languished, and burned, as God knows I have—'

'She was a weakly thing!' gasped Emma, struggling to a sitting position. Still it was as if she hardly saw Stagg at all. 'Don't you see, Charles? Poor Catherine – the springs of life ran so low, she would have been no good to you, it would have been a wretched, half-hearted existence for both of you. Whereas you and I – oh, we were perfect together. Remember? The warmth, the strength of it – everything cried out that this was *right*. You married the wrong sister, Charles, and you know it, and *I* put it right . . .'

'Yes: you were the strong one,' Fairfax said. 'And once you had established that it was not Mr Chilcott who wrote the letter – established it beyond doubt, when a *second* letter came on Tuesday, for by then Mr Chilcott was dead of a heart stroke – you set your wits to thinking who else it might be. Your visit to Mrs Chilcott here, where you tried in vain to get a look at her handwriting, was inconclusive. But there was another suspect. Tabitha. Perhaps the girl faked her reference herself! A plausible notion that seemed to be ominously confirmed when Tabitha made that shocking commotion outside your door that night. Tabitha was drunk, and destitute, and blamed you for her troubles, and suspected the real relation between you and your brother-in-law; and hurling stones and imprecations at your house probably relieved her feelings a little. She was not to know that it sealed her fate: hardened your suspicions into certainty; and sent you out that night to pursue and kill her. Charles had ridden off to fawn upon his uncle in London, and you were alone, and the decision was in your hands – just the way you like it. It had to be Tabitha: she had been a servant in the house, after all, when Mrs Porteous died; the girl was no fool, and must have put two and two together. In fact she knew nothing of it. She must have felt no real fear when you came after her down by Ebury Bridge: expected nothing more than a sharp exchange, perhaps; possibly it even occurred to her, seeing you there, that you had softened towards her and were going to offer her help. It was an unsuspecting girl, Emma, as well as an innocent one, that you clubbed down that night.'

Her breath came in quicker and quicker snatches, like a snared rabbit's: yet Emma Henlow put up a hand to brush back a lock of fair hair, with a neat, urbane motion, so that she might see him better.

'The end of it, you thought,' Fairfax said. 'You didn't come out and tell Charles you had done it, of course. He must have suspected – but then, why stir it up? Let it be one of those unspoken things, those unseen foundations of your intimacy. And after all, the threat was removed now: Charles must be glad of that . . . And then, today, a third letter came. You must have been at your wits' end, Emma: or were you still calm? Did you set yourself coolly to the problem again, realizing that you had killed an innocent girl for nothing, but putting it behind you as you returned to the puzzle of these damnable letters? Well, you came up with a solution after all. It must be *Mrs* Chilcott you had to fear all along. Perhaps she had written that reference in her husband's name: perhaps he had confided the matter to her; or Tabitha, who had been her maid, had let it slip to her. You discussed it, no doubt, with Charles: he still supposing that it was only your love affair that was threatened, but you with your darker knowledge, and a double reason to want this unknown correspondent silenced for ever. The urgency must have pressed upon you: this letter was grimmer yet, it said *Be sure your sin will find you out*. And the one person above all who must not know that sin was Charles – for then he would surely hate you, hate you unto death.'

And now a tear trickled down Emma Henlow's cheek, though her face was expressionless.

'No,' Porteous groaned, 'not hate – yes – oh God, I don't know . . .'

'All along, Charles, you had been the skittish one, inclined to panic,' Fairfax said. 'And when the third letter came, that panic truly overcame you, did it not? In your heart of hearts you must have wondered about Tabitha's death, even if you dared not frame the suspicion even to yourself. You were jumpy, haunted, fretted with feelings of doom. Everything seemed to be running out of control. This letter-writer was remorseless, and seemingly immortal: you could not get free of these toils. Unless . . . unless you ended the affair. Was that it, Charles? In your panic, did you say to Emma that you and she must end your ill-fated intrigue, and part? Even under normal circumstances, a horrible decision, like severing a limb. And when you are not meant to be together at all – when it is illicit, clandestine, magically secret – why then it is somehow even harder to contemplate . . .'

His eyes strayed to Cordelia, who met his glance with pale, helpless unhappiness.

'Is that when she made the ultimate confession, Charles, to bind you to her?' Fairfax said, taking a cautious step closer to Porteous. 'When she saw that you were drawing away from her, that she might lose you, did she throw down that confession as testament to her utter devotion? She had killed your wife, so that there would be just the two of you, together always. What the two of you had together was of her making – did she challenge you with that?'

'Yes,' sobbed Porteous, 'yes – but you didn't hear her,

Fairfax, you didn't hear her words. So hard and cold . . . not the Emma I knew . . .'

'I see. But that was the Emma you knew, Charles, if you had only let yourself see it. She threatened to implicate you in your wife's death, was that it? Drag you down with her?'

Porteous nodded, dragging his knuckles across his eyes. 'And she was so businesslike. She said we must deal with these letters, and then all would be well. She said I must be guided by her again . . . she believed Chilcott's wife must be the writer, she couldn't see that it could be anyone else, and so we must take steps. Her words . . . take steps . . .'

'If you had not been so very respectable,' Fairfax could not help saying, 'you might have known, both of you, that false documents of all kinds can be purchased, like everything else . . . And then, she had her horse saddled, and came over here, to call on Mrs Chilcott – to kill for the third and, she no doubt hoped, the last time.'

'I should have followed her sooner. For a while I was just frozen – lost – howling inside at the thought of Catherine in her sickbed, too weak to take our son in her arms . . . Oh, Emma,' Porteous cried stormily, 'how could you have done it? How—'

'Oh, Charles,' Emma said, very precise, but also with a tremendous weariness. 'How could I have done it? Because deep down, Charles, you wanted me to do it. In your heart, my darling, you wanted me to.'

'Emma . . .'

'Yes, Charles.' And when she repeated it, Fairfax did not for a moment catch on to the altered inflection in her voice. 'Yes, Charles. Yes.'

Too late, realizing what she was saying: too late, realizing what Porteous was doing as he reached into the pocket of his coat: too late, realizing that Porteous had brought with him not one primed and loaded pistol but a brace: Fairfax moved, too late.

It must have cost Porteous a good deal of pain to lift the pistol, aim it so steadily, and pull the trigger with his injured right hand, but he did it, neatly, and neatly shot his sister-in-law dead with a ball to her left temple. He had twice thrown off Fairfax and Stagg and Bayley, as if he had the strength of ten men, and was still struggling with powder and shot to reload, no doubt to shoot himself, when they finally overpowered him and held him down on the floor, a few feet from the fair broken head with its halo of blood.

Nine

To all Lovers of Sciences.

The greatest Prodigy that Europe, or that even Human Nature has to boast of, is, without Contradiction, the little German Boy WOLFGANG MOZART; a Boy, Eight Years old, who has, and indeed very justly, raised the Admiration not only of the greatest Men, but also of the greatest Musicians in Europe. It is hard to say, whether his Executions upon the Harpsichord and his playing and singing at Sight, or his own Caprice, Fancy, and Compositions for all Instruments, are most astonishing. The Father of this Miracle, being obliged by Desire of several Ladies and Gentlemen to postpone, for a very short Time, his Departure from England, will give an Opportunity to hear this little Composer and his Sister, whose musical Knowledge wants not Apology. Performs every Day in the Week, from Twelve to Three o'Clock in Hickford's Great Room, Brewer Street. Admittance 5s each Person. Tickets to be had of Mr Mozart, at Mr Williamson's, corset-maker, in Thrift-street, Soho.

The two Children will play also together with four

> *Hands upon the same Harpsichord, and put upon it a*
> *Handkerchief, without seeing the Keys.*

Fairfax had had to smile when he first read such advertisements in the London newspapers. He could hear in them the accents of Leopold Mozart, part justified pride, part exuberant pomposity: the Kapellmeister was certainly not dragging his feet in promoting his son's celebrity.

But when he attended one such concert, soon after moving back to London, his only smiles were of mystified delight.

Nannerl, who played for part of the concert, was an accomplished young musician. Wolfgang was something altogether more strange and unforgettable. The little boy, whose feet did not touch the floor as he sat at the harpsichord, and who made such a diminutive figure in that crowded concert room that people were craning and straining to see him over the ranks of hats and wigs, almost seemed to be silently laughing at his audience. Or not at them precisely: rather, laughing with delight at his own powers, as if he found them as inexplicable as everyone else. Fairfax was musician enough to realize that the tricks – the playing with the keyboard covered, the exhibition of perfect pitch in which a lady struck a random note and Wolfgang, his back turned, named it at once – were not exceptionally difficult. The marvel was that the little boy who had to scramble up to the harpsichord stool had already climbed to the eminence that most professional musicians laboured a lifetime to achieve. His playing had sensitivity and poetry as well as technical command: his own compositions sounded to Fairfax just as fine as those of Johann Christian Bach, who was the musical monarch of London that season. And when Wolfgang improvised, taking a theme and making it tender and melting, and then stirring and martial, and then turning it into a fizzing comic aria which seemed to mock all that had come before, he was even a little alarming. It was almost as if he had too much, and Fairfax found his view of the world staggering a little. Confirmed rationalist that he was, he was faced with the uncomfortable question of where this largesse came from, and could not answer it without recourse to notions like the Muses and God-given talents.

It was pleasing, at any rate, to see that this peculiar genius was recognized. The applause was loud and long, and that jaded townish audience could not stop talking about him as they filed out. Leopold, standing proudly behind the harpsichord, had caught Fairfax's eye earlier, and beckoned to him; and now Fairfax joined him whilst Wolfgang reluctantly received the caresses of two cooing ladies in turbans and sack gowns.

'Herr Fairfax, I am happy to see you, sir, and displeased with you. If I had known, you would have had admittance for free.'

Fairfax shook Leopold's hand. 'I would gladly pay more than five shillings, at any time, for such an experience,' he said, and then wondered if he shouldn't have, as Leopold murmured, 'Indeed, indeed?' with an interested glint in his eye.

'I would like to congratulate Wolfgang,' Fairfax went on, 'if he ever gets free of his female admirers.'

Leopold chuckled. 'He is tired of getting kisses from ladies, he says. Ah, a time will come when he will envy his younger self, I think . . . ! So: do you hear anything of our good friend Mrs Linton, I wonder?'

There might not have been any connection between those two remarks; but Leopold was no fool, and the look he gave Fairfax was shrewd and not unkind.

'Not of late. I am, of course, living in town again now, with my employers, and Chelsea is not in my way.'

'Of course . . . Wolfgang! Here is our old friend Herr Fairfax.'

The boy, breaking free at last from bejewelled caresses, hurried over and shook Fairfax's hand.

'Herr Fairfax, did you hear the concert? It went *magnifique* I think. I have played twenty or more since we came back into London—'

'Not quite so many, Wolfgangerl,' his father said.

'Well, lots: and always a big crowd. Better than Paris. Paris is *sch*—' The boy stopped himself with a blush. 'Not so good. I think we should stay in London, Papa. We can soon learn English, and we will always have enough money, and my friend Herr Bach is here—'

'Oh, we cannot stay away for ever, Wolfgangerl,' his father said. 'My Prince-Archbishop would not allow it: one must always have a care to one's responsibilities. Herr Fairfax, we have a private room here: step in, please, and take a little refreshment with me.'

'Cider?'

'The same. The recovery of my health has not altered my partiality for it – though I find I cannot get the same quality here in the city. We lodge at Thrift Street, and though it is very convenient, things come dearer and not so fresh as at Chelsea . . .'

There was a little panelled tiring-room off the concert room, and Nannerl was there, very shy over a large bouquet someone had given her. Wolfgang, full of high spirits, seized his father's cane and began riding it like a hobby-horse.

'And so, all that dreadful business at Chelsea is concluded,' Leopold said, pouring Fairfax a glass of cider. 'It is a strange thought that a note in my Wolfgangerl's *sinfonia* should have given you the clue to it, sir; and though you explained it to me, I am still a little puzzled by it all. But at least it is all over. I would say happily over; but I fear that cannot be.'

'No,' Fairfax said. 'Perhaps not.'

There was little to be salvaged from the whole tragical affair, he thought: though it seemed at least that the theme of death had been played through finally, and fallen silent. Charles Porteous had yet to stand trial for the killing of Emma Henlow on that ghastly evening last month; but in his last communication with Mr Yelverton, the magistrate, Fairfax had been given to understand that a manslaughter indictment, or even a plea of unsound mind on Porteous' part, would probably save him from the gallows. He hoped so. He had his own views about Charles Porteous, but there had been more than enough blood spilt.

Emma Henlow's, of course, had been the truly evil part in that drama. But as he thought about the people involved in it, all Fairfax saw was a pattern of common human flaws. Mr Gabriel Chilcott, that thrustful, overbearing, but perhaps lonely man who had sought to buy a wife as he bought a new harpsichord; Mrs Chilcott, an aloof woman who could love passionately, but not unselfishly; Giles Bayley, a clever young man probably capable of much, but just as capable of small, dangerous mischief; Jemmy Runquest, who surely was the father of Tabitha's unborn child but who saw no

271

great sin in shrugging it off simply because she was a woman, and like many a village Lothario he disliked women; Dr Stagg, who should have valued himself as an excellent doctor and a reliever of much suffering in the world, but fell into sordidness and self-loathing because he loved one unworthy woman who could not love him. A pattern of common human flaws; and Emma Henlow, murderess though she was, did not stand outside it. She had killed because she had thought she had good reason to – as most murderers did. That pattern of flaws only had to be altered slightly, its lines sharpened, its colours intensified, to create the state of mind in which killing another person seemed the only possible thing to do.

Well, it was concluded, as Leopold had said. Fairfax had remained in Chelsea only a few days after the shooting at Brockleigh House, helping Mr Yelverton with the practicalities of the case. Continuing to lodge with Dr Stagg – a man who would have to make peace with his own demons in his own time, if he could – was intolerably awkward, and so Fairfax had decided to come back to London. Good lodgings were hard to come by in Chelsea, and he was surely as fit now as he would ever be, and his employers were happy for him to return to his tutor's post if he wanted, and . . .

And there was nothing to keep him there.

He still did not know if that was bleak honesty or cowardly self-deception. He had re-created the scene a hundred times in his head since returning to London, as if by that means he might spot some clue in it that would tell him what to do and how to feel. But though he had teased out the identity of Tabitha Dance's killer, from this scene he could glean no meaning except the obvious one, the one that had made him come away from Chelsea pretty much like a man fleein the location of a crime.

The scene was simple. A few days after the shooting, he had called at Five Fields Row, and Frau Mozart had met him in the hall and asked him to walk up. And so he had done, agreeable enough but really longing to see Cordelia. And when he had asked after her, Frau Mozart had raised her eyebrows and said something about a visitor, and then led him to a bedchamber at the back of the house, with a window overlooking the garden below.

Walking in the garden were Cordelia and a man he recognized as George Linton, her husband.

Curious: he had always kept a very vague mental picture of Linton, a mere faceless sketch of enmity, a resented outline, but as soon as he saw that craggy, thick-set, pensive-looking man, it was as if he was as familiar to him as his own reflection.

Well, Linton had come to find his wife, and there they were in the garden, walking together between the straggling rose bushes, and no doubt talking over their differences as any estranged couple would. A thorny twig caught Linton's coat-sleeve, and he stopped to disentangle it. Cordelia stopped too, and after a moment put out her hands to help him. Once he was free, he looked at her without speaking for some moments, and then took hold of her hand, and held it.

Then they walked on, their hands still linked.

'Her husband, I believe,' Frau Mozart had said. 'It is good if they are to be reconciled.'

'Yes,' Fairfax had said; and then had come away.

For he should not be watching, after all: no matter what.

It was between husband and wife. *'Whom God hath joined let no man put asunder.'*

He had left her the briefest note possible, with the address of his employers, and returned to London that day.

Whom God hath joined let no man put asunder. Meaning no other man, no third party, no intruder. And that was how he had felt, watching the two of them together – an intruder. Never mind that his heart was tied to that woman's with bonds that hurt him, and defined him. Never mind the host of feelings that swept him, like ugly civil war, with hate there as well as love – hate of Linton, hate of her for not being free of him and for being so frailly human as not to know her own mind; and hate of himself, for the same reason. Feelings that seethed and clashed more darkly as the days passed, and there was silence from Chelsea. Never mind all that. He was outside, and he could only contemplate this conundrum that life had set him. His restless mind had to recognize, for once, the possibility that there was no solution.

'Ah – I have something for you, Herr Fairfax,' Leopold said now, setting down his glass. 'A memento. I hope you will accept it.'

'Oh, let me, Papa,' Wolfgang cried. He darted to the table where a portfolio lay, and drew from it a large paper. 'Here you are, Herr Fairfax: pray accept this with my compliments and those of my family.'

It was an engraving, a full-length portrait showing Leopold, Nannerl, and Wolfgang. In his gold-laced court costume, Wolfgang sat at the keyboard: Nannerl stood beside it, singing from sheet music; behind his son Leopold stood bowing his violin, looking down on the boy with stern benevolence.

'The original was painted last year in Paris,' Leopold said. 'I have had it engraved for purposes of publicity. And presentation to – special friends.'

'I am honoured,' Fairfax said. 'I shall not part with it, Wolfgangerl; and indeed it will be hard to say goodbye to the real article.'

'Don't, then!' Wolfgang cried. 'Come with us when we go back over the sea, Herr Fairfax. Leave those boys you teach – you could teach me! And you have very good French and German so you could help us on our travels, and then you could come with us to Salzburg—'

'Wolfgangerl,' his father laughed, 'you cannot push people around like chess-men, you know.'

''Tis a tempting notion,' Fairfax smiled. And it really was: fantastical it might be, but he thought of it for a moment with genuine longing. The longing of a man who knows he will be running away from something. 'But I am such a poor sailor, Wolfgang . . . and besides, it may not be goodbye. You may return to London some day. And I am sure, whatever happens, that I shall hear of you again.'

Wolfgang gave him an oddly adult look, a half-smile like the glint on a deep pool of sadness; then said, brightening: 'Oh, I shall make plenty of noise in the world before I am done . . . And not that sort of noise either,' he added with a wicked grin, lifting his coat-tails, and mimicking a monstrous breaking of wind.

'Wolfgangerl! You dirty monkey!' his sister cried, going off into shrieks of laughter.

Fairfax said his goodbyes, and left them still giggling, and went out into Brewer Street, taking his way by the Haymarket. The streets were busy, noisy, and malodorous under the afternoon sun: there was a hectic clatter of hooves and rumble of wheels, an enveloping bustle and jostle that seemed as if it would sweep him off his feet and carry him where it would. But Fairfax made his way through it with a dogged and purposeful step, like a man intent upon searching something out – elusive though it might be, a long and painful journey away perhaps; but worth the getting, and surely to be found at last.

Author's Note

The young Wolfgang Mozart's involvement in a murder case is of course fictional, but his visit to England from April 1764 to July 1765 is fact. So is the Mozart family's summer sojourn in Five Fields Row (now Ebury Street), Chelsea, around which I have constructed this fantasia.

As in the story, the recovery of Leopold Mozart's health led to their return to London, where young Wolfgang continued to make a sensation. When the family finally left England it was with regret, and Leopold gave serious consideration to the idea of settling here. It was the matter of religion that seems to have decided him against it. The Mozarts returned to Salzburg at the end of 1766, having toured the Low Countries and Switzerland on the way back; and though there were to be other travels for the young prodigy, he never came back to England.

Much has been made of the adult Mozart's struggles for security and recognition; and it does seem strange to us that the little boy who could command a hundred guineas for a concert should be reduced, in the thirty-sixth and final year of his life, to writing begging letters. Perhaps it was partly inevitable. The child prodigy was a novelty: the adult was a composer amongst composers. But the Mozart-lover cannot help speculating what might have been if, in 1791, he had returned to England. He had offers from London: his friend Haydn was going, and had a great critical and financial success there; Salomon, the impresario who brought Haydn over, was keen to land Mozart too. Instead Mozart chose to remain in Vienna, where, overworked, depressed, in debt, and progressively ill, he died in December. That last year broke him: perhaps it is too much to say that a return to England, a wealthy and music-hungry land, might have made him. Yet there are few historical might-have-beens so pleasant as the image of a prosperous, elderly Mozart presenting his latest opera at Covent Garden whilst the guns sounded at Waterloo, or directing a performance of his sixtieth symphony before the Prince Regent.

The Mask of Ra

Paul Doherty

His great battles against the sea raiders in the Nile Delta have left Pharaoh Tuthmosis II weak and frail, but he finds solace in victory and in the welcome he is sure to receive on his return to Thebes. Across the river from Thebes, however, there are those who do not relish his home-coming, and a group of assassins has taken a witch to pollute the Pharaoh's unfinished tomb.

Reunited with his wife, Hatusu, and his people, Tuthmosis stands before the statue of Amun-Ra, the roar of the crowd and the fanfare of trumpets ringing in his ears. But within an hour he is dead and the people of Thebes cannot forget the omen of the wounded doves flying overhead.

Rumour runs rife, speculation sweeps the royal city and Hatusu vows to uncover the truth. With the aid of Amerotke, a respected judge of Thebes, she embarks on a path destined to reveal the great secrets of Egypt.

'The best of its kind since the death of Ellis Peters'
Time Out

'A lively sense of history' *New Statesman*

0 7472 5972 0

HEADLINE

The Merchant's Partner

Michael Jecks

Fourteenth-century Devon . . .

Midwife and healer Agatha Kyteler is regarded as a witch by superstitious villagers of Wefford, yet she has no shortage of callers, from the humblest villein to the most elegant and wealthy in the area. But when Agatha's body is found frozen and mutilated in a hedge one wintry morning, there seem to be no clues as to who could be responsible. Not until a local youth runs away and a hue and cry is raised.

Sir Baldwin Furnshill, Keeper of the King's Peace, is not convinced of the youth's guilt and soon manages to persuade a close friend, Simon Puttock, bailiff of Lydford Castle, to help him continue with the investigation. As they endeavour to find the true culprit, the darker side of the village, with its undercurrents of suspicion, jealousy and disloyalty, emerges. And what is driving the young foreigner, son of a nobleman, who has visited the normally sleepy area only to disappear down towards the moors?

0 7472 5070 7

HEADLINE

A Rare Benedictine

The Advent of Brother Cadfael

Ellis Peters

'Brother Cadfael sprang to life suddenly and unexpectedly when he was already approaching sixty, mature, experienced, fully armed and seventeen years tonsured.' So writes Ellis Peters in her introduction to *A Rare Benedictine* – three vintage tales of intrigue and treachery, featuring the monastic sleuth who has become such a cult figure of crime fiction. The story of Cadfael's entry into the monastery at Shrewsbury has been known hitherto only to a few readers; now his myriad fans can discover the chain of events that led him into the Benedictine Order.

Lavishly adorned with Clifford Harper's beautiful illustrations, these three tales show Cadfael at the height of his sleuthing form, with all the complexities of plot, vividly evoked Shropshire backgrounds and warm understanding of the frailties of human nature that have made Ellis Peters an international bestseller.

'A must for Cadfael enthusiasts – quite magical' *Best*
'A beautifully illustrated gift book' *Daily Express*
'A book for all Cadfael fans to treasure' *Good Book Guide*
'Brother Cadfael has made Ellis Peters' historical whodunnits a cult series' *Daily Mail*

HISTORICAL FICTION / CRIME 0 7472 3420 5

Shroud for the Archbishop

Peter Tremayne

Wighard, archbishop designate of Canterbury, has been discovered garrotted in his chambers in the Lateran Palace in Rome in the autumn of AD 664. The solution to this terrible crime appears simple as the palace guards have arrested an Irish religieux, Brother Ronan Ragallach, as he fled from Wighard's chambers.

Although Ronan denies responsibility, Bishop Gelasius, in charge of running affairs at the palace, is convinced the crime is political; Wighard was slain in pique at the triumph of the pro-Roman Anglo-Saxon clergy in their debate with the pro-Columba Irish clergy at Whitby. And there is also the matter of missing treasure . . .

Bishop Gelasius realises that Wighard's murder could lead to war between the Saxon and Irish kingdoms if Ronan is accused without independent evidence. So he invites Sister Fidelma of Kildare and Brother Eadulf of Seaxmund's Ham to investigage. But more deaths follow before the pieces of this strange jigsaw of evil and vengeance are put together.

'The Sister Fidelma stories take us into a world that only an author steeped in Celtic history could recreate so vividly – and one which no other crime novelist has explored before. Make way for a unique lady detective going where no one has gone before!' Peter Haining

0 7472 4848 6

HEADLINE